KT-474-344

We hope you enjoy this book. Please return or renew it by the due date.

You can renew it at www.norfolk.gov.uk/libraries or by using our free library app.

Otherwise you can phone 0344 800 8020 - please have your library card and PIN ready.

You can sign up for email reminders too.

22
April

13/22

TONI JORDAN

DINNER
WITH THE
SCHNABELS

PIATKUS

PIATKUS

First published in Australia and New Zealand in 2022 by Hachette Australia
An imprint of Hachette Australia Pty Limited
First published in Great Britain in 2022 by Piatkus

1 3 5 7 9 10 8 6 4 2

A CIP catalogue record for this book
is available from the British Library.

ISBN: 978-0-349-43435-3

Printed and bound in Great Britain by Clays Ltd, Elcograf S.p.A.

Papers used by Piatkus are from well-managed forests
and other responsible sources.

Piatkus
An imprint of
Little, Brown Book Group
Carmelite House
50 Victoria Embankment
London EC4Y 0DZ

An Hachette UK Company
www.hachette.co.uk

www.littlebrown.co.uk

For Margaret and Ron, who taught me to be brave,
to think for myself, and how to box a quinella.

And for my sisters, Lee, Erin and Lauren.
If you are in the world, I can never be alone.

Prologue

In the reception of an office, high in a steel and glass skyscraper, a woman stood at the window and gazed down upon the city.

Up here, everything was quiet. From this gleaming eagle's nest, the noise of traffic and construction and the rush of pedestrians seemed the problems of lesser mortals. On the reception desk, a huge bouquet in pinks and whites was inappropriately cheery. *Nothing good happened in offices like this*, the woman thought. People only came here when things were going badly wrong.

The woman was in her late thirties, with tawny-blonde hair that rested on her shoulders. She turned and sat again on a beautiful chair designed without the smallest thought to comfort. She crossed and recrossed her legs. She'd been waiting for twenty minutes already. Her armpits were damp. She wished she'd brought a book.

The uncomfortable chair was covered in grey linen. The dot paintings on the walls belonged in a gallery. She couldn't detect any fragrance from the enormous bouquet. Everything was tasteful without displaying any particular taste. The chairs, the paintings, the flowers; these were meant to distract you from two things.

Bad news and exorbitant fees.

'Steve will see you now,' the receptionist said.

—

As Steve ushered her to a seat on the far side of the long table in the meeting room, she knew she'd made a mistake.

Oh, he was friendly enough. Delighted to see her.

'I can't get over it,' he said, clasping her hand in both of his. 'You're grown up. It must be twenty years.'

'More like thirty.' Her mouth smiled.

He whistled. He was a round man who wore braces – on his chest, not his teeth – and his head was strangely two-dimensional as though it were a colour photocopy of his actual head. 'I think of your father often.'

'That's kind.'

'And how's Nick? And your sister? What was her name?'

'Kylie. Nick's retired from football now, you probably know. Kylie's a pharmacist.'

'And your mother?'

'A danger to herself and others.'

He laughed. 'Nothing's changed, then. Clara, can you believe I bounced this woman on my knee?'

Clara, his associate, chuckled subordinately in her monochrome pantsuit.

The woman – the former bouncee – had agonised for weeks before making the appointment. It would have been easy to ask around for recommendations – she knew people who considered themselves experts in the field – but there was something concrete about that. Something committed. She would have had to put her thoughts into words. And soon, gossip would spread. Instead she'd done a little light googling and the name of Steve's firm had jumped out from the screen. She remembered Steve from her childhood: avuncular, patient with small children, smelling of tobacco and whiskey like her father. Logically, she knew Steve might well have retired by now, so she felt calmed by the sight of his name, by the memory of being small and having a wise grown-up to look after her.

Steve hadn't changed. He wasn't the problem. This whole thing had been a mistake from the beginning.

Steve was talking, she realised. Farewelling her. 'It's one of those days, unfortunately,' he said. 'I'll leave you in Clara's capable hands.'

Now that she was sitting across from Clara, everything seemed much more difficult. The walls were glass, as was the table. The receptionist had made her a latte in a glass and she wrapped her fingers around it. She wasn't alone, she told herself. All over the country, married women were sitting in glass offices just like this one, contemplating something they thought only happened to other people.

'Like I said, I'm not sure I want to do anything at all,' she said.

'That's fine. We're just having a preliminary chat,' Clara said. 'No obligation.'

'I might wake up tomorrow feeling completely differently.'

'It's smart to explore your options. To take your time. It's a big decision.'

'It's not just about me. There are the children to consider.'

Clara leaned forward and positioned a conspicuous box of tissues closer to the woman's chair. 'Of course. They're minors? You'll need a parenting plan.'

She didn't know what that was, a parenting plan. 'Perhaps we should start at the beginning?'

3

Clara smiled without showing her teeth. 'Of course. First, you'll need to make a list of all your joint assets. The house, particularly – the size of the mortgage and the estimated value. A list of all bank accounts with balances and any other liabilities, like personal or business loans. Any investment properties? No? You'll need to record how much both you and your husband have in super. Initial financial contributions to the marriage. And your husband's income, of course.'

She had wandered into a surgeon's office by mistake, she thought. Her skin was being flensed from her bones. Perhaps she should have brought her sister; every word that Clara uttered was blurring in her mind already. It occurred to the woman that she should make some notes. She fossicked in her handbag for a moment before Clara reached across the table to hand her a pen and a notepad emblazoned with the firm's logo: *MacArthur Family Law*.

Then Clara went on talking about the importance of mutual agreement wherever possible, to save them both in lawyer's fees – a practised joke here, about advising against her own self-interest. She talked about mediation, about give and take. Because of the ages of the children, arrangements for their custody would need to be formalised by the family court. Clara then gave her the number for a counselling support line in case she needed someone to talk to. She promised that this firm, Steve's, would provide an estimate of costs before each stage to eliminate nasty surprises. She talked about what the likely outcomes would be, should things proceed. Clara had reeled off these points to numb women many times before. This particular numb woman jotted notes as fast as she could.

'Does your husband have his lawyer organised?' Clara said.

'No. No, he doesn't.' Out the window, the sky seemed lower than at home. Heavy grey clouds were rolling in from the west. She resisted the urge to check the time; she'd told her mother, at home babysitting, that she had an appointment for a breast screen. 'I haven't discussed it with him yet. He has no idea I'm here.'

'That's not unusual, in couples where communication has broken down. Very frequently the wife does a lot of the processing by herself. The husband is quite likely to be blindsided.'

The woman made another note on the pad: *Simon likely blindsided.*

MONDAY

Chapter 1

At first glance, Simon Larsen looked like a man adrift. The hunch in his shoulders, the five-day stubble. He wore a stained hoodie and the trackpants stretched over his waist had seen better days. He was tallish without being quite tall, and beefy without being exactly fat. His eyes, once a sharp blue, were watery and faded with pouches underneath, like small, hairless caterpillars napping. His hair, already silver, was scruffy and his face was puffy and grey. He seemed aimless. That would be an understandable assumption, from the look of him.

But if you thought that, you'd be wrong.

Okay, he might not have a burning goal that ignited his energy and imagination and saw him leaping out of bed in the morning before the alarm. He'd had those in the past, yes. He was once driven and striving; he was once a person who made plans. That past Simon was someone he could barely recognise. But right now, there was something he did absolutely need to achieve.

He needed to landscape Naveen Patel's backyard.

This was not the kind of goal that poets immortalised in verse. It was unlikely to inspire a movie starring Steve Carell as

Simon. But the situation was urgent. If Simon fixed Naveen's backyard, disaster would be averted. And also – and here was the real motivating factor, he admitted – Tansy would get off his back. His mother-in-law, Gloria, would get off his back, his sister-in-law, Kylie, would get off his back, his brother-in-law, Nick, would get off his back. His wife and her entire family would get off his back if he fixed Naveen's backyard.

And once the backyard was fixed, Naveen would pay him. To be honest, they really needed the money.

All of this was incredibly motivating for Simon. See? He *was* a man with a goal. If he did this job by Saturday, he could be back to his normal life by Sunday.

And yet.

Right now, it was Monday morning. Early. Time was ticking. Simon had only one week to landscape Naveen's backyard, but he was not there, tilling and shovelling and planting. He was at Southern Cross Station with his wife, Tansy, waiting for a train.

Tansy was an apple-cheeked woman with tawny-blonde, shoulder-length hair and a dusting of freckles across her nose that looked like they'd been applied with a paintbrush. Her face was heart-shaped. She looked like a milkmaid from a fairy story, like someone who always drank eight glasses of water and slept eight hours every night. Simon still thought she was the most beautiful woman he'd ever seen.

They'd been sitting in the cafe at the station for all of three minutes when Tansy said she had to make a call. *Had to*. She fished her phone from the little pocket on the outside of her tan leather tote where it lived, snug as a Chihuahua, then she pressed the screen.

'It's me,' she said. 'The train's not in yet.'

Was a cafe inside a train station actually a *cafe*? It was more a food court sort of arrangement in this barn of a station. At this ridiculous hour, the takeaway-coffee line snaked along the glass cabinet of carrot cake and wraps all the way past the sushi place, but the seats were empty except for those occupied by Tansy and himself. The voice on the other end of Tansy's call was loud but indistinguishable. Tansy *uh-huh*ed and *mhm*ed and *gotcha*ed and nodded like a Russian sleeper agent receiving a coded briefing. Finally she hung up without saying goodbye.

'Was that Kylie?' Simon asked. 'Did you just call Kylie again?'

'Of course it was Kylie,' Tansy said as she finished her coffee. 'Who else did you think I would call?'

Several possibilities had crossed Simon's mind. Perhaps this urgent call was something to do with work: perhaps nervous owners of a house Tansy was trying to list or a tenant who'd woken up to find they had no hot water. Or perhaps she'd called Edwina Chee just to check the kids were okay, that Lachie had his library bag and Mia had her sports gear. Simon knew the kids had those things because he'd packed them himself. It wasn't every day that the kids were dropped at the Chees' to go to school with the Chee children, so it would be natural that Tansy wanted to check in.

How ludicrous, he thought. *Of course she would call Kylie.*

He pressed his lips together. The twelve years that Simon had been married to Tansy was long enough to gain some basic understanding of *when to shut up*. Simon was proud of knowing this. If he was in the Marriage Boy Scouts, he'd have a badge sewn onto his uncomfortably paramilitary shirt that said *Discretion is the better part of valour*. The less said, the better. There's no need to keep going on and on about something; part of the secret of a happy marriage was *don't sweat the small stuff*. Simon knew how to let things go.

'You just called Kylie from the car,' Simon said.

'It's the least I can do.' Tansy made a sad face.

Simon opened his mouth to say something that even now he knew he'd soon regret, when Tansy's phone rang. She held up one finger to him, then answered, 'Tansy Larsen.' Then she winked at him, which would have made more sense if she hadn't been Tansy Larsen.

'Not yet,' she said into the phone.

This time the voice on the other end sounded like someone who kept a supply of helium balloons at the ready, just in case they needed to give ransom delivery instructions at short notice.

'Relax,' she said. 'We're going to blend in to the crowd. She'll never even notice us.' And then she laughed, and looked at Simon and made a kissy face. Then she sang the beginning of the James Bond theme – *doo doodoodoodoo doo doo doo* – and listened for a while longer and when she hung up, laughing, she looked at Simon. 'What?' she said to him.

'Let me guess. That was Nick.'

'Of course it was Nick,' she said. 'Who else would it be? He says hi, by the way.'

'If only he was here at the station. At 7 am. Like we are. Then he could have said hi in person.'

'They both feel bad about missing out. Poor Kyles, and poor Nick.'

Where to start with a sentence like that? Missing out? Poor Kyles and poor Nick, *missing out* on getting up at five in the morning in the throes of a mild headache, listening to the kids moaning, propping them up at the sink and watching with one eye while they half-brushed their teeth while tugging a brush through Mia's hair with one hand and doing up Lachie's shoelaces with the other while your head continued to pound, then filling their pockets with muesli bars and yoghurt cups and half-carrying them, grumbling, and their bags (why does a child the size of Mia have a backpack the size of a small pony?) to the car while your wife is on the phone to her sister, again, then delivering your children, lids half closed, to the Chees', to be greeted by at the front door by Edwina Chee in a Hello Kitty dressing-gown that Simon would never have guessed came in adult sizes and slippers that looked like miniature schnauzers? ('Dad!' Lachie had said, all at once awake as he tumbled from the back seat. 'If they were real dogs, Edwina's feet would be up their *bums*!')

Or should he be thinking of *poor* Kyles and *poor* Nick, *missing out* on missing half a day's work this morning, which put Simon behind on Naveen's backyard already, on the very first day he was scheduled to begin. There was turf to be laid! Garden beds to be prepared, shrubs to be planted! The pavers hadn't arrived yet! It was perfect labouring weather: mid-twenties, only partly sunny. Very lucky, for February. Yet here he was, accompanying his wife to Southern Cross so that Tansy, who was actually the *poor* one, didn't have to do this on her own.

This was a terrible idea, he thought. He hated to think of her putting herself through this, being upset for no reason.

'It's not too late to go home,' he said. 'We could have a leisurely breakfast without the kids. I could make you an omelette.'

'I'm fine.'

'I don't like her already,' he said. 'I haven't even seen her and I know. She's a pain, I can tell.'

Tansy reached over and squeezed his hand.

The waiter approached their table.

'I'll have a shiraz, please,' Simon said. 'A double shiraz, with a side of vodka.'

'He means another long black,' said Tansy.

Simon shrugged. 'I guess,' he said.

Tansy and Kylie and Nick. Simon had always known they were a package deal. There was nothing more important, Simon reminded himself, than the relationship between siblings. In *concept*. In the corner of Simon's brain where all his logical, reasonable and sensible thoughts lived, he completely understood the value in Tansy being so close to her elder sister and younger brother. Having grown up with Gloria as their single parent, sticking together was a survival skill. He saw them as a three-person French Resistance or a rock band. *Rage Against the Gloria. The Surrey Hills Underground.* He loved Tansy's relationship with Kylie and Nick. Theoretically. And he also understood these relationships in a more personal way.

At night, when Simon checked on Mia and Lachie, he would look down on them sleeping like perfect angels: Mia, snoring softly with her rosebud mouth open, and Lachie, with his thumb suspended an inch from his perfect baby teeth. Parents never love their children more than when they're asleep. *I'll protect you forever,* Simon would think in that moment.

And in the next moment, in a spasm of existential dread so sharp he would bend forward like he'd been winded, he'd remember that he and Tansy would both die. At some point in the future, they'd be dead and neither of them would be here to look after Mia and Lachie – that Mia and Lachie would have to *look after each other*. In that gasping, paralysing moment, he would pray to the god he didn't believe in that Mia and Lachie had subliminally absorbed how much their mummy loved their Auntie Kylie and their Uncle Nick, and how much the three of them relied on each other. Simon wanted nothing more from life in that moment than some kind of heavenly assurance that Mia and Lachie would model Tansy's bonds with her siblings and would grow up to truly love and support each other.

At other times though, he wished Kylie would get a job in a new pharmacy far, far away. Perhaps she could be the pharmacist on the International Space Station. Surely those poor orbiting astronauts had enough to worry about – sufficient oxygen, peeing in zero gravity – without having to wait for the next resupply mission for fungal cream and knock-off perfume. And Nick could be promoted to headmaster of some primary school in, say, Wagga. Wagga wasn't as far away as the ISS, but it didn't need to be. Nick didn't have half Kylie's determination. *Even working on the ISS*, Simon thought, *wouldn't altogether rule out Kylie popping over for dinner when he least expected it.*

Simon's own phone rang. He looked down: it was Naveen, no doubt wondering where he was. He hit decline.

'Why is she arriving so early?' he said. 'Today is Monday. The memorial isn't until Saturday.'

'No idea,' said Tansy.

'She won't be as beautiful as you,' he said. He put his hand over hers. 'She couldn't be.'

Tansy smiled at him.

'But I still think this is a mistake,' he said.

'I just want to see what she looks like,' Tansy said. 'A little peek.' She dunked a corner of a serviette in her glass of water, and proceeded to rub a stain on her shirt, near the second button. 'Cereal and yoghurt,' she said. 'From Lachie, somehow.'

Lachie managed to spread yoghurt everywhere, as though he stalked around the house with the tub in his fist, blobbing it on every available surface. Lachie was the Jackson Pollock of yoghurt.

'You're just rubbing it in,' Simon said. 'I'll spray it tonight. In fact, we could scrap this whole mission and go home, and you could get changed.'

'Stop fussing. She doesn't know what I look like. She's probably never even heard my name. She might not know any of us exist.'

'But what do you hope to gain by it?' Simon said.

'I want to be forewarned. We're hosting the memorial — I don't want her to show up and for us to be . . . blindsided. Is this gone, do you think?' This, about the stain. Then Tansy said, 'That's the train.'

And it was. Past the single commuters in sneakers with headphones, past the pairs of elderly tourists dragging wheelie bags and some still wearing masks, past the gaggles of uniformed schoolkids — four tracks across, the 6.54 from Traralgon was pulling in, only twenty minutes late.

Tansy's phone appeared again as though it was on a retractable cord, and hovered an inch from her ear. 'It's me. The train's here,' she said. 'Let Nick know.'

Simon dropped his face to his hands.

Tansy had hung up the phone and was out of her seat and moving before Simon could finish his second coffee. By the time he groaned to his feet, checked he still had his wallet and keys, tapped the bill and gave a reasonable distance to passers-by, she was already in front of the perspex barrier, watching the train disgorge its passengers. When he caught up with her, she started walking towards the gates at speed. He followed.

'Look for someone who's just like me and Kyles and Nick, but different,' she said.

Considering that Tansy and Kylie looked nothing alike, and Nick was a man, that might be tricky. 'But she's younger, yes?' he said. 'How much younger, do you think?'

'But we all look young for our age,' Tansy said, squinting. 'And she's from the country. So.'

Simon had considered himself to be reasonably intelligent before he married Tansy. He was smart at school, smart at university – but now he saw his main deficiency. He spoke only English. Plain, normal, Australian English. Tansy, he'd realised over the years, was bilingual, because she possessed an entire other language that floated underneath her words. Sometimes Tansy talked a lot; at other times, her sentences contained only one word. Either way, the words that came out of Tansy's mouth often concealed a world of information that Simon had no idea how to decipher, as though Tansy's actual speech was a tip of a massive submerged iceberg of meaning. Best to simply nod as though what she said was obvious to him. No sense exposing his ignorance. That was another thing he'd learned.

'So . . . she'll look older, because . . . there are fewer beauticians in the country? So women who grow up outside of an urban area age quicker?' he said.

Tansy stopped walking so abruptly that a besuited businessman with a dusting of dandruff on his shoulders and a hiking backpack had to swerve around her. She tilted her head to one side and frowned.

'Beauticians? I've never thought about that before. I don't think so, but maybe,' she said, and Simon was left wondering which part was unlikely: that there were fewer beauticians in the country (empirically obvious, surely) or that beauty treatments kept women looking younger (which must be one of the reasons women went to beauticians in the first place).

Tansy started walking again. Simon followed. Ahead, there was a bottleneck at the gates: a shuffle of office workers and several construction workers were stuck behind a young woman with a number-two buzz cut trying to get through the gate while holding, for some reason, a huge floral pillow. They watched, still walking, until the pile-up cleared then Tansy stopped again, suddenly, and threw her arm out sideways, smacking him in the chest.

A woman had cleared the gates and was walking towards them.

'Don't look. It's her,' Tansy whispered.

What did this woman have that they – Kylie, Tansy and Nick – didn't? All these years of waiting, of wondering. Tansy had never mentioned it, but Simon knew she thought of it sometimes. As Kylie must have. And Nick. Finally, they were about to find out.

Chapter 2

'How do you know it's her?' Simon said.

Tansy turned side on. 'The hair!'

Don't look didn't mean *don't look*, Simon was fairly sure.

He looked.

The woman Tansy had spotted, Possibly-Monica, wore her tawny-blonde hair in a pageboy style; a cross between Tansy's colour and Kylie's cut. (Kylie had shiny black hair, and her pageboy cut made her look like the star of a German documentary on SBS about Nefertiti.) In short, the woman looked exactly like Tansy and Kylie, but different. He could see nothing of Nick in her, but perhaps that was to be expected. The woman was in her early thirties, maybe, which would make her a little younger than Nick – although Simon was hopeless at guessing women's ages. She wore white tailored pants and a blue sleeveless top in some kind of silky fabric, and carried a patchwork leather handbag on one shoulder.

'Quick, lend me your sunglasses,' she said to Simon. 'Mine are in the car.'

19

He handed them to her and, at once, stabs of glare entered his eyeballs and reached down into his brain where his headache nestled, dozing, and inconsiderately woke it up. He raised his sights to the weirdly curved ceiling and the escalators heading up to the mezzanine, where the woman clutching the huge pillow was now causing another traffic jam, and he felt a rush of anger towards public-space architects worldwide. Overpaid, overpraised, self-indulgent wankers. Why did there need to be so much *sunlight* in train stations? Were they expecting someone to perform surgery right here on the platform? Also, Monica had never met Tansy, as she said. Monica probably didn't know that Tansy existed. Surely a disguise wasn't necessary?

He didn't say any of this. Instead he followed Tansy, who was winding through the crowd, following Possibly-Monica.

'Well, you've seen her,' he said. 'Now we can go.'

'I just want to . . .'

Possibly-Monica had stopped. She was being greeted by a thin man in a shiny suit with a narrow tie, and two children. She picked the smaller one up and held the other one to her waist. Then they all began to walk across to Collins Street together.

'Bugger, it's not her,' Tansy said as she handed the sunglasses back to him. 'Maybe an aunt, visiting for the day. With only a handbag, no luggage. I should have twigged. Disappointing.'

They headed back to the other end of the station. It was properly busy now, though almost everyone was wearing headphones and, from the looks on their faces, could have been completely alone. He saw a cringe of hipsters, some with skateboards under their arms. He saw one or two students, loping and slouching, and out on Spencer Street, a barrister with a wig in one hand and a briefcase in the other. The buzz cut woman with the pillow was somehow still on the escalator, now halfway up, and no matter how far she stood to the left, no one could pass her because of the size of her pillow. They'd have no chance of finding one random person among all this.

'Hang on,' he said to Tansy. He walked towards the foot of the escalator. Once pillow-woman reached the top, she turned around and descended again on the other side.

'That's the biggest pillow I've ever seen,' said Simon.

'A European,' said Tansy. 'What on earth is she doing?'

How Tansy could tell the woman's continent of origin from this distance was beyond Simon, but what she was doing was obvious: she was riding the escalator up, then turning around and riding it back down again. It reminded Simon of a lava lamp he'd owned in his twenties, which he'd found similarly entrancing – but he smoked a bit of weed back then. Still, there was something hypnotic about watching her and the pillow descending, then ascending. It was relaxing.

Until the woman's next descent. For seemingly no reason, as Tansy and Simon watched, she shrieked. A high-pitched shriek, the kind to frighten pigeons. And as she shrieked, she dropped her pillow, which hit the head of the man standing below her on the escalator, who spun around and in turn hit the woman in front of him with his briefcase. And then the whole escalator was in an uproar, all except the woman herself, the cause of the kerfuffle, who considered the arguing people below her with a mild distaste. She was staring at them with one eyebrow and one hand raised.

Correction. Staring at Tansy.

Chapter 3

'Monica the mystery woman,' Simon said. 'You've never met her before, right?'

'Never,' said Tansy. She seemed stunned. 'But that can't be her. She's so . . . *young*.'

'And she's never even seen you?'

'Never met, never seen, never spoken to. There's no way she could know what I look like.'

Yet here they were, frozen in the middle of the station while a strange young woman almost skipped her way towards them.

'Oh. My. God, it's really you!' the young woman squealed as she approached. She then seemed to register that she'd been too loud, too enthusiastic. She calmed, visibly. Her lack of hair made her brown eyes seem enormous, like Bambi. She rearranged her face, dropped her shoulders. 'I mean, hey,' she said, laid-back now, as though she hadn't shrieked a moment ago.

Simon looked at Tansy. She had a smile plastered on her face as if she were being approached by a 5G conspiracist heading her way with a pamphlet. He could imagine her fingers itching to call Kylie and Nick.

'Tansy, right? It's you, isn't it?' the woman said. 'I can't believe you came.'

'We came,' said Tansy, somehow without her lips moving.

'Thanks. I mean, really, *thanks*.' She shook her head in wonder.

Simon could only stand there, watching the two women watching each other. The younger woman's face looked like that heart-eyes emoji, as though her pupils had changed shape in front of Tansy.

The young woman was the first to speak again. 'You are so much prettier in real life. Look at you. A real estate agent. Seriously, respect.'

'I . . . I just do rentals,' said Tansy.

'And those shoes! Do you wear them all day? The height of that heel, wow.'

Tansy's eyeballs darted towards Simon, although the rest of her face stayed immobile. 'You get used to them.'

Now that she was closer, Simon could see that she was a tall young woman. A tall *very young* woman. Early twenties, if not younger, wearing vivid pink eyeshadow, a black lace dress and heavy multicoloured boots. A silver ring pierced the corner of one eyebrow, and along one arm was a winding, climbing . . . well, it should have been a rose by the looks of the stem and the leaves, but the flowers were, for some reason, purple petunias. Her lashes were so pale as to be non-existent and her eyes were clear and soft, like an inquisitive rabbit. On her other arm were three supermarket single-use shopping bags, stuffed full. Were single-use bags even legal anymore? They were very likely *illegal, contraband* single-use bags. If Simon had spent weeks in a police station looking at mugshots of every person on earth who could possibly be Tansy, Kylie and Nick's half-sister, this Monica would be at the bottom of his list, below Edwina

Chee, below even Christos from the fish shop, and he was a fifty-year-old Greek man with hair growing out of his ears.

'You're Simon, right?' she said. 'I'm Monica.'

'Of course you are,' said Tansy.

Monica bent her legs open at the knees and thrust the pillow in there as though she were riding a very tiny horse, and offered her fist to Simon. He stared at it for a moment then did the same, and they bumped. Then she leaned forward and hugged Tansy like half of an A-frame, their heads touching and their bodies apart because of the pillow.

'It's lovely to meet you,' Tansy continued, with only the smallest pause and with her biggest smile, the smile that still made Simon's heart squeeze even after all these years.

Sometimes when Simon lay awake in the middle of the night, he would look over to see Tansy sleeping beside him and it seemed to him that she actually *glowed*. His rational mind knew the streetlight outside glinted on the broken slat on the venetians, which then bounced off the Ikea lamp that stood on the cardboard box they used for a bedside table. Simon knew his wife did not actually have a halo. At times like this, though, he thought that if anyone in the world should have a halo, it should be her. Monica was not family. Monica was not even a friend, but Tansy had decided to take the high road. She was genuinely warm to this person, and all Simon had to do was live up to her example.

On the other hand, it was tempting to hate her on Tansy's behalf.

Above all – and this was the important thing – be cool. Don't betray any kind of surprise, especially not about her age.

'Fucking hell,' said Simon. 'What are you, twelve?'

'Lol, no,' said Monica. 'It's so cool you're here. Mum said no one would meet me, but I knew you would. I was going up and down, up and down, looking for you. City people are too busy for common decency, Mum says. Up themselves. Wankers, she says.'

'We're not wankers,' Simon said.

'I know! You're not dickheads either. Mum was totally wrong,' Monica continued. 'I had a feeling you'd come. My own siblings wouldn't let me arrive here in the city and not know anyone and have to find my way to the hostel all by myself. Are Kylie and Nick here too?'

'They couldn't get time off work,' Tansy said quickly.

'Totally,' Monica said. 'So busy. With Kylie being a pharmacist and all. Pharmacists are super smart. And the famous Nick! A primary school teacher, responsible for, like, actual kids. I get it.'

'Right,' said Tansy. 'You seem to know a lot about us.'

'We're busy too,' said Simon. 'We should be at work.'

'Simon,' said Tansy.

But Monica didn't look offended. 'Oh totally, sorry. I can get to the hostel by myself, no drama.' She pulled the pillow out from between her knees and juggled her plastic bags, which had left red lash marks on her arms.

'Well, if you're sure . . . now that we've said our hellos, we'll head off,' said Simon.

Monica extracted a phone from one of the bags and shook it as though it was an extension of her hand. 'I am *totally* sure. Directions, right here. It's only seven blocks. And a city is just a big town, right? And it doesn't look like rain. Although it might. Rain. Anyway, if it does rain, I'm sure I won't get wet. Not *very* wet. It's all part of the adventure, right?' Monica clocked their expressions. 'It was just nice of you to come.'

That's the advantage of a relationship as long and solid as Simon and Tansy's – their joint understanding transcended speech. They were *in simpatico,* as though they communicated subsonically, like married bats. Simon couldn't hang around in the city all day. They were both late for work already. They'd achieved their goal: they'd seen Monica, the half-sister that Tansy had never met, and what's more, they'd spoken to her. *Tansy could report back to Kylie and Nick that their mission was accomplished,* thought Simon. *Nothing more needed to be done.*

'We're driving you,' Tansy said. 'We insist.'

———

After a bit of *Seriously, I'm good* versus *It's no trouble really,* Simon took Monica's bags, which were surprisingly heavy and stuffed full with what seemed to be mostly clothes, although a few sharp, heavy things whacked into his calf. Monica looked more than capable of carrying them herself of course, but he needed to do something, otherwise why was he here? Together they dodged the traffic on Spencer Street and veered around the homeless people camped against the buildings and passed the glossy windows artistically arranged with things Simon couldn't afford until they nipped around the corner to where he'd parked. It was a good thing that he was laden with bags and they were dodging and veering because no one knew what to say.

'How was the train?' Simon said eventually.

They made for an odd trio. Tansy, fresh and glowing in her tailored work suit and bag and black heels, Simon in his trackpants and hoodie and work boots and Monica in . . . young-people clothes, clutching an enormous floral pillow.

Monica wrinkled her nose. 'The cafe was out of egg sandwiches. Coffee was fine, though.'

'Still, it must be a big improvement,' said Tansy. 'The standing.'

'They don't make you stand all the way from Traralgon?' Simon had visions of the suburban trains he'd seen on the news years ago, in stories about overcrowding on the Frankston line. 'That's appalling.'

'Lol. It's a big improvement on the bus, she means,' said Monica. Her stride was long and confident next to Tansy's, who was tottering in her heels, legs scissoring in her skirt. 'Because you can stand up and walk around on the train.'

Great. Now this stranger was translating his own wife to him.

'How about this for a park?' he said when they reached the car, a third-hand Pulsar in metallic blue. Although it was Tansy's, he'd driven so she could speak on the phone. 'Right in the middle of the city. Hardly anyone knows this spot. See, no ticket.'

He waited for a reply from either of them, or perhaps a smattering of applause, but it didn't come. *A typical lack of appreciation for the beauty of this parking spot*, he thought – and then he realised he shouldn't have drawn Monica's attention to it. He didn't want *someone else* parking here – or worse, *telling other people* about it. He'd always imagined leaving its location to Mia and Lachie, perhaps in a sealed attachment to his will. It would be passed down to their children, and to their children's children. Perhaps as the years went on, it would become part of the folklore of the family. It would acquire a nickname. Simon's Spot, perhaps. Or Pa's Pozzie.

'Although sometimes you do get a ticket. An expensive one,' he said. 'It's definitely on the parking inspector's radar, that's for sure.'

That should do it.

He opened the passenger door for Tansy and the back seat for Monica and her bags and pillow, and Tansy opened an app on her phone and entered the address Monica gave her.

'I thought you were, like, an architect? Don't you have your own business?' Monica gestured to his trackpants and boots once they were moving.

'I'm doing a favour for a friend of Tansy's right now,' Simon said as he chucked a U-ey on Lonsdale. The engine made a grinding noise, and he thought of kebabs to distract himself from hearing it.

'Simon is helping my old friend Naveen with his backyard,' Tansy said.

'I *was* an architect. Before. I'm just weighing up my options right at the moment,' Simon said. 'It's temporary.'

Monica didn't reply.

'I wasn't the only person to go broke during the lockdowns,' Simon continued.

Still nothing.

'I'm between jobs right now, which isn't at all unusual if you read the papers, and Naveen has been Tansy's best friend since they were kids, and his landscape guy cancelled at the last minute, and the memorial service for David is supposed to be held there, in his backyard. The invitations have already gone out. He needed a hand. I'm just filling in. It's certainly no reflection . . .'

He raised his head for a better angle of the rear-view mirror and saw Monica with her head tilted to the side and her tongue out, taking a selfie. She was stretching her other arm forward and holding an aluminium packet. One corner was folded back and he could see fat chocolate squares peeking from underneath the foil.

'Fudge? It has nuts,' Monica said, still looking into the camera on her phone. 'So don't eat it if you're going to, like, swell up. Mum made it. When I was at school, she couldn't bake anything with nuts, because our school had this no-nuts thing? Now everything she makes has got nuts.' She shrugged.

'It looks lovely, thanks.' Tansy took a piece.

Simon took a deep breath. 'Nuts about nuts?' he said.

'OMG, dad joke,' Monica said.

'So ... you're staying here by yourself?' said Tansy. 'I was just telling Simon earlier, girls who grow up in the country are more mature. They drive cars earlier, they have part-time jobs. They're self-reliant.'

So nothing about beauticians, then. Simon cleared his throat.

'Dad's memorial is going to be in your friend's backyard?' said Monica, apparently not up for discussing Tansy's analysis of city versus country girls. 'Is that not a bit ... random?'

'He was having it landscaped anyway,' said Tansy. 'It's quite a big space. It seemed less ... formal than a reception place. More intimate. He offered, and we said yes.'

'And what do you do for a living, Monica?' said Simon.

'This and that.' Her gaze was fixed out the window. 'Oh my god, an actual tram. The size of it! You wouldn't want to be hit by that, RIP.'

The soundtrack of the remainder of the short trip was Monica looking out the window, giving a running commentary – everything from the shops to the street names to the fashions to the hairstyles. She had an opinion on everything. Simon had no idea that the downtown streets of Melbourne were so fascinating. Had she really never seen graffiti before? Or two miniature dachshunds in matching outfits? Or a man walking along King Street dressed as a pirate?

'We've ... never met, right?' said Tansy. 'I wouldn't have forgotten.'

'Right,' said Monica, staring out the window, goggle-eyed.

'You recognised us though? How?'

'I stalked you.'

Simon nearly veered into the next lane. 'You what?'

'Like, online. Your socials,' she added lightly.

'Oh. You mean Facebook?' he said. 'We don't post very much.'

'Facebook, yup. And the rest,' she said.

'What rest?' Tansy frowned at Simon.

Monica shrugged. 'There's lots of stuff around if you look for it. Nick is on everything and you guys are in some of his Instagram stories. Plus your photo is on your work website, Tansy. And *your* high school reunion committee posted the video from last year's nineties dance, Simon. Oh my god, so hilarious. And the school fete committee blog has lots of pics of both of you.'

'Really?' said Simon.

'Yep. And the Google review you wrote for your dentist, Simon. Painless extractions, they're a good thing. There's not much Kylie floating around, just a bit, but she has an excellent resting bitch face. Dad never told me anything about you guys; I asked and asked. So I had no choice but to stalk.' Then she leaned forward in a rush. 'Wait, slow down, it should be just up here.'

Tansy frowned at her phone. 'That's what it says, but I can't see a hotel.'

'*Hos*tel,' Monica said. 'Sssss.'

Simon pulled over.

'I can't see a hostel either,' said Tansy.

The phone had given them directions to a nest of three shops: a drycleaners, a heavy-metal nightclub and a sex-toy parlour called The Glory Hole, which had a bondage joint in the basement.

'Cool, it's right here,' said Monica. 'I really appreciate the lift.'

Sure enough, the word *HOSTEL* was spray-painted in black on the wall, together with an arrow pointing to a narrow open door between the drycleaners and the nightclub. Standing on the footpath to the left of the door were two men: one with a beard and dreadlocks wearing army-surplus khaki pants and no shirt, and the other in some kind of a poncho. They both turned to stare at the car as they pulled up.

'Are you sure this is the place?' said Tansy.

Monica peered out of the back window. 'It didn't look like this on the website.'

'I'm not sure . . .' Tansy began.

'Tans,' said Simon. 'I think Monica is capable of making her own decisions.'

Monica looked down at her phone, then up at the hostel. 'It's definitely the place. I'm only going to sleep there, right? No point wasting money on a bed. Besides, it had great reviews on Tripadvisor. And it's eco-friendly.'

'Which means what, exactly?' Simon said.

'They don't use any insecticides or pesticides or fungicides, not even in the bathroom or the kitchen,' Monica said. 'And they save on fossil fuels by not having any hot water and limited lighting.'

'It doesn't sound very hygienic,' Tansy said.

'I'm a pretty experienced traveller,' she said airily. 'I went to Bondi once, for a weekend.'

To Simon, though, she looked paler.

'Hostels are fantastic for meeting people,' Monica went on. 'Sixteen beds per room. No lockers though.' She lifted the plastic bags. 'That's why I haven't brought the *good* shopping bags. The *reusable* ones. They'd be nicked in a minute.'

Monica cracked open the door and stepped one leg out, and the undeniable stench of urine wafted into the car and assaulted Simon's nostrils.

'I'd better go ahead and check in,' she said. 'It's bound to be busy – Monday night is haggis night. Anyway, thank you so much for the lift.'

'Our pleasure,' said Simon, using up precious oxygen reserves.

Monica hesitated there, one foot in and one foot out, while Simon slowly suffocated.

'Look, Tansy. I need to tell you something.' Monica looked straight at Tansy, who had swivelled in her seat.

'Oh?' said Tansy. She glanced at her wrist where a watch would be, if she had one. 'Maybe we could . . .'

'Let me just tell you . . . here goes. I was an only child, right? I guess, I don't know, I idolised the three of you. You all seemed . . . awesome.'

'Awesome?' said Tansy. 'Us?'

Monica nodded and bit her bottom lip. 'I always wanted brothers and sisters. But Mum was like, how about a puppy? But a puppy is totally different.' She gathered her bags and stepped out of the car, then bent to speak through the open door. 'Anyway,' – she shook herself slightly – 'anyway, enough, right? I do not do drama. I guess I'll see you Saturday, at Dad's memorial? I can't wait to meet Kylie and Nick. And Mia and Lachlan, of course. My niece and nephew! I can't get over it. I'm Auntie Mon. How hilarious is that?'

She shut the door, wrestled the pillow under her arm and turned to walk towards the hostel.

Tansy wound down her window. 'Wait,' she called out. 'I've been thinking.'

Oh no, thought Simon.

Chapter 4

Simon had never loved their old house quite as much as he did now that they didn't own it anymore.

When he and Tansy bought their house some months after their wedding, he'd thought it was an okay house. It was fine. He remembered distinctly that his predominant feeling on the day they moved in was relief rather than joy. Property values were in the middle of one those cyclical spurts that seem as Australian as spiders and thongs.

Buying a property in any capital city back then was like playing musical chairs. At the beginning, you think it's a game. It's a joke, almost. How did you become the kind of person who bought a house? Wasn't that for old people, or boring people? When you were a kid, your parents' idea of a good time was to spend the weekend driving to Prize Homes and imagining a different life. So early in your house hunt, you cruise around on a Saturday afternoon with a vaguely ironic air because it's all a bit of a joke. *A pink pedestal bathroom sink? A brown ceramic tile splashback? Who are these people?* But then pink-pedestal-sink house sells, and the brown-splashback house sells, and you realise that the music has stopped and your bottom is hanging in midair without a supporting chair of any description while someone else's bottom is on the chair you'd thought was too daggy and now you're a chairless loser and there are fewer chairs than there were before and the next song will be even more competitive. Saturday afternoons ceased to be a joke and became a game of skill and strategy: *Risk*, but with the potential to ruin your life. Soon you were almost ready to let down the tyres of the other purchasers at inspections. The amount of money Simon and Tansy were borrowing was eye-watering, and yet every time they saw a house that seemed barely habitable but possibly affordable, it ended up selling for more than expected – and to a couple younger than them. And he and Tansy had a generous, unexpected deposit! How could people that age pay that much for a house? Had everyone in this entire country won Powerball except for him?

During those long months of househunting, Simon would wake on Saturday mornings with a feeling of pressure on his chest, thinking about the long day of inspections stretching out in front of him, feeling defeated before he began. It seemed that no matter how many houses they saw and how much they were prepared to compromise, they were fated to spend every Saturday until the end of time looking at houses and never buying one. Saturdays were gone forever. Their weeks and thus his life was now one-seventh shorter than it had been before. Where would that leave their future? Their as-yet-unborn children?

So when they'd finally bought a house, he felt relieved. The yard was a bit pokey, yes, and it was a little further from the train than he would have liked. There was some cracking on the outside walls and some damp on the inside walls. And the kitchen!

He'd never seen so much chipboard in the one spot, and in such a distinctive colour. What would you call that colour? Puce?

And the pressure of their planet-sized mortgage had replaced the pressure of possibly never buying a house, so he felt only marginally better than before.

But moments after they sold it nearly ten years later – when Tansy had stopped pretending she wasn't crying and had instead developed hay fever for the first time in her life, and Lachie had said goodbye to every plant in the backyard and Mia had packed her stuffed animals in her *Frozen* suitcase and the agent stuck the huge diagonal *SOLD* sticker over the board – in an instant, he loved that house. It was the only home his children had ever known. How could he have ever seen that yard as small? It was intimate, but there was plenty of room for the kids to ride their bikes. In fact, it was the perfect size for one of those *The Block* makeovers. If only he'd replaced the fence or at least painted it, and paved part of the yard, and made a fire pit. How much better their lives would have been, if only he'd built a fire pit! And it was a brick house! Brick was solid. He should have designed an extension and built a parents' retreat upstairs. The kitchen that he'd never touched could have been swivelled around and the wall between the dining room removed. He should have ripped that puce chipboard out with his own hands.

Now he couldn't bear to even look down their old street. If by some ill chance he was driving past on the way somewhere, he'd turn his head and deliberately look the other way because even seeing the street gave him an almost physical pain. The smallest reminder that they'd once owned a house, a family *home*, and now they didn't – well, it was like a dark cloud, and everyone knew that the only successful way to stop dark clouds from spreading and taking over everything was to fence them off in your mind and look the other way, both metaphorically and physically. For the last year, the four of them had been renting a two-bedroom, sixties cream-brick flat on the other side of town, far enough away so he wouldn't be faced with any reminders that some other little girl was sleeping in Mia's room, and some other boy in Lachie's room, and some other woman was sitting up in bed with a cup of tea in the room that was once his and Tansy's. The memory of their old house seemed impossibly perfect, like part of a dream he'd had long ago.

There was probably a German word for this, he thought. Nostalgia for a house you didn't appreciate at the time but grieve for once you've moved: *Gesundheitkindersurprisewurst*, or something.

Simon gripped the steering wheel. Without even looking at Tansy, he knew that his failure with this house – his failure at life – was about to be writ large. Up on a billboard, lit with spotlights. Even in their old house, the two words now foxtrotting in his mind would have made him shudder. Now that their home was a shoebox with a lid, they made him sick to his stomach. Those two words: house guest.

Monica was halfway across the footpath to the door of the hostel. She turned to wave at them.

A *two-bedroom* flat. That was the point. The four of them lived in a two-bedroom flat with a tiny balcony. Tansy surely hadn't forgotten that Lachie slept in the *dining room*. She'd been the one to thumbtack some curtains from Spotlight across the servery and buy a fake Japanese folding screen off Gumtree to give him the illusion of a room of his own. She also couldn't have forgotten that they ate their meals sitting around the kitchen bench, on stools. *Four* stools.

His wife was sensible. His wife was responsible. Simon had nothing to worry about.

'You should come and stay with us,' Tansy called out.

Monica looked stunned. 'That's too much, seriously,' she said.

'Not at all. I should have thought of it earlier. I don't know why I didn't,' Tansy said. 'It's a little crowded but we'd love to have you.'

Simon's heart sank. Tansy had now entered a phase of decision-making that he liked to call 'hand grenade with the pin removed'. This had been her state of mind when she 'volunteered' Simon to fix Naveen's backyard in the first place, and again she was warming up. She was becoming fully committed to her position. Possibly she even believed it herself – that it had always been her intention to invite Monica to stay with them and for some unknown reason she'd failed to articulate it before now. Short of throwing himself physically on top of her and smothering any further eruptions, at no small risk to his own personal safety, he knew from long experience that nothing could be done at this point. Even if he could pull her aside and remind her that, not half an hour ago, Monica was someone she'd just wanted to peek at.

There was no point even trying.

'Darling,' said Simon, 'I'm sure Monica has plans for her week, and I'm sure they don't include living in the 'burbs with an old married couple and two kids. She probably wants to catch up with friends.'

'No I don't,' said Monica.

'Monica probably wants to go to clubs, or to see some bands,' Simon said. 'It'd be selfish of us to keep her all to ourselves. We're terribly boring, Mon. I've been meaning to bring it up with Tansy before now.'

'I don't know what to say,' Monica said.

Simon knew what she should say. *Say no*, thought Simon. *Saynosaynosayno*.

'You guys are awesome,' said Monica. 'It's totally a yes.'

Chapter 5

'Earth to Simon,' Tansy said.

They were just coming along Heidelberg Road, about to turn into their street. How had that happened? Luckily for Simon, the Pulsar knew the way. Also if he'd been speeding, he was one million per cent confident that Tansy would have told him.

'I was listening,' said Simon. 'So interesting.'

He had about four minutes to work out how he could check Monica into a motel when their savings account contained exactly $159.72 until Tansy's payday, which was Thursday, and their credit cards were almost maxed out except for an emergency-only buffer. Beside him in the passenger seat, Tansy looked completely comfortable, as though she brought home random people every day. He could see her hand holding her phone close to her lap, her thumb darting across the screen at a ferocious speed.

'The problem is the hip joint itself,' said Monica, gazing out the window. 'Look, so many cafes. That one has a deli attached.'

'Can't they operate on her? Isn't it routine these days for older people to have their hips replaced?' said Tansy, her eyes on her screen.

'She hates the whole concept of rehab. Relying on other people, you know? Mum is just too independent. She needs to rest. Act her age. It's the linedancing. She's obsessed with every-thing country. Twang twang guitars. Songs about dogs.' Monica leaned her head back on the seat and looked up. 'But you can't tell her. She won't be told.

Tansy made a listening noise.

'Anyway,' Monica continued. 'Mum loves the country. You'd never get her to Melbourne, not ever. And Sydney! No chance. She loves the wide open sky. Out where we are, it stretches from horizon to horizon, not like the little slivers you see between the buildings in the city. Total deal-breaker. Even when she puts on a DVD . . .'

Puts on a DVD?

'I know, right? She loves them, it's devastating. Anyway, she thinks the cinematography is more important than the story or the actors. Vista, that's what she wants to see. Sky and horizon.' Monica held her hands in front of her in L shapes, like a frame. 'Her favourite is that movie . . . ? We must have seen it a dozen times. What's the name of it? Obvious sexual tension between those two handsome dudes? Lots of bum-slapping, holding their faces very close to one another like they're about to have a pash. So hot. And they're wearing the . . . whatsitcalled, on their heads?' She waved one hand, as though measuring herself for a huge potential afro. 'And sweeping shots of the sky?'

Simon opened his mouth to answer, when Monica continued. 'Helmets. *Top Gun.*' She nodded, satisfied. 'Totally.'

'Here we are,' Tansy said, as they pulled up out the front. They both parked on the street because the garage was filled with a few odds and ends: some tins of unopened paint from when Simon had decided to redo the study in their old house but never got around to it; some timber from when he'd planned to build the kids a cubby; an assortment of grow-your-own mushrooms kits past their expiry date left over from his self-sufficiency phase; and the plastic drum and bits and bobs from his attempt at home-brewing. His guitar case, containing the guitar he'd never learned to play. His Ab Trainer Pro, still in the box. And a tangled assortment of power tools in a pile, like an electrical-appliance orgy.

Simon helped Monica with her plastic bags. There were twelve flats in the block but only three others that shared their stairwell, but they didn't meet any neighbours on the way up to the top floor. Jock and James, both nurses, had married as soon as the legislation passed and were obsessed with Rube Goldberg machines. Every few months they invited everyone in the block over to stand tentatively against the walls and drink excellent wine while watching a golf ball trigger their latest invention to serve a slice of toast. Yulia, downstairs, was a tiny retired music teacher with frizzy grey hair and a Russian accent, and was a blessing – she gave Mia piano lessons at neighbour's rates and sometimes babysat. And the girls, Gemma and Erin, both PhD students (obvious by their drooping, haunted faces) didn't socialise much but were quiet and pleasant.

At the top of the stairs, Simon paused, keys in his hand. Perhaps it wouldn't be so bad. Perhaps it was his lucky day. Maybe a fire had swept through the flat while they were out and nothing was left inside but charred remains. Or they had been burgled by desperate and unfussy thieves, and he would open the door to find the flat completely empty with only the stained beige carpet visible.

Perhaps he wouldn't be forced into showing this stranger exactly how much he'd failed his family.

'Honey,' said Tansy, 'are you planning on opening the door sometime soon?'

He took a deep breath, in and out, and jangled the keys in his hand. 'We had to find something at short notice,' he said. 'It's only temporary. Don't expect a palace.'

'I am queen of couch surfing,' said Monica, moving her pillow to the other hand. 'High maintenance I am not.'

'You won't be sleeping on the couch!' said Tansy. 'We'll move Lachie in with Mia for a few days; he won't mind.'

Sure, Simon thought. The poor little guy – not only losing his own room in the move from their old house to the flat and being forced into the dining room, but now losing that also and having to move in with his big sister like some kind of rough sleeper. The injustice of it caught in Simon's throat but it was too late to say anything now.

'That's assuming that we can actually get inside, and we don't sleep here on the landing tonight. Simon?' said Tansy.

'Oh, right,' he said.

He opened the door, and all at once saw the flat from the perspective of a first-time visitor: cardboard boxes filled with toys lining the walls; four bikes wedged behind the front door – that he'd meant to put away in the garage – preventing it from fully opening; the stained couch; the few miserable shelves in the lounge room stuffed to overflowing with books and board games and family photos and his LPs. The kitchen benches, mostly visible from the front door, were crowded with appliances and Tupperware and food that wouldn't fit in the cupboards.

'Home sweet home,' said Tansy. She deposited her handbag on a bookshelf that was made of bricks and boards and looked as though it belonged in a uni share house.

Simon's face burned.

'You guys are the best,' said Monica. 'You won't even know I'm here. Just point me to your coffee machine and I'll sort myself.'

'We mostly drink instant,' said Tansy. 'Or tea.'

'Wow, seriously?' said Monica, eyes bulging.

'I wish I'd organised the day off,' Tansy said. 'I feel awful about dumping you here. Perhaps Simon could . . .'

Was there such a thing as a god? Did a divine intelligence control the universe and the lives of every one of us? It wasn't a topic that Simon thought a great deal about, except at that very moment, his phone rang.

'I'm sorry, I have to get this,' he said, and turned his head to answer.

It was Naveen.

'G'day Sime,' he said. 'How are ya, mate?'

'Naveen!' Simon held one hand over the phone for a moment. 'It's Naveen,' he mouthed at Tansy.

'Clearly,' she said.

'Just checking if you were coming by, mate,' said Naveen.

'Yes, still coming,' said Simon.

'Not a drama,' said Naveen. 'Just need to go out for a bit. I could leave a key somewhere?'

'Of course I want to do the backyard,' said Simon. 'I made a commitment and I will absolutely be there.'

'Yeah, no worries,' said Naveen. 'Just want to know about the key.'

'Mate,' said Simon. 'Please, there's absolutely no need to go off. Let's all be calm.'

Naveen *was* calm. As the conversation went on, however, Simon's replies grew increasingly out of proportion with Naveen's actually quite patient and reasonable questions. Simon also made a number of pained facial expressions, and occasionally bit his bottom lip and looked to the heavens in anguish.

In short, Simon *might* have exaggerated Naveen's displeasure for his own gain. Simon felt a little guilty, because Naveen quickly backtracked and began soothing Simon as though he had in fact gone too far, when he hadn't. But not very guilty.

'I'm sorry,' he said when he hung up. 'Naveen's ropable. Absolutely losing it. I really need to get there ASAP.'

'I can't believe he'd speak to you like that,' Tansy said. 'He's lucky to have you. I'll sort him out.'

'No,' said Simon. 'This is a business arrangement. I'm not having my wife intervening.'

'I worked at Red Rooster when I finished school,' said Monica. 'I am all over customer service. Give me two seconds with him, sorry not sorry.'

'I don't understand it,' Tansy said. 'Naveen never gets angry. He must be under a lot of pressure.'

'He's certainly got a temper,' said Simon. Which wasn't exactly a definitive lie. Naveen might indeed have a temper – it's just that Simon had never seen it. 'He really tore me a new one. Language like a wharfie.'

'I would slay him so hard. Like, RIP Naveen, *mate*,' said Monica.

'I'd better head off,' Simon said with a shrug of deep reluctance.

'Of course, you go ahead,' said Tansy. 'Poor darling.'

Mon wasn't fazed. She was restless from the train, she said, and wanted to stretch her legs and explore some shops, so she left her bags and the pillow and they all exchanged numbers and went their separate ways.

Finally, thought Simon, when he was safe behind the wheel of his own ute. He didn't feel even the slightest remorse for verballing

Naveen. By the time Tansy saw him again, the courtyard would be finished and their little chat would be long forgotten. And Monica would never meet him.

It was a teeny fib that would have zero repercussions.

Chapter 6

Simon had friends. Simon had *plenty* of friends. It's just that he couldn't recall *exactly* the last time he saw them.

Tansy, however, still saw her friends regularly. How did that work, exactly? Tansy had one friend specifically for online yoga (Davina, who lived two streets over), which they did on her back deck. Presumably you're not chatting all the way through your Sun Salute, so what is the point of doing yoga with someone? Tansy seemed to speak to Edwina Chee, who Simon suspected knew very intimate details of their lives, almost daily. And Tansy was always popping down to Yulia with biscuits when she and the kids were baking, or dropping a lasagna into Gemma and Erin. Not to mention how often she saw Kylie and Nick.

It wasn't only the *utility* of Tansy's friends that amazed him, but their longevity. She had met Naveen in primary school and still they saw each other all the time. When Naveen bought his takeaway chicken shop, Tansy dropped around with a Japanese waving cat, and in the early days after Naveen's divorce, he would often bring Lexie over on his weekends because he found the dynamic of the two of them eating alone to be weird.

Simon liked Naveen. He was a slender-limbed, soft-featured man with a mop of thick black hair that seemed to grow inches overnight, which left Simon, who inspected his hairline in the mirror every morning for signs of possible receding, pricked with envy.

When Simon arrived at Naveen's, he was surprised to find him home doing paperwork at the dining-room table, despite all that talk about the key.

This might be a little awkward, he thought.

'I thought you said you'd be out,' said Simon.

'I have to work up some new vegetarian dishes for a big job. Everyone likes eggplant, right?'

Simon shrugged. 'I guess.'

'Mate,' said Naveen, 'what was that about?'

'Sorry, sorry,' Simon said. 'I'm a little sensitive today.'

'Don't be so hard on yourself,' said Naveen. 'It's been a tough couple of years. Cut yourself some slack. Fancy a tea?'

Simon did fancy a tea. Naveen headed to the kitchen and Simon followed. Simon could see teen-girl accoutrements scattered around the house: a fluffy pink beanbag in front of the television, a white puffer jacket and an assortment of beanies on the rack near the front door.

Simon cleared some notebooks, gel pens and a balled-up pair of socks off a chair.

'Sorry,' said Naveen when he arrived with the tea. 'Lexie's only here every second weekend but I think her possessions breed while she's away. Although I can't talk – the socks are mine.'

He un-balled them; they were bright orange with a pattern of tiny yellow ducks in sunglasses.

Simon had both kinds of socks in his wardrobe: black and grey. He felt sad for Naveen. He considered novelty socks, and ties also, were the way that people with no actual personality overcompensated.

'At least you won't lose your feet in the dark,' he said.

'Lexie bought them for me.' Naveen ran a hand through his hair. 'She thinks my clothes are boring and I'll never get a date if I don't show a bit more spark. She bought me a pair with little hamburgers on them, and a pair covered in stormtroopers. I don't think women find that kind of thing attractive. Do you think women find that kind of thing attractive?'

Simon tried to imagine his serious, sensible Mia at Lexie's age, talking with him about his love-life. He tried to imagine only seeing her every two weeks. Both thoughts made him vaguely queasy.

'Lexie's worried about you,' Simon said. 'That's sweet.'

'Who thinks about their dad dating, at thirteen?' Naveen said. 'Besides, I don't think I'm ready to date. I'm terrified, to tell you the truth. Single women are terrifying. They're all so successful and confident and competent. I'm a single dad who owns a chicken shop. My daughter buys my socks.'

Simon had no idea how to respond to that.

'I mean, what do they want? How am I supposed to behave? How do you even meet them? On an app? And what should I wear? I don't have the headspace to think about outfits. I wish I could just throw clothes on and look reasonable. Like Nick does. How does he look so good all the time?'

Simon knew exactly what Naveen meant. Looking good was Nick's superpower. It was illogical, indecipherable. Simon could put on a shirt, say, or a sweater, and look like a spherical colourblind hobbit. Nick in the exact same shirt or sweater would look like a model. A *French* model. Who owns a vineyard and, in his spare time, pilots his own plane.

'You're either born with it or you're not,' said Simon.

'You got that right. Now that we're seeing more of him – oh,' Naveen said, at Simon's expression, 'you didn't know. He's coaching Lexie's soccer team, which is such a relief. I did it last year and it meant I had to pay someone an extra shift to cover for me at the shop. Which I did not need. Nick is a godsend. He's just started.'

'God, how much does that cost you?'

'Oh. Ha. Nothing. He volunteered.'

'Volunteered? To do something he didn't have to do? Nick? My brother-in-law Nick?'

Naveen sipped his tea and shrugged. 'Since he quit footy he's missed the team dynamic,' he said. 'The girls are beside themselves, the mums even more so. Mate, his clothes. Lexie knows all the brands. She loves fashion. At least she's interested in something, right? If only she paid that much attention at school. She knows all the Insta-influencers, she reads all the blogs about the right stuff to wear. I wouldn't have even known what an influencer was when I was thirteen.'

Simon refrained from saying that he still didn't.

Naveen made a face. 'The other day, Lexie asked me if I was using protection. She's just a kid! I dropped my coffee all over the floor.'

'I'm sure you set her mind at rest.'

'Considering I haven't slept with a woman since the divorce – yes, I did,' said Naveen. 'Perhaps I should ask Tansy to have a word with her. About boundaries, et cetera.'

So Naveen was thinking of delegating an important conversation with his own teenage daughter because he was uncomfortable with the personal direction it would take?

He wanted to palm off this crucial, intimate discussion with his child to Tansy because he found it too embarrassing?

That was a truly excellent solution, Simon thought.

'I'd do the same thing in your shoes,' he said to Naveen. 'I'm sure Tansy would be delighted to help.'

———

In the backyard, there was lots to do. Simon needed to scrub the old pavers with sugar soap and then scuff up the glaze with the orbital sander so the new pavers would adhere – whenever they finally arrived. This would work fine because the original pavers were sound. They weren't cracked or lifting or warping. Naveen didn't like the colour, that was all. He was covering up perfectly acceptable pavers and spending a fortune, all because the colour was a little bit . . . blah. He was also digging up a serviceable if sparse lawn and replacing it with new turf, and replanting the borders with fresh shrubs.

There was nothing wrong with any part of the backyard – in fact, it was better than the yard in Simon and Tansy's old house. The plants he was replacing weren't thriving or trendy, but they were fine.

It's all right for some, thought Simon, *paying for a new backyard*. He had long ago reached a stage in his life where he thought menial labour was behind him, yet here he was. He hadn't put himself through uni to dig up grass! After all these years, his life had boiled down to this. He wiped his face on the back of his sleeve.

As the afternoon progressed, Naveen went to work and Simon – well, he also worked. He laboured for a while, but planning was work too. Thinking, that was work. He might have made another tea, or two. This kind of drudge was just so demoralising compared with owning a business. Over the course of the afternoon, though, he began to feel better. His joints started out stiff, then eased. The creaks and groans began to diminish. Today's headache had also lifted. He no longer felt like his eyebrows were pulsating in time with his heartbeat. He could relax. There was no rush. He had the entire week.

And, good news! He received a text that the delayed pavers had arrived in the warehouse and would be delivered tomorrow.

And he felt more positive about their unexpected visitor. After all, Kylie was single and lived by herself in a two-bedroom semi-detached house. A whole house, for one person! Surely Monica could move in with her for a few days. Or rather, surely Monica could put up with Kylie for a few days without wanting to kill her. And while Nick did have a flatmate – Russell – that was easily fixed. Russell spent most of his waking hours at his parents' house anyway. Russell's parents adored him. He worked in their fruit and veggie wholesalers and all of his brothers and sisters still lived at home but, in a uncharacteristic fit of independence caused by listening to too much Katy Perry, Russell had moved into Nick's spare room only to regret it as soon as he was faced with a full laundry basket and an empty fridge. Moving back in with his parents for five days as opposed to only dropping in for meals and clean clothes would be no hardship for Russell. And if worst came to worst, there was always Gloria. She lived by herself in an *enormous* house, their original family home. She wouldn't even notice if . . .

Gloria. His mother-in-law.

Okay, Simon thought. *Possibly that was a little bit unlikely.*

He tried to imagine himself in Gloria's shoes. Thirty years ago, she had been happily married to David and comfortably off, with a big house in the suburbs. She was a full-time mother to Kylie, Tansy and Nick – then eleven, eight and six – and very involved at their schools. She played tennis several times a week; she took the kids to swimming lessons and cooked those elaborate nineties dinner parties that seemed like an Olympic event. Then, out of the blue, David comes home one day and announces that he's fallen in love with another woman and he's moving to Sydney to be with her. He packs and moves out then and there. David keeps paying the kids' school fees and maintenance and sends them Christmas and birthday presents, but after the divorce goes through, the kids see him only a handful of times over the next three decades.

Fast forward three decades to the first lockdown. Simon arrived home from the supermarket one day to find Gloria's car parked on the street outside their house.

Simon should have anticipated Gloria being at his house. He should have seen the black clouds circling from miles away, the violent stabs of lightning bracketing her convertible as it drove. He should have felt the drop in temperature, seen the small birds falling dead on the wing – he should have noticed his mother-in-law was on the move, like the edgy calm of an approaching cyclone.

But he hadn't noticed. He was surprised when he pulled up and saw her stalking up and down on the footpath. He was astonished to see her wearing a leisure suit. Designer, but still. Her cloak made from the skin of Dalmatian puppies must have been at the cleaners.

Simon opened the car door and stepped out.

'I don't know what you're saying, Mum,' Tansy shouted from the front steps, observing the distance rule.

Gloria was yelling and waving a sheet of paper. Tansy was in the front yard with the kids. This was back when they had a yard, when they still lived in their old house, and he was still holding on to his architectural practice. Barely, but holding on. Mia was still enrolled at her old school, and he still thought there was a chance they could afford for Lachie to follow her.

'This is ridiculous,' Gloria shouted as Simon got out of the car. 'I'm coming in. These are extraordinary circumstances.'

Gloria was a difficult woman to maintain eye contact with. Even from this distance, her gaze felt like Simon had a red dot on his forehead and any moment now, his head would explode.

'No, Nana!' yelled Mia. 'You're not allowed. It could be very dangerous!' She was holding Lachie around the waist to stop him running to Gloria.

'This is not the kind of news that should be yelled across the front yard,' said Gloria. 'I need to hold my daughter.'

Simon walked over to where they were standing and swung Lachie up onto his hip. Tansy was pale, he could see. He didn't know how long Gloria had been there but it seemed that they were at the beginning of something.

His thoughts went first to Gloria herself. Was she ill? Perhaps test results had arrived in the mail and she had some terrible cancer and OH MY GOD she would have to move in with them while she underwent treatment. He loved his wife. He would do anything for his wife, but please, *please* not that.

But Gloria didn't look sick. She looked like a steaming, bubbling volcano of human output, like she always did. Could it be Nick? Or Kylie?

'Just tell us,' he said.

Chapter 7

So she did. Gloria told them, across a two-metre space of air, that Tansy's father, David, had died.

Gloria had received a handwritten letter from someone who identified himself as David's 'best friend'. It was sudden, the letter said. David hadn't suffered. Because of the restrictions on funerals, he had been buried quietly in country Victoria where he had lived on a farm, with only a few friends and his *wife* and *daughter* in attendance. The news of his death would obviously come as a shock, the letter said. The family was aware there were many people who were unable to pay their respects due to the unusual circumstances. But when everything was back to normal, they would organise a proper memorial service in Melbourne so all of his friends and colleagues and extended family could attend.

Simon had met Tansy's father a handful of times. Simon remembered him sitting in the back of the church at their wedding while Gloria walked Tansy down the aisle. Simon couldn't remember him at the reception. He had met Mia and Lachie only a few times, although he sent them Christmas and birthday presents. David was tall, he remembered that. Fit-looking. He jogged. Bald, but wore it well. (Simon was envious of men with good-shaped skulls. He knew that if his hair fell out in the years to come, he would look like a kohlrabi with ears.) He hadn't thought of David in years.

He looked at Tansy. Her eyes were shining. Her arms had dropped loose to her sides, as though her shoulders no longer functioned, as though the tendons that controlled them had been cut.

'Mum, who's David?' Mia said. She took Tansy's hand with both of hers, and held it, despite Tansy's hand drooping, unresponsive.

'Your poppy, pumpkin,' said Tansy. 'He sent you that book about cats, for your birthday.'

'It's very sad, being dead,' said Mia. 'You go away for ever and ever. At school, the fish in the library were floating on the top and their eyes were like . . .' She goggled her eyeballs wide and cupped her hands around them.

Tansy still hadn't moved. Simon set Lachie back on the ground and took Tansy in his arms. She folded there, unresisting.

'I'm sorry,' he whispered into her hair.

Gloria was quiet, there on his footpath, and this in itself was some kind of miracle. The arm that held the letter had dropped to her side. When she was still, it was easier to remember that she was a woman in her mid-sixties who lived by herself, and that she hadn't been allowed to hug her children or her grand-children for weeks. It can't have been easy.

'There's nothing we can do,' said Gloria. 'We can't even hold our own ceremony at home, as a family. We have to wait for the memorial service and god only knows when that will be.'

Tansy roused herself then, and peeled her face away from his chest. 'Mum,' she said. 'We haven't seen Dad in years. We didn't even know he was married again, much less had a kid. And I don't want to bring this up, but you hated him. It's very sad, of course, but are you sure you even *want* to go to his memorial?'

'I was married to that man for twelve years and am the mother of his children. I didn't get to go to his funeral,' said Gloria in a soft voice. 'Of course I want to go to the memorial service.'

Simon knew that memories often become distorted, especially during such fraught times as lockdowns, but he was convinced he remembered this conversation exactly as it happened. Every word buried itself in his long-term memory, never to be forgotten, because he couldn't recall ever having been so shocked. Who was this strange leisure-suit-clad woman on his footpath, and what had she done with his mother-in-law? Perhaps he'd misjudged her. She'd obviously been deeply hurt by her divorce. Devastated, even. Tansy had told him stories about Gloria in the weeks and months after David left – frightening snippets of episodes of drinking and bouts of sobbing and recreational drugs and Gloria cutting her own hair with kitchen scissors in a rage – that were terribly uncomfortable to hear. Simon always tried to change the subject whenever Tansy brought it up, because it must be even more uncomfortable for her to talk about.

But, Simon thought, *look at Gloria now*. He'd been vaguely terrified of her since he first started dating Tansy, but all at once, Gloria didn't seem so scary. She still remembered how much she'd loved David long ago. She'd softened over the decades and gained the wisdom and perspective of life. The vulnerability and grief she was showing now was a side of Gloria he hadn't even imagined. She wanted to stand beside David's grave and farewell him, and pay tribute to their younger days when they meant the world to each other. Simon was moved.

Momentarily.

'I will not be deprived of this,' Gloria said. 'Do you know how often I've dreamed of that man in a shallow grave?

'Mum,' said Tansy.

'Or maybe he was cremated. Even better. I would have given a thousand dollars to light that match.'

'Rise above it, Gloria,' Simon said. 'It's all water under the bridge.'

Gloria looked at him, two laser beams extending from her eyes and melting the flesh from the bones of his face.

'Water under the bridge?' she said, smiling like a Bond villain. Then she stomped right up to the fence, crushing the already half-dead lavenders underfoot. 'WATER UNDER THE BRIDGE?'

From the corner of his eye, Simon saw Mrs Hopkins from next door twitch her curtains. Gloria saw it also and, true to form, considered it a provocation. He knew what she was thinking. *Oh, am I too loud for you? Am I disturbing your precious peace and quiet? That. Was. Nothing.* She prowled up and down the footpath in front of the house, shouting to the ground then at the sky, as though every molecule of air needed to be informed of the injustice of it all.

'And did you see what they called us, in this letter? Extended family! That's what it says!' Gloria said, and she screwed up the paper in her hand. 'Tansy, Kylie, Nick and me – we are not *extended*. Oh no. We are *immediate*. We will host this memorial service, whenever it happens. This wife and daughter – whoever the fuck *they* are – they are *extended*.'

'Now you have to put a dollar in the swear jar, Nana,' said Mia. 'And Daddy's here, which is bad. When he's at work, we're not supposed to tell him that you swore in front of us.'

'What?' said Simon.

'And we have to change the swear word to an animal for Lachie because otherwise he'll get expelled from kinder and it will go on his permanent record.' Mia squatted down beside him. 'Lachie, what does Nana say?'

'Nana says, "What. The. Fox",' said Lachie.

'Good job!' Mia high-fived him.

'And besides, what kind of seventy-year-old has a *best friend*?' Gloria continued.

'I have a best friend,' said Mia, looking up. 'Her name's Daisy.'

'You're allowed to be infantile, you're practically an infant,' said Gloria. 'They are grown men. It sounds very gay to me.'

'Mum,' said Tansy.

'What? Don't give me that face. I don't mean lovely modern gay, like Ottolenghi-gay. Linen and baking and adorable dogs and/or children. I mean old-fashioned, *repressed* gay. KingGee shorts, steel-rimmed Aviators, moustaches that look like little brooms.' Gloria clutched at the few remaining lavender spikes that were still in flower and mangled them beyond recognition. 'Honestly, that would explain a lot. Let me tell you, the bedroom skills of that man left much to be desired. Over the entirety of our marriage, I could count the number of orgasms I had on one hand.'

Simon cleared his throat.

'Half the time I had to begin without him,' Gloria continued. 'I had to have a head start if I was ever going to get anywhere. Like a handicapped race, but in reverse. It's a miracle I had any children at all. Once—'

'Who knows when we'll be allowed out again?' Simon blurted, as fast as he could. 'They might have forgotten all about this memorial service by then. It might never happen.'

'Oh, it'll happen,' Gloria said. 'Mark my words. I will not be deprived of this. I will be there. We will *all* be there! My successful, handsome children and my adorable, perfectly behaved grandchildren. And you too, Simon. It's important you're there. Because you can drive us. We – David's *immediate* family – will host the most elegant, charming and tasteful memorial service ever conceived.'

'If that's what you want, Mum,' said Tansy.

'And I'll tell you something else,' Gloria continued. 'I will look *fantastic*. If I have to never so much as look at a carb again, I will walk into that memorial and everyone will think, *You idiot, David Schnabel. You stupid, dead, bald idiot.*'

Gloria had left not long after that to tell Nick about David's death. He was a sensitive boy, Gloria explained, bound to be upset. He was the kind of person who felt bad for strangers. Losing a parent could be unmooring, even as an adult. It was important that she broke it to him in person. She might pick up a few bits and pieces for him – or perhaps make a casserole. It wasn't every day a boy lost his father.

As for Kylie . . . Gloria had shrugged. David wasn't a young man. People die every day. Gloria couldn't be expected to go all the way to Kylie's work – and besides, pharmacies freaked her out. They're always full of sick people! Kylie was a grown woman, and a health professional besides. *Suck it up, buttercup.* Gloria would phone her later in the afternoon, if she found the time.

'Some people coddle their grown children,' Gloria called out as she got back in her car. 'I've never understood it.'

—

Simon didn't believe in psychics, but in the first few years after meeting Gloria, he did wonder. She showed remarkable accuracy about future events, it couldn't be denied. Now he thought that her gift wasn't prognostication; it was command. The very universe itself was nervous about going against her wishes.

Sure enough, almost two years later, the week of the memorial service had arrived. Gloria had organised it by email with David's 'best friend', Noah. It was to be an elegant, tasteful event in Naveen's newly renovated backyard. Neither Simon nor Tansy had the energy or courage to suggest that perhaps the whole thing was a mistake.

At least David's widow wouldn't be attending. Gloria was disappointed – she'd wanted a clear-cut comparison so she could be declared the winning wife, as though the funeral was a *MasterChef* finale and the mourners would be holding up scorecards. But the Widow Schnabel had found the first funeral draining and emotional, and felt that 'one service per husband was plenty' and also she didn't like the city and, besides, she had a dodgy hip. This, in Simon's view, would diminish, though not eliminate, the possibility of a hideous scene. David's daughter Monica would be there though, and was planning on arriving in Melbourne on the Monday beforehand, on the first train from Traralgon.

Now said Monica was here, in their flat, and he had to admit that it was unlikely Gloria would put her up in her spare room.

Still, Simon thought, *it wouldn't hurt to ask.*

Chapter 8

For the whole of Simon's drive home, he thought about beer. As he pulled out of Naveen's driveway, he thought about pale ales and bitters, and as he merged onto Punt Road, he thought about IPAs and pilsners. He could almost see that rich colour like liquid gold or that lighter, softer amber like threshed wheat from a sheath held by a toga-clad Greek maiden. He thought about a head of white foam not too tall, but not too flat either, and he thought about his own father pouring a glass from a longneck after work and the way he'd taught him to tilt the glass just so when he was far too young to drink or to associate beer with anything so weighty as the very essence of being a working man. He thought about that bitter fizzy crispness that made every cell in his mouth feel alive. And the smell! Beer smelled like the way Simon felt the first morning he woke up with Tansy lying beside him.

Simon was thinking about beer because it was a Monday night, and Monday and Tuesday were beer nights. This was a strict rule he'd put in place for himself. Wednesdays to Saturdays, he moved up to wine, because the week invariably required tools of a higher calibre as it progressed, as though he were a hunter and Mondays were quail but Fridays were wildebeest. Sundays were his alcohol-free night.

Except, of course, if Kylie came over for dinner. Then a beer night could be moved up to a wine night, and a wine night could become a whiskey night. But not a *neat* whiskey night. A whiskey with soda night. Whiskey neat was reserved for celebrations and medically diagnosed shock, and there hadn't been many of either of those in the Larsen household for quite some time. If Nick came over, upgrading from beer to wine or wine to whiskey and soda was optional, though lately it had happened more than not. And of course if Gloria came over, or all of Tansy's family came, he reached straight for the whiskey, even on a Sunday. Dinner with the Schnabels. It could be the title of a horror movie.

The secret to responsible alcohol consumption, Simon knew, was absolutely firm limits.

He thought about this as he arrived home, turned his key in the lock and opened the door. He could hear voices inside.

'And that's why if you jump off a roof, you should put down *two* mattresses,' Monica said.

His children were sitting on the couch, one on either side of Monica, looking at her with rapt attention. When they saw him, they scrambled up and rushed for the door, calling out 'Daddy' and each grabbing a leg. He dropped to his knees and hugged and kissed them both. And then Tansy lifted her head from where she stood in the kitchen and blew him a kiss, and she was wearing the blue velour hoodie which she didn't overly like but which he loved because the pile was soft, like the fur of a small blue dog.

This was what Simon lived for. It didn't matter that his wife's half-sister had been sprung upon him – when his children greeted him like that, and his beautiful wife was happy with him, nothing else mattered. All was right with the world.

'Nick and Kylie will be here soon,' Tansy said. 'We're having spag bol from the freezer.'

'Mum,' said Lachie. 'I'm starving.'

'And the fridge is making a funny noise,' said Tansy. 'And could you get the kids a piece of cheese? I've been flat out.'

'In a minute.' Simon kissed Tansy and said hello to Monica.

'How about now?' Tansy said. 'I've got my hands full.'

'Sure,' he said, and he took his stubby into the poky bathroom and drank it in the shower, which was really a rose positioned so low that he had to bend his knees to wash his hair, over a pink bath with an Ikea shower curtain. He waited while the cold beer and the hot water worked their magic.

When he came out, Tansy was finishing a green salad. The kids were sitting next to Monica on the couch again.

'And that's why you shouldn't eat yellow Lego,' said Monica.

'That's amazing,' said Mia. 'I can't wait to tell Daisy.'

'What Monica means—' said Simon.

'Her name is Auntie Mon,' said Mia. 'Look at her pretty shoes.'

'Yes, they're very nice,' Simon said, but then he saw that Monica was wearing an entirely different outfit from this morning: faded blue jeans, a white singlet with some logo, and sneakers made of a patchwork of different colours and textures of suedes and leathers, like they'd been sewn together by a colourblind person, in the dark. Her eye makeup had changed also and was now dark and smoky, as though she was an alien assassin from a movie, and she wore huge hoop earrings. 'What Auntie Mon means is that you shouldn't eat *any* Lego,' he said.

'But if you're thinking about eating some,' Monica said, 'the yellow ones are the worst.'

'But don't think about it,' said Simon.

'Hello?' said Mon. 'Are you sure you want your children to eat things without *thinking* about it?'

Tansy came out of the kitchen and began arranging stools and cushions. 'Mon's been such a help,' she said to Simon. 'She's had the kids spellbound.'

He imagined his children soaring from the roof and landing in a narrow strip between two mattresses, a stream of Lego of every colour except yellow exploding from their mouths. He went to the fridge for another beer.

'Dad,' said Lachie, trailing after him. 'Dad, Dad, Dad, guess what? I get to sleep with Mia tonight.'

'I know, buddy,' said Simon. 'It won't be for long.'

'Mum said we could. We're going to both be in Mia's bed! It's going to be just like a sleepover and she's going to read me a story. But no giggling, Mum says. Because it's a school night.'

Lachie could barely keep his feet still, and he was wringing his hands.

Brave little tyke, thought Simon. *What a soldier.*

'There are conditions,' said Mia.

Lachie held out a piece of paper. Written in Mia's deliberate hand was a list in purple pencil:

no kicking
no using my pillow
no pinching
no unnecessary farting
ABSOLUTELY NO touching
my piggy bank or my skissors or my Frozen suitcase.

At the bottom of the page was a complicated squiggle which could have been anything, but was apparently Lachie's signature.

Skissors, hey? Still, she was miles better at spelling than he was at her age.

'Did Mummy help you with this?' said Simon. 'It's pretty great.'

Mia shook her head. 'I'm not seven anymore,' she said, with her hands on her hips. 'I can draw up a basic contract.'

At school events or Mia's playdates, Simon looked at other eight-year-olds and their parents with smug generosity. Look at the way they played games on their iPads, or watched television, or wheeled their dolls in miniature strollers. Bless!

Childhood was not a competition, he knew that. But if *were* a competition, there was no question who would win. Mia did little other than write and draw; she filled pages with notes and had what seemed like hundreds of pens in a multitude of colours, and topped every subject and seemed to spend hours on her homework. At first, he was concerned. Surely children in Year 3 shouldn't have so much homework? He'd almost resolved to discuss it with her teacher, but Tansy seemed unperturbed. Besides, what kind of a complaint was that? *My child loves doing hours and hours of homework?* Simon sometimes wondered what he and Tansy had done so right to deserve Mia. Lachie was adorable, but he could be a terror. When he was toddling, he drew on the walls with crayon and loved nothing more than opening the fridge door whenever their backs were turned in order to smash eggs. With Mia, it seemed their only responsibility was feeding, clothing and washing her, as though she had made a decision in utero to do the rest of the bringing-up herself. Simon imagined her sitting at the miniature table in her room where she spent hours, pencil gripped in her fist, tongue between her teeth.

'Mate, you should never sign something without having a lawyer look at it,' Simon said to Lachie.

'Auntie Mon is my lawyer,' said Lachie.

'The conditions are quite clear,' said Monica. 'My client understands his legal obligations and has waived his rights, habeas corpus, ipso facto.'

'Did you chat to Naveen?' Tansy said. 'What was he so upset about?'

'Still totally happy to sort him,' said Monica, blowing on her nails.

'He's fine now,' Simon said. 'I don't want him to feel self-conscious about it – everyone has bad days. Best not to mention it.'

Tansy nodded. 'If you say so. The kids and me and Nick will sit up here,' Tansy said, setting plates and napkins along the kitchen divider. 'And you and Kylie and Monica can sit on the couch.'

'Kylie and Nick?' he said. 'They're coming? Tonight?'

'Mum already told you that,' said Mia.

Kids and their vivid imaginations! He would certainly have remembered that both his sibling-in-laws, as well as his half-sibling-in-law, were going to be here for dinner, because that was something that was impossible to forget. He sighed and felt his muscles sagging on his bones but after a moment, he steeled himself and tousled Mia's hair, wistfully, wishing for a quiet dinner with just the four of them. Mia looked up at him, excitement in her eyes. Seeing her aunts and uncle was thrilling at her age, he supposed. He strained his ears towards the front door. The silence sounded menacing, its timbre unmistakably ominous.

Chapter 9

There was a chilling knock at the door and when he opened it, there they were: Kylie and Nick.

'Yay,' said his children, jumping on the spot.

Monica stood and wiped her palms down the front of her jeans; she seemed nervous, which made Simon's heart squeeze for her. *Of course* it was good for Mia and Lachie to have a half-aunt staying with them, and aunts and uncles dropping in all the time. He resolved to be more patient and make more of an effort to see things from Monica's perspective. Kylie looked stiff and high-shouldered in navy, and Nick wore designer jeans designed to look shabby.

'Oh my god, hi!' Monica leaned in and – unbelievably, to Simon – wrapped her arms around Kylie's shoulders.

'Oh boy,' said Nick. 'That's brave.'

'Oh, so we're hugging,' said Kylie. 'That is a thing we're doing.'

She wore an expression that reminded Simon of a documentary he'd seen about exposure therapy, in which a woman was forced to stand still while a tarantula crawled between her clavicles. Then she patted Monica twice on the back with one hand.

'Of course!' said Mon. 'We're sisters.'

'Half, but who's counting?' said Kylie.

'You don't look so scary close-up,' said Mon. 'I don't know what Dad was on about. And such a cool name. I've never known an actual Kylie before. It must have been very popular, back in the day. Like Kylie Minogue.'

'"Back in the day?"' said Kylie. 'Kylie Minogue is much older than me. *Much.*'

From her severe dark hair to the tips of her polished black boots, Kylie was taller than both Tansy and Monica, and thinner. There was a slender gap between her two front teeth, the kind of space that would make a different woman look vulnerable but made Kylie look as if she'd been in a bar fight. Kylie was pressed and pleated and starched. If your life depended on a prescription, accurately filled, you were in the right hands.

'Don't I get a hug?' said Nick when Monica released Kylie.

'Of course, man,' said Monica as she complied. 'The famous Nick! Wow, you're really tall.'

'You're so young,' said Kylie. 'I mean, you're really young. How young are you, exactly?'

Mon said she was twenty-six.

'You look much younger than that.'

'You're sweet. It's the shaved head,' said Monica. 'I looked way older when I had my dreads. I loved them. Mum hated them. In the end, it was the smell, you know? Like a dead possum sitting on your shoulder. So I shaved them. Anyway, twenties is old in East Gippsland. Or it's young. The whole place is filled with people under fifteen or over sixty-five. I'm in a class of my own.'

'Twenty-six! The old boy was quite a dog, wasn't he?' said Nick. He smiled his thousand-watt smile, the one that had seen him considered for *The Bachelor*. 'Which bodes well for me in the decades ahead.' Nick bent down and picked up Lachie, who was pulling at his jacket. 'How was school, little buddy?'

'I still can't read,' said Lachie. 'It's not fair.'

'He says that every day. I tell him he has to be more patient,' said Mia, rolling her eyes.

'How about you, Miss Brainiac?' said Nick.

'Good. I've decided that I'm going to be an astronaut when I grow up. Or else a magician,' said Mia.

'Simon, mate,' said Nick. 'What is growing on your face? Is it deliberate, or have you been shipwrecked on a tropical island with no one to talk to except a basketball?'

'See, it isn't just me,' said Tansy. 'It really is getting out of control, Simon. The neck, especially.'

'I love Daddy's beard,' said Mia. 'It's soft, like a kitten.'

'Thank you, Mia,' said Simon. 'Someone in this family has good taste.'

'And what do you do, Monica?' said Kylie.

'I have what is called a portfolio career,' Monica said.

Kylie narrowed her eyes.

Simon thought of his recent resolution to be more generous in spirit to Monica. Now would be the perfect time to intervene and change the subject, because Kylie had that look. Only one thing was distracting him: over Kylie's shoulder was a massive leather bag that even Simon could tell was expensive, and as he lingered at her side like a puppy waiting for a Schmacko, she extracted from it two bottles of red wine, the labels of which were covered in gold medals. He took them and audibly sighed.

'What does that mean exactly? A portfolio career?' Kylie said.

'I have a few things on the go.'

'Right. And what are they?'

'Oh, you know.' Monica rolled her eyes as if she was vaguely hopeless and she couldn't even recall her line of own work.

'I see,' said Kylie, in a way that made clear that in respect to this topic, she did not. 'And do you have a partner?'

'Me?' said Monica. 'No. No no no no. Only Keith.'

'Keith?' Kylie folded her arms.

'He's not my boyfriend, as such. We've been hooking up since I split up with Tracey. I'm pansexual, obviously.'

'Obviously,' said Nick.

Monica continued. 'But it isn't serious. I guess I always imagined having the kind of relationship where you finish each other's –'

Simon nodded, thinking of Tansy.

'– chips,' said Monica. 'But Keith covers his in barbecue sauce. Deal-breaker.'

Just then, Tansy came out of the kitchen and hugged Kylie and Nick.

'Jeez, Tans,' said Nick. 'I love what you've done with the place.'

'We're *renting?*' said Mia. 'It's *temporary?*'

The grown-ups all laughed and looked away.

'You know what they say. Less is more,' said Tansy, kissing Mia on the head.

'I once dated a man who used to say less is more,' said Kylie. 'He had the smallest penis I've ever seen in my life.'

Simon had nothing against sex. Of course he didn't. He had absolutely nothing to be embarrassed about in that area. Before he met Tansy, he was quite the *dog* himself. He'd kissed a lot of girls in his single years. Lots. His success rate with actually getting them into bed wasn't *quite* ideal, but the way Tansy and he had thrilled each other from the beginning was proof that he was simply a late bloomer. And yes, perhaps things had slowed down in the bedroom department lately, but that's because of the rapid alteration in their circumstances. What if Lachie was unsettled in the dining room during the night and needed them? Also, this apartment was a rubbish build. The wall between their bedroom and Mia's was like paper. Tansy didn't notice these things; she wasn't an architect. But Simon noticed. What if Mia heard them? What kind of long-term trauma could that cause her? But mostly he was trying to be respectful of Tansy: her new job as a leasing agent was exhausting, with long hours. It was his duty not to pressure her. Even when she instigated things, even when she seemed quite keen ... it was a sacrifice he was prepared to make.

What he would never understand was how Tansy's family seemed to think that sex, in all its technicolour detail, was an appropriate topic for casual conversation, in front of strangers or children or anyone. Simon's parents, two hardworking dentists from Canberra who were astonished and a little bemused by his late arrival, believed that talking about politics, religion, money and sex was distasteful. Meeting Tansy's family was like arriving in one of those cultures where it's seen as the height of good manners to burp at the table. Halfway through his and Tansy's wedding reception, Gloria had turned to Simon's mother and casually said, 'Lucky you, being married. I haven't been laid since November.' Simon thought he'd have to carry his mother out on a stretcher.

'Seen Mum lately?' said Nick.

'I went around on Saturday arvo, to help her with the garden,' said Tansy. 'It's becoming too much for her.'

'Nothing is too much for her,' Kylie said. 'She's just bored with it. She's playing you.'

'Was she in a good mood?' said Nick. 'For her, I mean.'

'Please don't tell me you want to hit her up for another loan,' said Kylie. 'I think you'll find the bank of Mum is closed.'

'You could help her a bit more, Nick, on the odd occasion,' said Tansy. 'It wouldn't kill you.'

'All right, I'm just asking. Simon, mate,' said Nick. 'I'm outnumbered by women here. Give me a hand, will you?'

'Let's eat,' said Simon. 'The kids are starving.'

'If only someone had given them a piece of cheese earlier,' said Tansy.

Simon poured wine and Tansy served from one end of the coffee table. The conversation was slow at the beginning but, despite everyone's very different styles – Tansy, loving if sometimes incomprehensible; Kylie, sharp and to the point; Nick, charming and a little shallow; Monica, kooky and unpredictable – after a while, things started to flow, mainly due to Kylie's insistent questions. They learned about Monica's mother, Jackie, who had met David at a wedding between David's former assistant and Jackie's nephew on one of her rare trips to the city. This was many years after he left Gloria. (The grand romance that spurred the separation hadn't lasted six weeks, according to Monica.) Jackie had thought David unbearable at first: a typical suit, in some blindingly boring job in a heartless multinational corporation. Corner office, Qantas Club, blue ties – all the things she despised, but he had won her over. Jackie still lived on their hobby farm and bred rare pigs and grew vegetables and had a house cow and chickens, like she was Amish.

'Mum would never eat a battery egg, not in a million years,' Monica said.

Simon opened his mouth to suggest, gently, that that was an utterly privileged comment, that not everyone had the ability to keep chickens and for some families the dollars between the cost of battery eggs and free-range fancy-schmancy eggs made a substantial difference to their weekly budget; and that while he was of course a supporter of improving animal welfare, and while *of course* he tried to teach his children kindness above everything else – especially towards those who couldn't protect themselves, like chickens – not everyone lived in an Agrarian paradise and some of us lived in the real world and that kind of food fascism was unlikely to inspire anyone to make more humane choices. Instead he poured himself another glass of wine. A big glass.

'Simon. Is that your third?' Tansy raised her eyebrows, and he knew what that meant.

'And what kind of a father was David?' said Kylie. 'I'm curious, that's all. Because he wasn't much of one to us.'

Chapter 10

A silence descended but Monica didn't seem to notice. She kept eating as though she was in a restaurant or among friends, as though this question wasn't at the heart of everything that mattered to Tansy and her siblings. She sat there as though she was one of them. She wasn't one of them. That was obvious in the way she ate: she twirled a monstrous tornado of spaghetti around her fork and unhinged her jaw like a boa constrictor to hoover it in. Kylie, Tansy and Nick used a knife to cut around the outline of the pasta, severing any dangling strands, before eating.

'I wouldn't know,' she said. 'I've got nothing to compare him to.'

Simon felt all his good intentions towards Monica melt away. She was the child that David stayed for and she was sitting there, among the children that he left, nonchalantly eating spaghetti. Simon imagined that Kylie and Tansy and Nick had thought of that question a hundred times since they learned of her existence: *What was it about us that made him leave, and what was it about you that made him stay?*

'We're curious, that's all,' said Nick.

'Dad was always busy with work. Travelled a lot. A real high-flyer. When do you think I'll get to meet Gloria? Dad talked about her all the time.'

Gloriá. Nick looked down as though he had never seen spaghetti before and could not figure out what these long white worms were on his plate. Tansy spat on her serviette and leaned across to became entirely focused on wiping around Lachie's mouth; he squeezed his eyes and lips closed and resolutely offered up his face. Simon took another gulp of wine.

Kylie looked at Monica as though she were some unknown drug to be dispensed and the description on the box didn't match the appearance of the tablet.

'And you work on the farm too?' said Kylie.

'I chip in a little,' said Mon. 'I'm not great, but. Chickens and me, we don't see eye to eye. Mum has this gift with animals. Keith helps a bit.'

'And you've stayed in East Gippsland all this time?' Kylie said. 'You didn't come to Melbourne for uni, or anything?'

'Uni!' Mon looked down at her plate. 'Dad was on me to finish Year 12, and I barely managed it. Good on him, but honestly. I could never live up to you three. You got all the brains. It used to drive him nuts.' She bit her bottom lip. 'I'm a bit thick.'

The father in Simon raised his head. No young person should think that about herself. Whoever had made her feel that way – they had some explaining to do.

Tansy cleared her throat. 'School isn't everything,' she said.

'Absolutely,' said Simon.

Mon shrugged. 'It's okay. You know what they say: the early sperm is the good sperm.'

'I have never heard anyone say that about sperm in my life,' said Kylie.

'Sperm,' said Lachie. 'Sperm sperm sperm.'

'It's a kind of whale, sweetheart,' Tansy said to him, while twirling her fork in her spaghetti. 'Humpback, blue, killer, sperm.'

'Spermy spermy sperm!' said Lachie. 'Blue killer sperm, attack!'

Simon topped up his glass.

—

Some nights, getting Lachie to sleep was a kind of nightmare, but after Kylie and Nick left, Lachie crawled into Mia's bed without the usual drama of glasses of water and checking under the bed. Simon went to tuck them both in.

'Dad, Dad, Dad, guess who's in Mia's bed?' Lachie had called out. 'Me!'

Mia positioned Lachie against the wall – so you don't fall out, she said. She looked so serious and responsible, and Lachie so awed that Simon could have wept.

'Are you going to read to us?' said Lachie.

'Not tonight, buddy,' said Simon.

'A joke? Just one? Please?' he said, with the covers pulled up to his cheeks.

'Okay, ready? Because this is an excellent one, so you'd better be ready,' Simon said.

Lachie nodded. Mia shrugged.

'How many tickles does it take to make an octopus laugh?' He paused while they shook their heads. 'Ten tickles!'

He kissed both their foreheads and wished them goodnight, then left them to their groaning. Out in the dining room, Tansy had made Monica as comfortable as possible in Lachie's bed, between his Buzz Lightyear sheets, her head on her enormous pillow and her feet sticking out the end. When he and Tansy finally fell into their own bed, it was past eleven – which wasn't very late just last week, because he usually napped on the couch after he got the kids off to school. But now that he had to start working in Naveen's garden at seven, it seemed like stoner hours. He held Tansy in his arms, as he always did before they slept, and as usual he marvelled that someone with skin that felt like hers, who smelled like her, with hair as soft as hers, was lying beside him.

'How long is Monica staying?' he said.

'It didn't come up,' said Tansy. Then she leaned forward and kissed his neck. 'Let's not talk about Monica right now.' Then she burrowed her hand under his pyjama top and walked her fingers across his chest.

He wiggled one arm under her and rubbed her back in a way that he hoped would seem companionable – but not too companionable. Then he shifted her around until her back was pressed up against him so he could spoon her from behind, and he kissed the back of her head.

Tansy, however, wiggled her bottom back into his crotch.

'You're not going to give me that speech about the thin walls again, are you?' she said. 'The kids won't hear a thing. They're exhausted. Dead to the world.'

'So am I.' He moved further back so she was no longer touching him. 'Back to Monica. So you have no idea when she's planning to leave?'

Tansy was facing away from him now; he had to strain to hear her. 'After the memorial service, I guess.'

'Perhaps we should clarify.'

And then he thought about the memorial itself, and what would happen. And he started to have the smallest feeling of foreboding, one of those dark clouds that hovered at the edge of his mind.

'Has anyone talked to Gloria?' he said. He knew that Tansy or Kylie or, rarely, Nick, tried to call her almost every day. 'She knows about Monica, right? That she's staying here? With us?'

'No,' Tansy said. Her voice was small.

Simon's parents were still alive and living in Canberra; there had never, to his knowledge, been the slightest marital discord between them. No marital *accord*, in his memory – they were like long-term boarding-house residents who nodded companionably when they passed each other in the hall – but no *discord*. He knew, though, that first wives and second wives and half-sisters were very much part of the way we lived now. *This is what modern families look like*, he thought.

But for some unknown reason, he thought there might be a slight chance that Gloria would be a teensy bit put out if she knew that Monica was staying here, and that all of her children had met Mon, and that no one had mentioned one word of this to her. Possibly he was being over-sensitive. That was probably it. He'd seen so many of Gloria's dramas over the years that he was expecting the worst. Half-siblings usually had some kind of a relationship, he'd gathered from the opinion pages, and frequently good and close relationships. What was happening right now to Tansy and her siblings was utterly unremarkable.

'Do you think one of you should?' Simon said.

But Tansy was already asleep.

TUESDAY

Chapter 11

The stages of a man's life could be marked by his changing fantasies. It seemed to Simon that only moments ago, all his fantasies involved serendipitous sex in complicated scenarios like *car runs out of petrol in the middle of nowhere so he knocks on a stranger's door and two girls in lingerie invite him in*, or *minding his own business hiking in a national park when a naked girl steps out from behind a tree*. The specifics of the plot were important to him back then; the character motivations, less so. Now it was all he could think about. Why, he couldn't say.

Was he really the kind of irresponsible person who'd run out of petrol on such a deserted stretch of road? And why on earth was the girl naked in a national park? Exposing vulnerable skin in the Australian bush for any length of time was worrying. There were more scary insects than were known to science! At the very least she should be wearing sensible hiking shoes. And the sex itself would have to be vertical – or else leeches would attach to your private parts, a thought unparalleled in its horror – and without any means of support, or her bare back would be lacerated by pressing against a tree. Simon doubted he had the core strength for that kind of manoeuvre, even when he was in his twenties. It was as if his younger fantasy brain lived in an alternate universe where the rules of gravity and entomology did not apply.

But everything changed when he met Tansy. From that day forward, Simon's fantasies became less plot-driven and more sensory in nature: he and Tansy, swimming around their over-water bungalow in Tahiti, or he and Tansy, buried in furs in a snowbound chalet. His skin had been inert until he first touched Tansy. When they started dating, he couldn't get over the feel of her: the brown tautness of her triceps and the silken wobble of her inner thigh. Her skin felt like no other woman's. If Simon was a deaf and blind witness to a crime, and if the criminal had brushed up against him while committing said crime, and if Tansy was said criminal, he could confidently pick her skin out of the police line-up using only his fingertips. When he first started making love with Tansy, he felt like the world was a richer and more textured place than he had ever guessed, like that moment in *The Wizard of Oz* when the black and white of Kansas blossoms into technicolour Oz.

After their years of marriage though, his fantasies had changed again. In his wildest imaginings, he is in a tuxedo, sitting beside Tansy in a grand auditorium. In this fantasy, Tansy is not giving him a surreptitious hand job while they both pretend to focus intently on whatever's happening on stage. There's no sex what-soever in his fantasies anymore. Instead, he and Tansy are both watching as Mia is awarded the Nobel Prize for Medicine or Lachie tearfully dedicates his Oscar to his parents. Simon felt himself becoming emotional just thinking about it.

Now that Simon was home while the kids were getting ready for school, it would be a fantasy come true if his children could be quiet in the mornings.

Wrangling children was such an enormous undertaking, he was surprised someone hadn't made a billion dollars by designing an app. He went through the rigmarole every morning: first, he was woken by the sound of Tansy struggling the children to their feet as though raising the dead. Then listening while she fed and dressed them while one (okay, Lachie) got distracted by a song on the radio or had an urgent need to resolve some long-standing philosophical problem like whether flies were disgusted by other flies. *One fly might go to another fly: Phil, you are way too clean today, you're making me wanna spew. Roll in some poo right now. That would happen, wouldn't it, Mum?* And what does Tansy say to that? *I'm sure Dad knows the answer,* is what she says. Why does she refer Lachie to him? He's clearly trying to sleep. She knows the same amount about flies as he does, which is precisely nothing. Simon hasn't secretly been Jeff Goldblum all this time.

Then there's the packing of the lunchboxes, where parental effort was inversely related to reward. Tansy spent hours painstakingly cutting vegetables into interesting, kid-friendly shapes that attracted zero interest. When she had an early meeting, Simon would slap together Vegemite and cheese on white bread with a side of pretzels and the kids were so keen they'd scoff it on the way to school. And fruit! What a waste of time and money. Parents pack fruit, apparently, so that the fruit can enjoy a leisurely few hours out of the house.

Then once the kids were physically at the front door and the door was opened, the 'just haftas' began. *I just hafta get my hat.*

Or *my jumper*. Or *my library bag*. Or *my lightsaber*.

Simon once ran a business! With clients! And staff! He spent literal decades waking up before the alarm and heading out the door as dawn was breaking. Now he couldn't seem to force himself awake. Now the very idea of the day and what it might hold seemed . . . more than he could handle. If he stayed in bed, which was preferable, then nothing else bad could happen. So that was how he spent his mornings before Naveen's garden was dropped on him – he was dragged to consciousness, either unwittingly by his noisy children or by an extreme act of will because Tansy had left early and it was his turn to act as incompetent butler slash cook slash fly-philosopher.

It had, in fact, been a long time since Simon had felt competent at anything.

—

It had been almost six months actually, and even then the achievement was so modest that the rush of satisfaction he'd felt quickly turned to embarrassment.

It was a Thursday night, he remembered. Gloria was over for dinner and had paid for a pizza delivery as a treat for the children. It was almost bedtime so Simon asked Lachie to brush his teeth. (Mia didn't need to be asked.)

'Already?' Lachie started his zigzag wander to the bathroom, touching every surface he passed with his fingertips, when he turned. 'Oh,' he said. 'I forgot. It's Book Week. I'm supposed to dress up like a Minion tomorrow.'

'A what?' Simon said.

'An onion?' said Gloria. 'What kind of school asks children to dress as root vegetables? This is why people go private.'

'A *Minion*,' said Mia. She searched on the iPad and showed them a picture of a spherical yellow cartoon character with goggles and Mardi Gras overalls. 'There's a letter on the fridge. Lachie brought it home weeks ago. I'm Jessie from *Toy Story*, because it's sun-smart to wear a hat.'

Simon had a vague recollection, but there always seemed to be so many letters from the school.

'Don't look at me,' said Tansy. 'I have an early staff meeting tomorrow. Ask your father.'

'Tomorrow? As in, *tomorrow*?' said Simon.

'Yep,' said Lachie. 'And the best costume gets a sticker.'

'Well,' said Simon. 'Lucky for you I always keep a spare Minion costume for exactly these circumstances. I ran it up on the Husqvarna as soon as I found out your mother was pregnant, because you can't be too prepared.'

'Really?' said Lachie.

'No,' said Simon. 'I'm kidding.'

'Oh,' said Lachie.

This was an example of why being a primary caregiver for small children was more stressful than running a business. Were Minions even *in* books? Or was this a flaky book-alternative costume? In the years ahead, would Lachie become one of those teenagers who never actually *read* the book they're meant to study but instead watched the movie? And would Lachie subsequently fail English right through high school because the ending of the movie was different from (and almost always inferior to) the ending of the book? And would this be extrapolated into his adult life: skipping classes at university, missing deadlines at work, standing people up on dates and failing to file his tax return for years at a stretch?

'Okay then,' Simon said. 'A Minion it is.'

'Yay!' said Lachie. 'I'm going to be a Minion!'

Simon sat back in his chair and was surprised to feel a surge of adrenalin gurgle through his veins. It was like the old days: an urgent job for a demanding client on a tight deadline.

He felt alive.

'Don't worry about a thing, buddy,' he said to Lachie. 'Dad'll look after it.'

First he found a tape measure in the old sewing basket under Tansy's side of the bed, and he measured Lachie's height, shoulder width, waist and hips. While Tansy and Gloria put the children to bed, he made some rough sketches. Then he grabbed Tansy's car keys.

Kmart in Barkly Square was open until 10 pm. He was there in twenty minutes.

—

When he arrived back home with his supplies, Gloria and Tansy were still on the couch where he'd left them, chatting, with a glass of wine each. While they watched, he started work.

First he covered the coffee table with a towel, then brought out his supplies: a domed food cover, the mesh ones that keep flies out. He'd also bought cardboard, yellow material, wool and Velcro. And a hot glue gun.

They stared at him, agape.

'Simon,' said Gloria. 'I hope you know what you're doing. That little boy is relying on you.'

'Too easy. This is just like when I was an architecture student, making models.' He posed with both hands on the hot glue gun, then did a quick draw from an imaginary holster on his hip. 'Do you feel lucky, Minion punk? Well, do you?' he drawled, Eastwood-style.

—

When Lachie woke in the morning, he stared at the costume with stunned wonder. 'You are the best dad in the whole entire world,' he said finally. 'I'm going to be just like you when I grow up.'

He *was* the World's Best Dad. It had taken half the night, but the costume was – there's no point being modest – a triumph. The sides were a little lumpen, yes, and the overalls were slightly off-colour, but still.

'I'm with Lachie,' said Tansy, kissing his forehead. 'That is wonderful.'

'Dad,' said Mia, 'this could be your new job! Ring up the Minion people and ask them!'

It fitted Lachie perfectly. He walked like a huge yellow blueberry with eyes. Negotiating his way down the stairs was a challenge and he barely fit in the back seat of the car, but he won the sticker for best costume. It was the first time Lachie had won anything at school. It was a highpoint of Simon's parenting, and one of the few highlights of his life over the last couple of years. Tansy was proud of him. He floated through the rest of the day in a SuperDad glow, doing the interminable laundry without collapsing on the couch to nap, as though the World's Best Dad had no need for sleep. Oddly, though, Lachie's response wasn't the strangest thing about the whole affair.

He remembered back to those early morning hours leaning over the costume, concentrating as it came together way past midnight. Tansy had gone to bed, but for some reason Gloria had remained where she was, sipping her wine on the couch, and had let herself out sometime later without him noticing. Simon remembered the keenness of her expression, the way she narrowed her eyes as she watched him work.

'Well, well,' Gloria said. 'That is actually very impressive. Some people respond better to deadlines and emergencies than planning and strategy, I suppose.'

—

But that was months ago. Now, he had only one week to finish Naveen's backyard and it was already Tuesday morning. Twenty per cent, gone.

There was no escaping it – he was running behind schedule. Just a few very short weeks ago, he'd been at home, unemployed. Before he started on Naveen's garden, his days had been his own once he finished the housework, and he spent them in his pyjamas with a whiskey, surfing the internet, maybe watching that hidden-camera video of the beagle playing the piano and howling, or doing quizzes like *Tell us your favourite Avenger and we'll tell you how to distract yourself from your existential crisis!* That dog was compelling viewing. Sometimes Simon howled along with the beagle – it was surprisingly soothing. And that Catahoula that talked by pressing buttons on the floor! *We live in an age of miracles*, he thought. In hindsight, those predictable, sleepy days of his recent past had a lot to recommend them.

Today, the day dawned warm and bright; it was forecast to hit the low thirties, which would make for uncomfortable labouring.

When Simon woke, Tansy was lying beside him, tousled, with one curvaceous leg sticking out from under the cotton sheet. Not entirely unrelated, his morning stiffy was proving unusually persistent; he had to walk around the flat a few times thinking about Gloria before he could pee.

Then he looked in on the kids, who didn't need to be up for another hour. Mia was on her stomach near the edge of the bed with her hands on her hips and elbows splayed like teapot handles. Lachie, in his ladybird pyjamas, was facing the other way in a horizontal sitting position, Mia's thigh as his chair. It was as though they were miniature WWE wrestlers frozen on the mat seconds after some complicated takedown. Simon straightened them and pulled up the covers. They didn't stir. That ability of children to sleep through anything – it was a beautiful constant in this changing world. Simon remembered his father carrying him inside the house after he'd fallen asleep in the back seat of the Volvo when he was Lachie's age; he'd done the same with his own children. Times like these, he wished they would stay this age forever. He'd even forgo the Nobel prize and the Oscar. Simon would give everything he owned just to sit and stare at them for the rest of the day.

But Naveen and his delayed pavers were waiting, so instead he went out to the kitchen. He mixed oatmeal with water and put it in the microwave, then he heard a phone ping from the other side of the folding screen, behind which Monica was sleeping. To be honest, Simon had forgotten she was there. Had he been too noisy?

In another moment, the screen moved and Monica appeared. She was wearing a knee-length cotton onesie in rainbow stripes, with a matching hood with ears and a soft white unicorn horn.

'Good morning,' he said. 'I'm trying to be quiet, Tansy's still sleeping.'

'No worries,' she whispered. 'I'll just get the door.'

'Door? I didn't hear anyone knock?'

'Knock. Hashtag old school.' Monica held her phone up to Simon's face, showing him a text that said *Here*.

Chapter 12

She opened the door to a man in a hi-vis shirt with three cardboard boxes at his feet.

'Monica Louise Schnabel?' he said.

'Yo.' She thanked the delivery man, closed the door softly and carried the largest box to the coffee table.

'Oh. You're receiving deliveries here,' said Simon. 'And at this time of the morning. Which is fine. Of course. We said make yourself at home.'

'It's super fast, right? It's who you know. I only ordered it yesterday morning.' She pulled a set of keys from the pocket of her onesie and ran one along the tape on the top of the largest box. 'So much packaging.' She shook her head. 'Sad face.'

She pulled out some white foam and lifted a plastic bag from the box. She unwrapped that to reveal a small silver espresso machine. 'Coffee, though. Happy face. The grinder and the beans are in the other boxes. You'll still need a knock box, I forgot about that.'

Simon stared at the machine in wonder. He longed to fill the filter basket with soft, warm grounds that smelled like heaven;

he longed to take the tamper and compact it smooth. He lifted the milk wand with one finger, as though it would snap.

'How can you afford all this?' he said.

'I got it wholesale. Plus I'm not staying at the hostel, so I'm saving there.'

Wholesale? How does one get a coffee machine delivered overnight, wholesale? And what would a night at that 'hostel' have cost? An espresso machine, grinder and bag of beans divided by the cost of a bed at that hostel was ... Jesus, how long was Monica planning to stay? Because in Simon's mind, that worked out to seven months.

He took a deep breath. He had questions – but he also had a job to do.

'I'll leave you to it,' he said. He went back to the kitchen and heaped instant coffee into his thermos and took the milk out of the fridge while waiting for the kettle to boil. Then he tipped the milk into his thermos. Out came a stream of curdled lumps.

He felt the plastic container. It was quite warm. He opened the fridge again. It was quite silent. Then he noticed a spreading pool of water on the kitchen floor.

'I hope you don't take milk,' he said to Mon.

'Oat,' she said. 'I'll nip out for it later.'

Simon tilted his head back until his neck creaked. How did other people manage to exist in the world? Was he a particularly fragile, delicate petal? Why did this kind of thing leave him so utterly unmoored? When he was a child, his father seemed to be in charge of everything. He had an aura of competency that Simon never doubted. Had he guessed what it was really like being an adult – that you never felt in control of anything – he'd never have slept. His ancestors had survived plagues and pestilence and famine and being shipped across the globe chained in the bottom of a leaking, flea-infested ship for stealing a handkerchief, so he understood intellectually that, in the grand scheme of things, a broken fridge was not a problem of monumental proportions.

That's not how it felt though. All these little hurdles of modern life added up until they reached stress levels of convict-ship proportions. A broken fridge meant food needed to be replaced and he hadn't budgeted for that, and also that someone had to wait around for the fridge repairer – or worse, it meant the purchase of a new fridge. Where was he supposed to get the money? It seemed to Simon that modern capitalism was only masquerading as a conservative force. It was actually a radical movement bent on overturning the traditional family by pushing everyone towards a ménage à trois. It wasn't actually *possible* to run a family with only two adults. If only a marriage had another wife (preferable) or even another husband, things would work so much better. Family life would be more efficient if one spouse concentrated on earning an income, another one ran the house and stayed home with the kids during holidays or illness and rostered on for tuckshop duty, and a third had a flexible job that allowed them to wait at home for the fridge repairer.

'I don't suppose you're staying home today?' he said.

'Nope.' Mon was flicking through her phone – the espresso machine manual online. 'Breakfast meeting soon.'

'What is it you do again?'

'Right now? Espresso appliance installation technician.' She pulled the unicorn-horned hood over her forehead, stuck out her tongue and bent her head low to take a selfie with the machine.

—

Living in a block of flats like theirs meant that waiting for a tradie or a delivery was normally no problem. But today, Jock and James were both working and Gemma and Erin were both at uni. Yulia, who rarely seemed to leave her flat, had somehow chosen today for her monthly trip by bus and train to Dandenong, where the only hairdresser in all of Melbourne mentally and constitutionally equipped to tackle Yulia's crowning glory operated from her garage. ('She is genius,' Yulia often said. 'She is Shostakovich of hair.')

Consequently, Simon spent the day at home, by himself, passing through the Five Stages of Waiting for Tradies.

First, denial. When he called the emergency repair people at the dot of nine, he begged the woman for an appointment today and she agreed with the air of someone condescending to give you a kidney. When he further pressed her for a window, she ummed and ahhed before telling him with sighing reluctance that the fridge repairman would be there sometime between 10 am and 4 pm.

'With any luck,' she said. 'Probably definitely.'

Which probably meant between 10 am and 10.15, Simon thought. He'd *definitely* be on his way to Naveen's in no time. And if the fridge repairman wasn't here by, say, 10.30 am, Mon would probably be back soon. After her breakfast 'meeting', she'd told Simon she was going shopping for the day. He was sure she was exaggerating. Who could shop for an entire day? She'd be gone for an hour at most, then she'd take over waiting here. She could read a book or something. He'd be a little late to Naveen's, that's all. There'd be plenty of time to start preparing the new garden beds.

By midday, he'd progressed to anger. Instead of finishing the backyard that was hanging over his head like a judgement, he kept himself busy by sorting the overflowing laundry hamper into piles.

'*Hand wash only*,' he read aloud from a care label attached to a skirt of Tansy's. 'This is mostly cotton! "Tell 'em they're dreaming".'

Simon had a system for the laundry. He found it soothing, organising the loads, making educated guesses based on the specific fabric and construction of each individual piece rather than merely relying on the overly strict washing instructions, which in his view were useless and designed only to prevent manufacturer liability for catastrophic garment failure. He felt resourceful, like a chemist, choosing from the assortment of sprays and potions lined up under the sink for stains of every description.

There was a small chance he was overly invested.

He separated Tansy's blouses to handwash in a bucket later before filling the machine squeezed in the corner of the bathroom. When the first load finished, he slipped his feet into a pair of Tansy's old slippers – purple and fluffy – kept outside the front door and clomped downstairs, carrying the basket – so heavy! – to the drooping line in the backyard. The backyard was indifferently tended by a franchised gardening business once a month in winter and fortnightly in summer, and consisted of struggling grass, studded with bindies, encircled by a bedraggled fence half-pulled down by ivy. Along the side of the fence was a long and wide weed-infested garden bed where Yulia composted, and in the back corner was a gnarled, twisted apricot tree, still netted, improbably heavy with fruit in summer. The yard needed a basketball hoop, a paved area for chairs, a barbecue. A lemon tree. It was depressing even to be there.

Then he had to go upstairs again, because he'd forgotten the pegs.

Then down to the backyard again. He hung everything – even the kids t-shirts, even the undies – smooth and evenly, so they would dry uncreased. How could four people, two of whom were only half-sized, generate so many dirty clothes? What did Lachie *do* all day: just dive headfirst into every muddy/oily/crafty substance in a ten-kilometre radius? And the toothpaste! How did Lachie manage to get toothpaste all down his pants, from waist to cuffs? Did he actually have teeth on his ankles? How did people with three children cope? God help them, some people had *four*!

Today, though, even the laundry failed to calm him and instead he felt ever more hopeless. This was how far he'd fallen! From running his own company, with staff and clients, managing huge projects, to his current grand achievement: keeping his family in clean clothes.

He was glad his father couldn't see him now.

If the repairman would only come in the next twenty minutes (bargaining), Simon hereby vowed that he would not drink at all tonight. He would have only water with his meal, even if Monica was here. Even if both Kylie *and* Gloria dropped by. He couldn't be more reasonable than that. By 2.30 pm, he was depressed. He phoned Tansy; she didn't answer, so he left a message on her mobile to explain that she'd have to leave work early to pick up the kids then take them back to the office with her.

At 3.30 pm, he had at last reached acceptance when the phone rang.

Simon stared at it. It was a number he didn't recognise. It was either the fridge repairman calling to say he couldn't make it until tomorrow, or to say he was just around the corner and would be there in seconds.

As he held it in his hand, Simon felt like that clueless philosopher who didn't know whether his cat was alive or dead until he opened the box.

Chapter 13

'Simon Larsen,' he said, softly, into the phone.

'Simon! Flora Horvak. Man, how ya doing?'

Simon's architectural firm had never been huge. At its peak, there were only ever half a dozen employees, but Flora had been a constant. As she spoke, Simon had a series of vivid images of her: Flora in her mid-teens on work experience, socks down around her ankles, chewing gum; Flora as architecture student, helping out in semester breaks; Flora on her first day as a graduate architect, strolling in to the office with all the confidence in the world. Flora was one of those weirdos who always knew what they wanted to do with their lives, and who methodically went about achieving it from infancy. When Simon was a teenager, he was barely aware of architecture as a profession. He liked drawing furnishings and buildings; he had an affinity for shapes and for the way things fit together, and his maths grades were too poor for engineering. Architecture had grown on him slowly. He grew to believe that the spaces that humans inhabit can influence their lives, and that it was his privilege to make the world a more beautiful and functional place. Architecture was the most democratic of professions. It was art for ordinary people. For *all* people, because you didn't have to own a beautiful building, or even go inside one, to have it change your outlook on the world.

Now, it hurt to think about his life as an architect. He'd given decades of his working life and so much of his energy to architecture as art, as craft, as concept. It had been the biggest part of who he was. The day he'd signed the bankruptcy papers, he felt betrayed. He didn't know what he believed or who he was without his profession, his business and his income. If he'd met Tansy now instead of all those years ago, would she still agree to go out with him?

Flora, on the other hand, was born an architect. At four, she pitched any toy that wasn't Lego or Meccano out of her bedroom window. At fourteen, she took to regularly dropping her resume in to all the architectural firms within a three-suburb radius of her home. Simon was just starting his firm then, and he needed all the administrative help he could get. After that, she just stayed. Hiring Flora full-time when she graduated was one of the best decisions he'd made, and letting her go had been among the worst moments of going broke. He had failed as her mentor as well as her employer. Flora was another in the long list of people he'd let down.

'Great, great. Really good,' he said. 'How are you?'

He should already know the answer to that question, Simon thought. He should have followed her up over the last two years, made sure she found another job, been her shoulder to cry on – but somehow, he felt like he'd infect her bright, optimistic youth with his failure. Flora hadn't even asked him to be her referee for job applications, although he'd offered. Which made sense. Having worked for him would hardly be a feather in her cap. Perhaps she'd found work in an unrelated field. Flora, who was in love with everything about architecture, the history of it, the politics. Flora, who pored over design magazines from the library, studying the way Zaha Hadid made concrete flow like water, or how Ole Scheeren allowed buildings to tell stories. He tried not to think about Flora riding a food-delivery bike or as a barista, putting all her passion for design into making someone a latte heart.

'Crazy busy, you know how it—' Flora said.

'I know, I know,' Simon said, interrupting. 'I'm flat out. It's ridiculous.' He shut the door of the bathroom and walked towards the kitchen. Their washing machine had a spin cycle you could hear from space.

'But listen, Simon. I've got this thing happening. I'd love to have a chat with you about it? How—'

'Sure, of course, anytime,' said Simon, interrupting again, and then mentally kicked himself for it. *You are cool, you are relaxed*, he told himself.

'Great! It's short notice, I know, but any chance of a coffee tomorrow?'

'Tomorrow. Tomorrow, tomorrow . . .' Simon said, and paused for a period of time that he hoped would indicate that tomorrow was only a vague possibility, and he was flicking through his overflowing diary as he spoke. Any thought of Naveen's garden, already behind schedule, evaporated from his mind. 'Yep, sure. I can manage that.'

Flora went on to talk a little more about a job vacancy. It was a great job, she said, with an excellent path for promotion. The role needed to be filled urgently.

'I hate formal interviews but I just want to get everything back on track, you know?' she said. 'It's a fantastic opportunity. Everything's been a bit of a mess up until now, to be honest.'

A bit of a mess! He'd thought as much. Poor Flora. Simon made agreeing sounds while counting his breaths and keeping one ear out for the fridge repairman.

'A job interview!' he said. That was excellent; he couldn't be happier for her. He would do anything to help. They made a time to meet tomorrow and when Flora suggested a cafe not far from his old house, Simon didn't blink. He was happy to drive across town for this. And if Flora accidentally thought he still lived around there, that was fine with him.

When she rang off, he felt good about the whole thing. Flora wanted career advice before this upcoming job interview. She wanted to talk about how best to present herself; some ideas about how to handle tricky questions; whether she should enrol in a short course to update her skills. Perhaps she wanted him to role-play as the interviewer so she could practise – after all, he'd hired plenty of people in his day. He knew exactly what to ask. More than anything, he was thrilled she was applying for jobs. It was natural she would turn to him. He had been her first boss and had many years more experience than she did. He wasn't washed up, far from it. He was a vital, not-nearly elder statesman who still had lots to contribute.

Then the front door rang. The fridge repairman, at last! Everything was working out, see? Simon, newly restored mentor and dispenser of wisdom to young architects, opened it with a Zen calmness, expecting a sincere apology that he would magnanimously accept. Instead the man thrust a digital reader and stylus at him and said, 'Sign here.'

Simon signed – because that's what you do when someone thrusts a reader at you. Then he looked at the man more carefully. He was only holding the reader, nothing else.

'Where are your tools?' Simon said.

'What tools?' the man said.

'The tools for fixing the fridge.'

'You wouldn't want me to look at your fridge, mate,' he said. 'I can't even remember to shut the door of mine, bloody thing beeps like it's reversing through the kitchen. I've unloaded your pavers downstairs in the driveway. Have a good one.'

Simon was frozen for a moment, processing what he'd just heard. Pavers? Driveway? Surely that man didn't mean the court-yard pavers that should have been delivered to Naveen's place? Why on earth would they have been delivered to his place instead of Naveen's?

Simon raced around the flat to find his keys and phone, then bolted downstairs in time to watch the delivery truck pull away.

Sure enough, blocking the common driveway to the garages were two stacked pallets wrapped in plastic. He looked closer. The missing pavers.

Bloody hell. If he slashed the plastic and attempted to carry the pavers up the stairs to the flat by himself, his hernias would have hernias. And he had nowhere to store them upstairs anyway. But he couldn't leave them down here. Someone would nick them – not to mention the complaints from his neighbours when they couldn't access their garages. Honestly, the incompetence of people these days, it was breathtaking. He had a good mind to complain to somebody.

He was still standing there when a refrigerator-repair van pulled up on the street.

'Hope you haven't been waiting long,' said the man as he lifted his toolbox out of the back. 'I told head office it'd be my last job, hey.'

Simon checked his phone: it was 3.57 pm. He noticed his fingers were white where they gripped the phone, which didn't strike him as a symptom of calm. He could conquer this. He could. *Breathe, Simon. Just breathe.*

Then as he went to put the phone back in his pocket, it rang. It was a weirdly insistent ring, with a different timbre than usual. As though the phone was trying to warn him of something.

He glanced at the screen. Gloria.

His lower intestine twinged. He was incredibly thirsty. He might pay for this later, but for now, he pressed decline.

Chapter 14

By 6 pm, the sneaky whiskey he'd had earlier was working. Simon felt his shoulders dropping almost back to their normal position, and the pain in his neck begin to ease.

All of today's problems had been, if not solved exactly, then at least postponed. The fridge was fixed, although the repairman warned Simon that it wouldn't last long. He'd also split the fee across three credit cards so the emergency buffer remained intact, and he did it without giving Simon the kind of look that made him feel like a loser. Tansy had managed to leave work early and arrived home with the kids and a bag of replacement groceries she'd squeezed onto her credit card. And when Gemma and Erin arrived home from uni, they helped Simon move the pavers against the retaining wall, out of the way. And the best news of all – Naveen had been relaxed about Simon's no-show today. He was picking up Lexie from her judo tournament soon, on this side of town, and he'd be happy to swing by in his SUV to pick up the pavers and take them back to his place. *No drama*, Naveen said.

The cherry on the top: Gloria had neither left a message nor rung back.

It was probably an 'urgent' but unimportant call – Gloria's specialty. She was the chair of fundraising for the tennis club and was planning an enormous extravaganza next month: a hundred people for a catered buffet-style dinner. Tennis wasn't Gloria's sole reason for living, like it was for so many of her contemporaries, but it was certainly in the top ten. She never stopped talking about it. To everyone, but particularly to Simon. For a woman with three children and seemingly hundreds of friends, she phoned Simon a lot. She was always asking him to pick something up or drive somewhere to help. And there were the run-of-the-mill questions that just kept coming: *Simon, I'm watching a movie now – that hirsute man who plays the maestro, what's he been in?* Or *Simon, where do I buy a burqa?* Tansy would have received those calls back when she worked part-time in their business, but now Gloria considered that he was the family member with nothing better to do. This week, though, Simon was busy. Whatever it was Gloria wanted, she'd have forgotten about it by tomorrow.

And now Simon was sitting in the front yard of the block of flats in a folding lawn chair with a stubby in hand. Tansy, Mia and Lachie were sitting on their picnic rug beside him, eating the tacos that Tansy had made and the kids had carried downstairs so they could have dinner while babysitting the pavers. This was peak Tansy. She took everything in her stride.

When Simon did the grocery shopping, he prayed he wouldn't run into anyone he knew. He dreaded the sight of his trolley, filled with mince and sausages and home-brand everything, next to someone else's fillet steak and artisanal ice cream and bags of roasted cashews. Cashews! He thought of all the cashews he'd gobbled over the years, before the grocery budget was even on his radar. He hadn't realised that cashews were apparently grown in the Versace resort, tucked into silk sheets at night and picked by vestal virgins before being strapped in their seatbelts and driven, one per Tesla, to Coles.

Tansy, on the other hand, didn't seem affected by their sudden change in shopping habits. She knew how to make a list and stick to it; she could substitute ingredients and use leftovers and be cheerful while doing it. It seemed as though she knew two dozen ways to make mince edible for kids, and not too tedious for Simon either, and she could throw together tacos (which were just corn chips in a different shape, let's face it – what's not to like?) using packet seasoning mix while emptying school lunchboxes and putting away last night's dishes. Then find the rug, dig out the plastic glasses and make orange cordial as a treat for the kids, packing the taco components into Tupperware as if they were heading to a manicured park instead of sitting in the common front yard, a struggling strip of grass studded with dried lumps of dog poo, surrounded by dead sticks planted vertically in tan bark. All of which was within view of the street, so that they were stared at by passers-by as they ate. Tansy was a miracle worker.

'We should do this more often,' she said. 'I texted Yulia to invite her but she was exhausted from her hairdo and is having an early night. Gemma and Erin have gone out, and Jock and James have a work function.'

Simon leaned over and kissed her cheek while reaching for another beer. 'You're a wonder.'

She bit her bottom lip. 'I'm worried about Naveen's garden. You were late getting there yesterday, and you missed today entirely.'

'Hardly my fault,' said Simon.

She held up both hands. 'I know. And you know my policy – I absolutely refuse to nag. I refuse to become that kind of person. But will you finish on time? We've booked the chairs and hired waiters and glasses, and Mum wanted columns and a podium and an arch of white roses. It's all being delivered to Naveen's on Saturday morning. And sixty or seventy people have RSVPed. If we need to contact everyone to tell them we've moved the venue, I need to start now.'

'Trust me,' Simon said, leaning back. 'I got it covered.'

'Are you sure? Because—'

'Dad, Dad,' said Lachie. 'We had mince last night too. We're having mince two days in a row.'

Yep, they were. Eating mince, again, and out in the open like this. Simon grew up in a proper house, not a flat, and couldn't remember eating anywhere but the dining-room table with shining cutlery and a napkin on his lap. He tried and failed to imagine his father eating a taco for dinner. Or his father eating anything at all with his hands, unless it was a sandwich, which was strictly lunch food. He couldn't help but worry about his children's memories of their childhood.

'Which is awesome. This is so much fun,' said Lachie. 'Dad, Dad, I know! Let's eat here every night!' As he spoke, a glob of taco mince landed on his leg. He bent his neck and slurped it up.

'That's the way, buddy,' said Simon. 'Look on the bright side.'

'We'll be back inside tomorrow,' said Tansy. 'This is a special occasion.'

'How was school?' Simon said.

'Awesome,' said Lachie. 'I went to the toilet and then, guess what? I washed my hands! And no one was even watching!'

'Well done, Lachs. How about you, Mia?'

'Good,' she said.

'Francesca in Mia's class got a iPhone for her birthday,' Lachie said. 'A brand-new one. She was showing everyone.'

'Francesca is a lucky little girl,' said Tansy. 'In this house, we think that eight is a bit young for smartphones.'

'I don't want one ever. It's an unnecessary extravagance.' Mia pursed her lips, like a child little old lady.

'That's only if you buy it with *actual* money,' said Lachie. 'Not if you put it on Afterpay. Afterpay is *magic* money. Everything's free.'

'Ah, that's not how it works, buddy,' Simon said.

'Dad, I have to go upstairs soon,' Mia said. 'I've got homework.'

'Homework, again?' Tansy said. 'Are you sure? Perhaps you're misunderstanding the instructions. I think it's time we talked to your teacher. You're doing too much for an eight-year-old.'

'No!' said Mia. 'It's good practice for high school.'

'Mum, Mum, I was good at school today too!' said Lachie. 'Mrs Falvey said my art project was *outstanding*! And I never even *did* it!'

Simon took another long drink of his beer.

'Where's Auntie Mon?' said Mia.

Simon and Tansy looked at each other. 'I've texted,' Tansy said. 'She's having a holiday, after all. She must have a long list of things to do.'

As if on cue, a car pulled up and Monica got out of the back seat.

An Uber! They were only fifteen minutes' walk from the station.

'She must be made of money,' Simon whispered to Tansy, then wondered how his father's words had wound up in his mouth.

Monica stood with the door open, leaning in to chat to the driver, hands full of shopping and a large leather-look bag she didn't have yesterday. Women and their bags! Simon rarely saw women outside of their homes with nothing in their hands.

He frequently walked out the door with his wallet and keys in his pockets but Tansy's handbag weighed as much as a small child – it was a miracle one of her shoulders wasn't three inches lower than the other. Tansy often said that the entirety of her life could be reconstructed by careful forensic analysis of the contents of her bag. How women must hate those burdensome instruments of torture! It was a wonder that handbag burning wasn't a thing, like bras.

The kids ran towards Monica. 'Look at you guys!' she said. 'Are you having a picnic? I'm starving.'

'We're having tacos, which is good except for the lettuce and the tomato and these green bits,' said Lachie. 'But you can pick those out and throw them in the garden when nobody's looking.'

'Those bits are my favourites,' said Mia. 'They're very healthy.'

'Aren't you a bit young to be thinking about health?' said Monica. 'Kids your age should be scoffing lollies like nobody's business.'

'I am, I am!' said Lachie. 'I promise!'

'I'm *not*. I have to be healthy to look after Mum and Dad when they get really old.' Mia sat down again. 'I mean, even older than they are now.'

'Good to know, sweetie.' Tansy kissed her forehead.

Mon and Lachie sat too, and Lachie wriggled to be closer to her. He poked her in the arm. 'Are you *really* made of money?'

Tansy cleared her throat. 'Would you like some dinner?' she said to Monica. 'There's plenty. I couldn't eat another bite.'

Which was weird, because Simon had noticed she'd only had one taco of her own, then half of one of Lachie's. Women had a different metabolism but he'd still be hungry after one and a half tacos. Perhaps Tansy was dieting. She certainly didn't need to. That slight tummy she'd never managed to lose after having Lachie only made her more cuddly. It was important for a husband to really *see* his wife, to notice specific parts of her without being instructed to. Men weren't mind-readers yet women loved setting little tests that they were predestined to fail. Being observant was one of them. Had Simon told her recently how much he liked her little tummy? He resolved to let her know tonight, as she was getting ready for bed. Meanwhile, his beer was already empty. He reached for another.

'Are you sure? I'm ravenous,' said Monica as she took a taco. 'Look at this! Hard shell, so retro. I love it. I have had *the* best day,' she said between bites. 'Living here is going to be awesome. I should have done it years ago.'

Living here? What did that mean, *living* here? *Here*, here, as in his dining room?

Chapter 15

For a moment, the inside of Simon's brain was quiet – the kind of quiet that precedes someone in scrubs on a television medical soap opera standing in front of a devastated family, saying, *I'm sorry. We did everything we could.*

'You're moving here?' Tansy said. 'I didn't realise.'

'Moving where, exactly?' said Simon.

'Here. Melbourne,' Monica said. 'I have a brand-new family. I want to get to know you all. And the shopping is ace. I bought so much. Mostly clothes. A few handbags.'

Handbags, plural? Simon frowned. A woman can only carry one handbag at a time, so why would she have more than one? Perhaps they're gifts. He hoped she wasn't planning to give a handbag to Tansy. She already had *three*!

'I can't really shop at home,' Monica continued. 'I'd never hear the end of it. Mum thinks consumerism is evil and we should all knit our own shoes from our own hair and weave handbags out of toilet-paper rolls.' She reached forward and helped herself to more grated cheese. 'I never tell her how much I buy.'

Simon cleared his throat. 'But you should never keep secrets from your parents, right, Monica?'

'Of course you should,' Monica said. 'Shopping, prime example.'

'I mean,' Simon jerked his head in the direction of Mia and Lachie, 'keeping secrets from your parents is wrong.'

'Nah,' Monica said. 'Some things are on a need-to-know basis. Have you got something in your eye, Simon? It keeps blinking like crazy. The right one.'

'What Monica means – Mia, Lachie – is that lying to your parent is a really bad thing, in general,' said Simon. 'Children who lie to their parents usually come to sticky ends.'

Mia was sitting cross-legged on the picnic rug next to Simon in his chair, and she spun around to look up at him. Her face was a mess of tension: her small forehead, normally smooth, was furrowed and her mouth was a grimace. She looked as though she was going to cry.

Simon leaned forward in his chair. 'What is it, sweetheart?' he said.

'Dad,' she whispered. 'I . . .'

Just then, Naveen's SUV swung into the driveway, heralded by toots.

Simon felt the relief flow through him, erasing the last remnants of stress for the day. Everything had worked out. If Naveen hadn't show up, Simon would have had to stay down here all night, protecting the pavers from being nicked. But here he was, on time! The kids were fed, the fridge was fixed, there was nothing to worry about. After they loaded the SUV with the pavers and put the kids to bed, the day would be over without any major disasters. Crisis averted. Simon could breathe easy.

'It's Naveen and Lexie!' said Lachie.

'This is the guy with the anger-management issues?' said Monica.

'No, no,' said Simon. 'He's fine, really.'

But Monica was already standing and wiping her hands on her jeans. 'No one speaks to my brother-in-law like he did yesterday. You guys are putting me up; it's the least I can do.'

'I appreciate the offer,' said Simon. 'But no.'

Monica began bobbing on her feet, jabbing like a boxer. 'You're working in his yard, that makes you labour. Labour standing up to capital, it hardly ever happens. Are you in a union?'

'Naveen is my oldest friend,' said Tansy, waving towards the car and smiling. 'I can't tell you how supportive he's been over the years. I don't know how I would have coped without him. He wouldn't have meant anything, honestly. He was probably just having a bad day.'

Naveen, oblivious to his new *capital* status, was waving back from behind the wheel but he still hadn't opened the door. Lexie was deadpan in the passenger seat, arms folded across her chest. They were talking. Simon couldn't read lips – but he knew Naveen, and he knew Lexie. *Why don't you pop out and say hello?* Naveen was saying. *Because I don't want to*, Lexie replied. *I didn't even want to go to a stupid judo tournament, it's lame. Why do I have to visit your friends? Mum never makes me do this. You could have dropped me off first. This is boring.* Lexie was certainly a handful. Simon felt sorry for Naveen, and relieved that Mia and Lachie would never behave like that when they became teenagers.

After a little back and forth and much pouting, Naveen and Lexie got out of the car. Lexie was short for her age, and wiry – all elbows and knees. She was still in her *gi*, orange belt tied across her waist. Her hair, inherited from her father, hung down her back in a thick black plait. Naveen's impossible hair looked thick and wet and was sticking up at an odd angle, and he was freshly shaved. He wore a dusky pink linen shirt and light grey jacket, evidence that he'd been dressed by Lexie and highly suggestive of his ex-wife, Caroline, being present at said judo tournament. Naveen was at that stage of post-divorce life where it was vital to him that his ex-wife believed that he was doing well. Without the possibility of Caroline judging him, Naveen rarely paid any attention to what he wore.

'Hi, hi!' said Naveen. 'Can't wait to check out those pavers.'

'Hi, little weirdos,' said Lexie as the kids clambered around her. 'Got any tattoos yet?'

'Draw one on me!' both Mia and Lachie said, bouncing around Lexie as though they were spring-loaded.

'Naveen, this is Monica, my . . . sister,' said Tansy.

'Your sister?' Naveen blinked and looked from Tansy to Monica and back again. 'Kylie is your sister.'

'I'm her other sister.' Monica folded her arms. 'Her younger sister.'

'Her what?' said Naveen.

'My half-sister,' said Tansy. 'You know. From Dad's second marriage.'

'I didn't know you had a half-sister,' said Naveen.

Mon turned to Tansy. 'I thought he was your oldest friend. Did you not tell him about me?'

Lexie's attention had shifted from the kids. 'Ooh, drama. Popcorn. Please,' she said.

'I did tell him, of course I did,' said Tansy. She scrambled to her feet. 'Naveen's just forgotten.'

'I'm not sure I would have forgotten that.' Naveen rubbed his palm around the back of his neck. 'I've known you since we were five. I know how many sisters you have. One. Kylie, Warrior Princess.'

'That's what we called her at school,' Tansy said to Monica. 'We meant it affectionately.'

'Irregardless. We need to talk about your behaviour towards Simon, Na-*Veen*,' said Mon, with a weirdly aggressive inflection.

'No, we don't,' said Simon. 'We don't at all.'

'See?' Naveen turned, blinking, to Simon. 'Women are terrifying.'

'Is this about lying?' Mia looked up at Simon. 'Is Naveen getting in trouble for lying?'

'Look, if I did lie—' said Naveen.

'Mon, please,' said Tansy. 'You're embarrassing us.'

'We were *there*.' Monica stood in front of Naveen, with her hands on her hips. 'You stand here in your knock-off Paul Smith shirt with your cute hair, flashing those dark eyes, taking advantage of a defenceless average run-of-the-mill working man like Simon.'

Naveen pulled at his sleeve. 'The man at the market said it was genuine.'

'To be honest, Monica, I've never really seen myself as defenceless,' said Simon. 'Or average. Run-of-the-mill, also, is not flattering.'

'Whatever,' said Monica.

Surely an innocent man shouldn't sound so defensive? Considering that he hadn't said one thing wrong to Simon, that Simon had made it all up, Naveen should be more indignant.

Instead, he was turning red and shrinking in front of them, holding up his hands like he was backing away from an escaped tiger. He looked guilty, almost. He straightened his collar.

'Look, I wasn't being a dick,' he said. 'I was only trying to help. It was Tansy's—'

All at once, Lexie shrieked at the top of her lungs, as though she'd seen a snake. 'Oh. My. God. Wait,' she said. 'I know you. You're Santa Monica.'

Only Monica seemed aware of what was going on.

'You are, aren't you? Oh. My. God. You're Santa Monica. You're her. Oh my god, I follow you. I'm dead. I'm literally dead. You are iconic.' Lexie was looking square at Monica.

'What?' said Naveen. 'Lex, English, please?'

Mon bowed her head and smiled at Lexie, before she nodded and gave a small curtsy. 'Busted,' she said.

'You're who?' said Naveen.

'Dad, you are such a dag. If you didn't spend every second worrying about the chicken shop, or your new vegetarian eggplant and chickpea whatever, you'd actually learn something about life? Don't you know who this is? I've told you about her a million times. I. Am. Going. To. Faint,' said Lexie, who had never looked less like fainting in her life. Her hands were clenched tight and she was rising and falling on the balls of her feet.

'What on earth is going on?' said Simon.

Chapter 16

People were complex, Simon knew. They had depths and layers. Everyone had heard those stories about 'happily married' women who found out by accident that their husband had an entirely separate family only streets away. There wasn't a murderer in the world who wasn't described by his neighbours as 'a bit quiet but a lovely bloke'. Every day, those people-you'd-least-suspect successfully hid gambling addictions, Valium addictions and Candy Crush addictions. Was it ever possible to really know another human being?

At first, it seemed that Lexie was speaking gibberish but gradually he pieced it together: she knew who Monica was, because his wife's half-sister was, if not exactly famous, on the road to becoming so. The world seemed to stop spinning for a moment. Stars appeared before Simon's eyes. He went to take another sip but his stubby was mysteriously empty. He must have accidentally spilled the rest on the grass.

'She's a what?' said Simon.

'An influencer,' said Lexie.

Monica was a social media ... person. On Instagram and YouTube, with a feed and a channel about fashion and country life and skincare and makeup. And shoes. Lots of shoes.

'I started it for a bit of fun because lockdown was super boring, but then Jenny Ong liked one of my posts about Mum's chickens and I got more and more followers ... and it just kind of went from there,' she said.

What 'it' was precisely and exactly where it 'went from there' was lost on Simon. It sounded suspiciously like one of the modern made-up jobs young people did these days. God knows how poorly it paid, how much they were being exploited.

'The gig economy.' Simon nodded sagely, pleased he remembered the phrase from the headline of a *Guardian* article he'd seen on Facebook. 'Just don't do things for free. You can't pay rent with exposure.'

'OMG,' said Lexie. 'It's a real business. The top influencers make thousands.'

'Thousands?' said Simon. 'Of dollars?'

'I'm not that big yet,' said Monica. 'But my subscribers and followers are super cool. And my views are growing every week.'

'Your blog –' began Simon.

'"Blog",' said Monica. 'Lol.'

'– about country life and makeup and shoes? It doesn't sound very high-tech.'

'So something has to be high-tech to be exciting? Dying.' Mon raised her eyebrows and smiled. 'Shoes, for example, are about more than just fashion. Shoes are us – our lives, our priorities. What happened during the lockdowns? No one wore shoes. People went around in socks and slippers for weeks.' She shuddered. 'That's because shoes are about industry, productivity, energy. The faster you move, the more you're engaging in a fast-paced modern world, the more pairs of shoes you need. Plus, I only promote things that are ethically made, or vintage. People want *authenticity*. You can't fake that.'

'I'm loving your whole outfit, by the way – the mini-skirt, the tights, the lace-up blouse, the long tailored jacket. It's amazing,' said Lexie. 'I think you wore that skirt with double denim a few weeks ago, right? I saw it on your feed. I'd give anything for a wardrobe like that. And I love your pumps! They're gorgeous!'

Mon stretched her legs out in front and bent her ankles from side to side. Her shoes, Simon saw now, looked like something that Minnie Mouse would wear if she worked in a Regency-era Parisian brothel. 'A leopard-print mini goes with just about anything, in any season.'

'They're funny looking,' said Lachie. 'They're like cartoon shoes.'

'Can I have a selfie?' squeaked Lexie, moving to kneel behind Monica. 'Please?'

'Of course!' Mon squeezed her face next to Lexie's in a practised way, while Lexie snapped. 'And another one with the shoes?'

'How fascinating. What's the name of your channel?' asked Tansy. Lexie told her and she looked it up on her phone, the kids huddling beside her. 'Would you look at that? All those lovely photos of you.'

'You. Are. Awesome,' said Lexie. 'Wait till I tell everyone at school.'

'Would you all excuse me?' said Tansy. 'I need to make a couple of urgent calls.' She stepped across to the other side of the driveway, pressing buttons as though the building was on fire and she was calling triple zero.

'You *are* made of money!' Lachie said. 'Dad was right!'

'Not a lot of money yet,' Mon said, giving Simon a grin. 'I'm just starting out.'

'It doesn't sound like a very sensible career path. Can you actually make a living from that?' said Simon.

'God, you sound like my dad. "You'll never get anywhere with grades like these, grow up, try harder, blah blah." Money does not make you happy, Simon,' said Mon. 'You need a certain amount, for sure, but beyond that? Nope.'

'I. Am. Freaking. Out,' said Lexie.

'Wow,' Tansy called out mid-stride, holding the phone away from her ear. 'That's amazing, Mon. Good on you. Anyone else for another taco? Help yourself.'

No, Simon did not want another taco. He would possibly never want another taco again. He wanted Tansy to get off the phone from Kylie and/or Nick and come back here and show him how to behave. Look at her over there, pacing and chatting, throwing her head back in laughter and talking nine to the dozen. He could just imagine what she was saying. *Oh my god, you'll never guess what I just found out!* Meanwhile, his children were buzzing around Monica as though she was the coolest person they'd ever met.

Simon remembered when his children had thought that he was cool, but that was long ago. Now Monica was cool. Monica was young and free and excited about the world. Once Simon had also possessed huge dreams, wide horizons, a belief in the endless potential of his work. Looking at her, he felt a hundred years old. He'd felt that way since his business went bankrupt and he lost their home. There was so much stacked against normal people: Simon had no family money, no upper-class connections. He was a battler. He'd given it a good shot but he was just one normal person trying to build something.

Everything was unfair: the virus, the banks, the government. He never got a break. The system was impossible to defeat. How did he expect things would turn out? He reached for another beer then felt Tansy's hand on his arm.

'It's a Tuesday night, remember?' she said.

He put the beer back.

Lachie was pulling his sleeve. 'Dad, Dad, Dad,' he said. 'This is really boring. Can I get the iPad?'

'And can I go upstairs and do my homework?' said Mia.

'Sure, have fun,' said Simon, who had no idea what they'd just asked and hoped it didn't involve swallowing tablets they'd found on the street.

'Yes, this is all so interesting!' said Naveen cheerily, though his eyes darted from side to side as though Monica was a rabid dog about to bite him. 'Let's get these pavers loaded!'

'Yes. Simon? Honey?' Tansy said. 'The pavers?'

'I've got to get Lexie back to her mum's,' said Naveen. 'She's got homework. Now that Kylie's tutoring her, she's got more work and I'm saving a fortune. The tutor she had last year, I can't tell you what she cost.'

Kylie was tutoring Lexie? *Kylie?* Simon felt a surge of sympathy. Lexie was going to end up like one of those Von Trapp kids who lined up like golden retrievers when they heard a whistle.

'Are you joking? Santa Monica is here! I'm not going anywhere,' said Lexie.

But she did. As people Lexie's age knew all too well, they were rarely in command of when they can arrive and when they can leave. There were pavers to be loaded and dishes to be washed and put away and kids to be put to bed. Besides, Simon was feeling a little woozy. Something he ate, probably.

He must have helped Naveen load the pavers and helped Tansy pack up. He must have waved goodbye to Naveen and Lexie, and said goodnight to Mon. He tucked in the kids; he didn't read to them, he was sure about that, and he had no memory of the joke he told them. Perhaps he said, *Why did the oyster never share his toys? Because he was shellfish.* He brushed his teeth. He distantly recalled doing the dishes. He definitely told Tansy he was having coffee with Flora tomorrow to help her prepare for a job interview, because he had a vague memory of her saying *That's wonderful! What a delightful girl; we should have stayed in touch. Give her all my love.*

Only one conversation stood out over the rest of the evening, and he wasn't even a part of it. He was standing in the short hall off the bathroom, wondering if he should put his pyjama bottoms on first, or the top. Tansy was in the kitchen getting a glass of water. Mon stuck her head out of the dining room.

'Thanks for dinner,' she said. 'It was really yum.'

From where Simon stood, he could see Tansy resting her glass back on the kitchen counter and folding her arms. 'Why didn't you tell us about your work?' she said to Mon.

Mon looked at the carpet. 'What about it?'

Tansy didn't answer. That was a mother trick.

'Because there's nothing to tell. It's not a big deal.'

'The fact that you kept it a secret actually confirms that it is a big deal.'

Mon inhaled in a way Simon recognised; it was the inhalation of someone who felt a judgement approaching. 'Dad didn't think it was a real job. He didn't understand social media. He wasn't a digital native. He thought I was' – she made bunny ears with her fingers – '"wasting my life", that I had "no prospects for the future". I wanted to show him that I did. I really wanted the feed to take off.' She ran her hand over her scalp. 'But then he died and I didn't get a chance to show him anything.'

There was quiet for a while. 'That sounds tough,' said Tansy.

'I guess. But it made me think.'

'What did it make you think?'

'That I had sisters and a brother somewhere in the world and that is incredibly cool. And that I should do something about it. I was going to tell you about the social media thing eventually. I just wanted you to get to know me first.'

'We certainly know you now,' she said.

The rest of the night was a blur. Simon's actual brain cells felt depleted, like they were each little muscles nestled inside his skull that had done too many reps with tiny little dumbbells. He couldn't remember feeling this level of exhaustion when he had his own business. Possibly it was something he ate.

At least the day would soon be behind him and he'd be in the blissful realm of sleep. Simon couldn't wait to drift off in peaceful, gentle slumber. His eyes were literally closing while he changed into his pyjamas, bottom half first. Tomorrow was a big day. Naveen's garden must be finished this week and he was way overdue, and then there was the coffee with Flora. Everything would make more sense in the morning.

Chapter 17

11.48 pm:

Instagram posts about country life and makeup and shoes? Simon never would have thought there was that much interest in shoes. Everyone wears them, obviously, but they weren't expensive like mobile phones or cars. What did a pair of designer shoes cost? Fifty or sixty dollars, tops. Not much of a profit margin in that. And Mon blogged . . . or whatever . . . about shoes in *Australia*. Not even French or Italian. What are intrinsically Australian shoes, anyway? Thongs with a lid? And what kind of person would buy shoes or clothes online, without trying them on? No one, that's who.

12.15 am:

He'd better get to sleep. Immediately. Soon. If he didn't get to sleep, he wouldn't wake up when the alarm went off. Big day tomorrow. Go to sleep. Now.

12.17 am:

Back when Simon was first starting his architectural practice, he went to a huge house in Malvern to talk about a possible renovation. He couldn't remember how he met this potential client, but he was distinguished and obviously wealthy; fit and greying in a retired-and-has-a-personal-trainer way. There was a young woman in a bikini in the backyard by the pool, and the prospective client introduced Simon to her while they toured the house. And then as Simon was leaving, he said, 'Great to meet you and your daughter.' That's what Simon, an adult who voted, with an allegedly functioning brain, actually said. *Daughter*. It came out of his mouth as easy as breath. Of course, the young woman was his wife. Of course, he didn't get the job. Sometimes he thought he shouldn't be allowed out of the house without a chaperone.

12.47 am:
Should they get a cat? Cats were excellent apartment pets, he'd heard. Cute, playful. Perhaps it would be good for the kids. Feeding them, brushing them, emptying the litter box – chores built responsibility in children. Mia already had that in spades, yes, but Lachie could probably do with a top-up.

1:02 am:
Why did that daughter/wife memory pop up every time he couldn't sleep? Yes, it was utterly humiliating, but it was years ago. The prospective client was someone Simon had never seen since, would probably never see again, and wasn't obviously vulnerable. Surely over forty-two years of life, Simon had embarrassed himself worse than that, in more harmful circumstances?

1.15 am:
For your viewing pleasure, here is a visual retrospective of a curated selection of some of Simon's most shameful moments.

All his greatest hits are here: congratulating a Rubenesque young woman who was not actually pregnant; calling his first boss 'Dad' in the middle of a meeting; falling off a moving treadmill in a hotel gym in front of a spin class. Enjoy this collage of more than thirty years of social faux pas, professional blunders and familial misjudgements!

1.31 am:

If only Simon had been nicer to that kid in Year 5, the one who had no friends. What was his name? Herbie? Harvey? The one who smelled. Simon had never been mean, never bullied him – but that was nothing to be proud of. Not actually bullying someone was a low bar of human behaviour. He should have been nicer. Why couldn't the teachers see that Herbie/Harvey had dyslexia or something, instead of punishing him for failing and making fun of him? Why didn't they *know* things like that, back then? Why didn't Simon invite him over or share his lunch or take the time to tell him he wasn't stupid? Why didn't his parents encourage him to be kinder?

1.39 am:

It was all right for Mon. It's easy to be excited about the future when you lived at home with your mother. He had a family to support, rent to pay. Do you know how expensive children are? The actual cost of their clothes and food and toys and education, not even counting all the wine you have to drink to get through it? Children are like small, messy cocaine habits.

1:50 am:

But what was here *before* the Big Bang?

2.32 am:

Does everyone see colours exactly the same? Was his green, for example, the same as everyone else's green? How would you ever know?

2.56 am:

If you were to die alone in a flat, how long would it be before your cat ate you?

2.58 am:

And there was so much work still to be done on the garden. He could just imagine the reaction if it wasn't finished: Tansy's disappointed face, Gloria's paint-stripping glare. Not to mention the money! They needed a new fridge. Finish the garden, make wife happy, get money, buy fridge, return to former life on couch. Simple. But for right now, sleep.

3.08 am:

Now. Go to sleep now. Immediately.

3.10 am:

And don't sleep in, whatever you do. Get up the moment the alarm goes off.

3.14 am:

His children went through so many pairs of shoes. People without children don't realise how fast kids' feet grow. They grow like the national debt, like nose hair. Lachie needs new shoes every four months and Mia's not much different. They *needed* new shoes, it wasn't optional – their little toes jam up against the front. That kids' shoe caper, that's a licence to print money.

3.42 am:

Anyway, who cares about Mon and her exciting plans for the future? What mattered was family: Tansy and Mia and Lachie. They were all safe and well. Look at them! Mia was so smart, so conscientious. And Lachie, such an adorable little tearaway. So loving, so much spirit. Simon's legacy wouldn't be some dry-as-dust balance sheet. Two things would show his worth as a person: Lachie's winning personality, creative endeavours and love of life, and Mia's perfect behaviour, report cards and future success.

No pressure.

WEDNESDAY

Chapter 18

It was all very well for Simon to consider the important moments in his life to have been inevitable. Important moments *did* seem that way, in retrospect. Back on that chilly Saturday night in 2005, though, he'd felt no sense of manifest destiny. He'd felt annoyed, mostly. He was dressed in his best cargo pants and military-style jacket with a six-pack of VB under his arm, and he was standing on the footpath with Brock, his housemate, while they considered the house across the street.

'Uncool, man,' said Brock. 'First you didn't want to go to a club, then you didn't want to go to the pub. And now I've found you this *rad* party and you don't want to go inside.'

'It's after eleven,' said Simon. 'It's too late, don't you think? They've probably gone to bed.' He could be home himself, having an early night after watching a repeat of *Iron Chef* or the episode of *Lost* he recorded on Thursday night. Simon simultaneously loved *Lost* and also couldn't wait for it to end. He was absolutely certain that the final episode would be entirely fulfilling and logical and all the loose ends would be tied up in a singular act of narrative genius.

Brock flipped his Motorola Razr open and closed, open and closed. 'Man,' he said. He took Simon's shoulder and squeezed it. 'Do you think I spend the weekend trying to drag you out of the house for my own amusement? Do you think I lack mates? I do not lack mates. I have hundreds of mates, thank you very much. I'm doing this for your own good.'

It was all very well for Brock to go out every night. Brock was a 35-year-old part-time chef slash ecstasy dealer, so going out was part of his job. It was practically a tax deduction. Simon, on the other hand, was a 25-year-old cubicle jockey. He had worked his way through his university years as a labourer for a landscape gardener on weekends and the long holidays, but now he did nothing physical at all yet was exhausted all the time. He was a junior architect in a huge firm, and months had turned into years since his graduation while he made models and designed air-conditioning systems for office blocks using CAD. But mostly his job seemed to be sorting out the software problems of the older senior architects, who would sometimes throw their hands up and have Simon physically sit in front of their computer and adjust plans to their directions. He had irregular weekend sex with Stacey, a plump closet punk in accounts who ignored him if they crossed paths during the day and stubbed out her post-coital cigarettes on his bedside table. Brock was forever offering him mate's rates on molly, but Simon always declined. This was his life with his brain operating at full capacity! Imagine how rubbish he would be with any kind of mental impairment. Besides, he was saving for an iPod.

Across the road, the house seemed quiet. Normal. Suburban. Possibly there was no party at all.

'Okay, all right,' Simon said. 'One quick drink.'

'I'd have more fun going out with John Howard,' said Brock. 'Come on then.'

The night was still but as soon as Brock opened the front door, the doof-doof from the sound system seemed to radiate through the soles of Simon's shoes and up his legs to his skull. And so many people! People of all ages, squeezed into corners and cluttered in doorways, drinking or dancing, smoking and making out. The house, Brock explained, was somebody's grandmother's, currently uninhabited, a tired brick-veneer with floral carpets, and pine panelling in the kitchen.

'It's a going-away party for Siobhan, yeah?' Brock said to him, over the bass. 'She's off backpacking with a girlfriend. Europe. Crazy, right? Best country on earth, right here.'

Brock, Simon realised long ago, was more patriotic than the average chef slash drug dealer. He also knew more people than Simon thought possible.

They found the bathroom and the bath, filled with dirty ice, VB, floating Bacardi Breezers and flaking cardboard boxes of wine.

'One quick drink,' said Simon. He reluctantly surrendered his six-pack to the icy water.

'Or two,' said Brock. 'Let's find Siobhan.'

They squeezed their way through the crowd, down the hall and past the dining table filled with open pizza boxes and bamboo bowls of Doritos to a small cement yard surrounded by a border of bark chips but no plants. The Hills hoist in the middle was strung with lights and assorted t-shirts, stiff with sun and age.

'Siobhan!' Brock said to a solidly built, short-haired girl in a purple tie-dyed skirt, clashing top and Doc Martens, sitting cross-legged under the Hills hoist.

Siobhan was already at the enormous-pupils, stuffing-pizza-in-her-mouth stage of the night. 'Brock! Drugs?' She looked up at him hopefully.

'Fresh out, love,' Brock said. 'I've been busier than Myer. Besides, you might have had enough.'

She turned to Simon. 'How about you? Any drugs?'

'Holy shit, is that Nick Schnabel?' Brock nodded to a tall man in a leather jacket in the centre of a circle in the far corner of the yard. 'Number one draft pick last year? Or was it the year before? He had a fantastic season. Out right now. Groin.'

Simon turned to look at Nick Schnabel, but then, on the other side of the yard, he saw a girl in a green dress. She was leaning against the purple brick wall that separated the house from a lane. The arms on that girl. Her brown, lithe arms.

First, Simon felt a jolt. Then a shiver spread over his skin. His heart almost jumped from his chest. He felt – and this was such a cliche, he could hardly believe it – as though he had been struck by lightning. Like every self-respecting bloke, he'd never believed in love at first sight, yet here it was. Unlikely as it might seem, all those romantic poets and sixties balladeers had been right all along. Simon felt his gut drop away into a yawning cavern, as though he'd eaten nothing since Tuesday and stomach acid was burning its way through his intestines. Then his head began to boil, as though someone was using his scalp as a Weber. He felt his forehead with one palm and held the other over his lips. *I'm sick*, that was his first thought. He ought to leave this party right now, get home to bed, beg Brock to bring him soup and penicillin. His second thought: the girl with the arms belonged with Simon, and he would cross every river and climb every mountain until she could see it.

'That girl,' he said to no one in particular, 'she's my future wife.'

'Mate,' said Brock. 'You should not say something like that in jest. Marriage is a sacred institution.'

'That's Tansy,' Siobhan said. 'My travel buddy. She hasn't got any drugs. I already asked her.'

Then Simon noticed that Tansy's arms were around the neck of a man. Simon didn't know him. In the future, he would come to know him as Jeff the ex, but at that moment, Simon felt only pity for him. *That poor bloke*, thought Simon. To be so close. For the rest of that stranger's life, Tansy would be the one who got away.

'I need to talk to her,' he said, then straight away, 'I can't talk to her.'

'You'd better make up your mind, sunshine,' Siobhan said. 'We leave for Budapest tomorrow night.'

'What?' he said. 'No. No.'

'Mate, you're looking a little off-colour,' said Brock. He turned his head to make sure Siobhan wasn't watching, then he slid a joint into the pocket of Simon's jacket. 'Here. Chill, Simon. It's on the house.'

Simon wasn't known for being decisive. He was easygoing, non-competitive, non-confrontational. He couldn't remember ever having felt this certain about anything, not even when he was in grade twelve and his father wanted him to study accounting instead of architecture. His father, who rarely lost his temper, was aghast and furious at Simon's career choice. He thought Simon would face a lifetime of unemployment if he insisted on becoming 'a fashion designer for ridiculous houses, working for people with more money than sense'. Architecture was everything his father loathed; he saw it as celebration of style over substance, part of the glorification of appearances and the subjectivity that sounded the death knell for Western civilisation. Dentistry wasn't like that. Teeth were either full of cavities, or they weren't. Simon had stuck to his guns, but the fight with his father had upset him for weeks. It was possible that it was his father's opposition that drove Simon through those difficult early years when he wasn't sure he'd made the right decision. He'd allowed himself to be backed into a corner; he couldn't give up. His father's disapproval had also been one of the reasons that Simon had moved to Melbourne to study.

'Maybe I should propose to her now,' Simon said.

Brock extracted the joint from Simon's pocket. 'No more for you, son. You should have said you were already flying.'

'You're right,' said Simon. Then he opened his mouth as though he was going to say something else, but no words came out. He just stood there, gormless.

'Earth to Simon,' said Brock. 'Are we going over to talk to the future Mrs Larsen or not? If she chooses to change her name. Which is, like, entirely her prerogative.'

'Yes,' said Simon. 'No.'

'First answer's the best answer,' said Brock, and took his arm.

'Wait.' Simon put down his VB. He needed a clear head; he wanted to remember everything. He and Brock approached them.

'You must be Tansy,' Brock said. 'I'm Brock. I'm an old friend of Siobhan's.'

'Jeff,' said Jeff.

Simon shook his hand with focused, warm control, nodding to convey his sympathy.

'This is Simon,' Brock said.

'I'm Simon,' he said.

'So I hear,' said Tansy, and she smiled at him.

'Nick Schnabel's over there,' said Brock.

'He's a dickhead,' said Tansy. Then she yelled across the courtyard, 'Yo, Schnabel! You're a dick!'

Nick turned and clocked Tansy. Then he proceeded to itch a spot on his cheek using his extended middle finger.

'He's her brother,' said Jeff.

'Is that right?' said Brock. 'Do you think I could ask him about the AFL's drug-testing regime? Professional curiosity.' Then to Jeff, 'Could you introduce us?' Without waiting for an answer, Brock threw his arm around Jeff's shoulder and guided him over to Nick.

'Is he actually a dick?' said Simon.

'Occasionally,' said Tansy. 'He's not just my brother, he's my *baby* brother. It's my solemn duty to stop him getting a big head.'

'Does athletic ability run in the family?' he managed. The rest of the party had turned into a blur around him.

'It's from Mum,' she said. 'Passed me by. Our sister has the same competitive streak as Nick, but she thinks sport is frivolous.'

'Ah. I thought maybe you were going to Europe to join the international bullfighting circuit.'

She smiled. Her freckles danced across the pink of her cheeks. 'I'm going to Europe because . . . I don't know why I'm going. My sister is very serious about her career. Nick is . . . Nick is Nick. I'm going to Europe to work out who I am.'

'You can't do that here?'

She nodded towards Nick. Brock was gesturing with both hands towards his groin – either discussing Nick's specific injury in some depth, or illustrating the hydraulics of the AFL's drug-testing regime.

'My family,' Tansy said. 'They're intense. Mum especially. I mean, I love them, but they're a lot. I'm in the middle. I just need a little space.'

'I can see that,' said Simon with a glance back at Nick. 'But when you *do* find out who you are, I'd really like to know.'

She turned her hazel eyes on him. 'Why?'

Simon had realised in mere seconds that she was that rare book entirely capable of being judged by the cover: she was as perfect as he'd imagined from across the room.

'It's just a guess,' he said, 'but I expect the answer will be spectacular.'

—

That was it. That was all they said to each other; in another moment, Jeff and Brock were back. Simon didn't crowd her or overstay his welcome. Nothing he'd ever done in his life so far had been as important as this. He would not stuff it up by overplaying his hand.

The next morning, Brock forwarded him an email: Tansy's details, sent at her request by Siobhan.

He kept in touch with Tansy while she was overseas in a friendly, genuine manner, asking her about each of her stops: Berlin, Majorca, London. Their emails grew longer, more detailed. He felt the thrill of her impressions in each new city. It's easy to say that he was patient but it was more than that. He was interested in everything she saw and everything she did. He saw each city through her eyes. He loved the process of corresponding with her, like they were courting in the Victorian age. If he was worried about her meeting someone over there and falling in love and staying in Europe and never coming home – if he ever woke up in the middle of the night, hyperventilating and convinced that he needed to hop a plane that second and find her and never let her out of his sight again – he never acknowledged it, not even to himself. Tansy would come back to Melbourne in a year; she had to. Some things were meant to be.

Hold your nerve, Simon.

When she did arrive back, he sent her a casual, cheery message. Then he heard she broke up with Jeff, who'd found someone more available in the year she was overseas. Simon instantly asked her out. She said yes. He was exhilarated – and yes, triumphant. In all these years he'd never lost that feeling of certainty. He and Tansy had rarely been apart and now, all these years later, she was still the love of his life. They were aligned, in sync.

There was nothing about Tansy that Simon didn't know.

Chapter 19

Observe Simon Larsen in bed: he's kicked the covers off so you can see him, top to toe. Five foot ten and three-quarters, or around 180 centimetres in new money. Solid build. It's almost impossible for a grown man to look dignified in pyjamas and these were cotton with long sleeves and long pants in a pastel blue stripe, and no exception. And how long had it been since he'd shaved? Too long. Reasonable head of hair for a man of his age, if greyish. If you didn't look closely at his eyelids you might take him to be at peace.

When he woke, the flat was quiet. Which was normal. What wasn't normal was that it was light. He rolled over and checked his phone.

Nine thirty! He should have been up hours ago. There were holes to be dug and plants waiting in their pots and black plastic bags and pavers to be laid. Timber to be cut and sanded and nailed, a watering system to be installed. He needed to get moving.

He checked Mia's room, the lounge, the dining room. Everyone was gone. There was a note on the kitchen bench: *You looked so exhausted, we couldn't wake you! Don't forget we're at the Chees' for dinner tonight. xx T.*

Did he already know they were invited to the Chees' for dinner? Was there anything he was supposed to bring? He must have slept like the dead not to wake when they all left. And where was Monica? She can't have gone out shopping again? She was at it all day yesterday; she must have already been to every shop in the city. He wondered for a moment how Monica slept. Not like a normal person, that's for sure. She'd sleep like someone with no commitments, who never had to worry about the cost of a new fridge . . .

—

Simon caught himself a good twenty minutes later, still standing in the kitchen in his pyjamas, frozen in time and space. Instead of rushing to shower and dress, he'd been sucked into a vortex of thinking of all the things that Mon didn't have to worry about: rent, children's education costs and working out how much super she should have at her age, which sounds like a simple question but has no simple answer. A large number of small things took up all the space in Simon's brain: like what if the rent went up and they couldn't pay it; and the pinpoint timing of the cancellation of the rotating free trials of all the streaming services under an assortment of email addresses.

No, Simon thought. He refused to be an envious person. It was an emotion he refused to entertain. What mattered now were his values and being a good role model for his children. Whatever Mon had or didn't have, that was no concern of his. He needed to snap out of it.

Then he heard keys in the lock – the front door opened. It was Mon, in blue cloud-print leggings and a midriff top, carrying a water bottle.

'Yo, Simon,' she said, closing the door behind her. 'I've been to Pilates! Live! So different to Zoom, it's unbelievable. Hey, I'm getting Korean delivered. You want in?'

Simon looked at the floor. The floor was really the only place he could look, because the flat plain of Monica's stomach would be unavoidably in his field of vision if he looked at her face.

'Hello?' said Monica. 'Are you okay?'

'Fine, yes,' he said to the carpet. 'No Korean, thanks.'

'I got a new filter that turns you into a puppy. Wanna see?'

'I'm good.' He needed to talk to Tansy. She didn't answer on her mobile, so he was forced to try her office landline. The trick to phoning Tansy at work, Simon knew, was to carefully count the number of rings to avoid the call being redirected back to Meg, the receptionist and office manager. He needed to hang up after exactly eight rings.

Or was it seven?

'Greeves and Stamos Real Estate, how may I be of assistance?' Meg said suddenly. *Seven. Damn.* Meg had the rare ability to sigh heavily while speaking yet, at the same time, to sound as though her nose was completely blocked or even non-existent. It was as if Voldemort had a job answering the phone for a suburban real estate agency.

Simon's mouth went dry. There was no hanging up now, his number would be on the screen.

'Meg! Simon Larsen here. Just calling for Tansy.' He sounded as casual as he could.

'Huh. Good luck with that. She's not in.'

'Thanks, Meg.'

'You could try her mobile but I'm not promising anything. I don't know why she even bothers carrying one. You can never get through to her.'

Simon didn't say that he'd already tried. That would sound pathetic. 'Will do, thanks. Anyway, I'd better—'

'I've got a pile of messages for her already,' said Meg. 'She's hardly ever in the office lately. I'm not sure what I'm expected to do about it. Stick a GPS on her forehead? I'm not a miracle worker. If it was anyone but Tansy, I'd be suspicious.'

'Suspicious? Of what?'

'That she was going to job interviews. But there's not a chance. She loves her job. It's pretty annoying.'

Simon frowned into the phone. Tansy loved her job? The job she was forced to take because, thanks to Simon, she no longer had the luxury of staying home with the kids? 'I think you'll find she hates her job, like any normal person,' Simon said. 'I know her a little better than you.'

'Er, no. She loves it, trust me. You can't fake that. But why wouldn't she love it? Driving around, never letting me know where she's going,' said Meg. 'God knows what she's up to. It's impossible to keep track of her yet I'm the one who's supposed to take messages. When is she going to get back to me, that's what people ask. How should I know? Is that fair? Honestly.'

'She works very—'

'It's all right for some. I'm never allowed out of the office. I sit at this desk all day. Never see the sky.' Nasal sigh. 'It's not healthy. The cubicles are bigger at Pentridge. I have a vitamin D deficiency, I'm pretty sure. I need one of those lamps.'

'I hear you,' he said.

He looked at the clock on the microwave . . . but it was Simon's lucky day. Meg received another call, so he managed to hang up.

Monica was gone. The bathroom door was closed and the shower was running.

Great, he thought. *She'll be in there for ages.*

Next he phoned Naveen.

Who wasn't answering either. Simon left an apologetic message. This was the third day in a row that Simon hadn't shown up when expected. If Naveen were a normal client, there'd be hell to pay. Simon needed to pick up his game. Be more professional.

He had to focus, get on with his day. Simon stood in front of his wardrobe, thinking about possible outfits for his coffee with Flora. Perhaps he should wear jeans? Jeans were casual, hip. He would look vital, connected to youth culture. Actually, no. Jeans would look pathetic, like he was having a midlife crisis. Which he certainly wasn't. Or it would lead Flora to assume that he wasn't working in an architectural office. Okay, he wasn't, but he didn't necessarily want Flora to know that. He should be practical and sensible and wear his outdoor work gear, for going straight to Naveen's afterwards. Actually, nope. No, no, no. How would that look? Like he was hopeless, that's how. Like he was working in his wife's friend's garden because he couldn't find anything else. At the back of his wardrobe were his business suits, unworn for a couple of years. He pulled out a pair of tailored pants and held them up to his waist. They seemed weirdly small. Perhaps the drycleaners had shrunk them. He decided on a slightly fancier outfit – a crisp patterned shirt and a sports coat, an outfit he might have worn to take Tansy somewhere nice for dinner back when they did that – because he had no other options.

Both Tansy and Naveen would call him back any minute, Simon thought. That's why, when his phone rang a little later, he answered it immediately, without looking at the screen.

Rookie mistake.

Chapter 20

'Finally,' said Gloria, after Simon said hello. 'I was beginning to think you were dead. Though if you were dead, I'm sure someone would have let me know. Eventually.'

An image of her on the other end of the phone filled Simon's mind: Gloria, in her glossy black helmet and sweeping cape, stalking the corridors of the Death Star, mobile to her ear, her voice rasping like an asphyxiating asthmatic while she telekinetically suspended gasping underlings by the throat.

'Not dead,' said Simon, although if he could slip into an induced coma for the duration of this conversation, he would. 'Thanks for asking, though.'

'The reason for my call,' she began, 'is to check where you're up to with Naveen's backyard.'

He sat heavily on the bed. The backyard, the backyard. Everyone was on his case – first Tansy, now Gloria. He refused to be micromanaged. He was a grown man, not a child.

'Fine,' he said. 'I'm exactly on schedule.'

'What does that mean, on schedule?'

'It means I have everything under control. How are you, Gloria?'

She snorted like a distant dragon. 'How am I, Simon? How sweet of you to ask. I'm frustrated, that's how I am. I've been trying to call Tansy but it's impossible to get through. What on earth is that girl up to? We need to work out a plan of attack for Saturday.'

Simon scanned his memory for their plans this weekend. A school fundraiser? A party? Some kind of human sacrifice Gloria had organised to reinforce her demonic powers? He had no idea. 'Saturday?'

Gloria made a noise in the back of her throat; it sounded like a dog, vomiting. 'It must be nice to be you, Simon. You do remember Saturday? David's memorial service? Wake up, Australia. I'm extremely busy. I'm also organising a fundraiser for the tennis club and the caterer has insufficient vegetarian options. I need to put all the arrangements for Saturday behind me.'

Of course. How could he have forgotten? That was why he was finishing Naveen's backyard. That was the point of all that work.

Now he could hear an odd rhythmic tapping through the phone, as if there was a hostage on Gloria's end of the line sending a desperate plea for help in morse code. There wasn't a hostage, of course. That was a ridiculous idea. Gloria lived alone. The sound was Gloria's long painted fingernails, staccato against the dashboard of the Death Star. Women's nails were one of the many subjects that Simon knew nothing about but Tansy had explained that Gloria's nails were a thing of wonder: they looked for all the world like gel (which, despite the name, was anything but gel-like) but were actually natural. Gloria's nails had the tensile strength of steel, as though the bones of her fingers and toes were continuing to grow straight out through the tips of her appendages. She could tighten screws with her nails. Open letters. Skewer cherry tomatoes. Even the slightly larger cherry tomatoes. The ones that were testicle-sized.

Oh yes. The memorial service. That's right. 'I thought everything was organised? Tansy said so?' Simon said.

'Hello? I don't mean the chairs and the flowers, et cetera. I've instructed the caterers – we're not having those funeral mini sausage rolls that stay pale regardless of how long they're in the oven. How do those vampire sausage rolls so comprehensively defy the laws of pastry? Regardless, I don't care about those extraneous details. What I mean is: what we're going to *do*. Our plan of attack.'

'I'm not sure we have to do anything,' Simon said.

Gloria laughed in the same way that a doll might, if it were a doll in a Stephen King novel. 'Oh Simon,' she said. 'Poor, sweet, naive Simon.'

'I'll ask Tansy to call you, if you'd like,' he said. He made a mental note to also ask Mia to show him how to set individual ringtones on his phone so he would never make the mistake of answering Gloria's call again. Tansy could have 'Lady in Red'. Gloria could have the theme from *Jaws*, perhaps.

'I've already left her a message. This is urgent. We need to coordinate what we're going to wear, for a start.'

'Maybe Kylie would be the best person to—'

'Right. If I wanted everyone to look like a news anchor from the 1980s. Are the shoulder pads a form of armour? And her hair! Don't get me started. We need to find her a boyfriend. Naveen will be there on Saturday, right? He was a dreadfully whiny little boy but I expect he's grown out of that. He's single now? With a child? Which is perfect, because Kylie's over forty, so that ship has sailed.'

'Ah, Gloria. I really can't see any romance there. They've known each other since they were children. They're friends.

I mean, Kylie's not as close to Naveen as Tansy is, but you'd definitely categorise them as friends.'

'Friends?' Gloria laughed again. 'Men and women cannot be friends, Simon. The genitals get in the way.'

'That's not true at all. Tansy and Naveen are a prime example. They've been friends for decades.'

'Is Kylie gay, do you think? If she were gay, why wouldn't she say something to me? I'd get one of those t-shirts, the ones that say *Proud Mum of a Lesbian*. I'd wear it everywhere. I'd go to all the marches. And if any ill-advised person tried to homo-shame my child, they'd wish they'd never been born. I have lesbian friends now, I'll have you know. They weren't easy to find out here in Surrey Hills. Surrey Hills is not Northcote. But I persevered. I can't tell you how often I had to go to the farmers' market and initiate conversations about goat cheese. Anyway. Kylie just needs to be honest about her sexuality. With me. I've asked her repeatedly if she's a lesbian and she won't even answer! She's repressed. Takes after her father. It's ridiculous. I've been nothing but supportive of that girl for her entire life.'

'Anyway.' Simon pressed one temple with his thumb. 'Perhaps you could chat to Nick about what we should wear to the memorial service?'

'Certainly not. The poor baby has enough on his plate without worrying him with something like this.'

'I'm not sure I can help,' said Simon. 'I want to help, don't get me wrong. But I'm not really a fashion person.'

'I'm aware of that, I'm not blind,' said Gloria. 'Anyway. I was thinking of us all in black, and me and Tansy and Kylie in little pillbox hats with veils. Mia and Lachie will be the star attractions because they're adorable. Gorgeous grandchildren are the best revenge, that's well known. I want them in peacoats, Simon. Just like JFK Jr and Caroline at the funeral.'

How stupid would that look, at a memorial service? Lachie and Mia in little jackets covered in long, multicoloured tail feathers. It sounded inappropriate to Simon, and probably cruel. 'I—'

'And I want us all to wear fuck-me sunglasses,' continued Gloria. 'If I'm going to buy Nick a new black suit, it should be today. Luckily, with his physique' – she pronounced *physique* with a heavy French accent, like a television chef who speaks normally until they say *Parmigiano-Reggiano* like a seventy-year-old Umbrian who's never left the village – 'it won't need alterations. Nick is a perfect specimen, so we can save a bit of time there. You, on the other hand. We'd need the trousers taken up, the sleeves let out and the chest . . . altered. Which would be fine, if the funeral was next year. If you'd shown a bit more foresight, Simon, you could have joined a gym. Is it too late, do you think? You could start today. This minute. What do you think?'

What did Simon think? He thought Gloria was unlikely to buy *him* a new black suit, and he certainly wasn't buying a new suit, and he certainly wasn't having this non-existent suit altered, and he wasn't joining a gym *this minute*. As to fuck-me sunglasses – he didn't even know what they were, but he was positive he didn't want his children to wear them. 'I—'

'You do have a black suit, I assume? Never mind, you can always wait in the car. I think we're going to look amazing. In fact, I think you should organise those YouTube people to come out and film us. Can I leave that to you, Simon? Excellent, one fewer thing on my plate.'

'Actually, Gloria, that's not how it—'

'Simon.' She paused, and an even greater gravitas than normal came into her voice. 'It's past ten o'clock in the morning. Are you still in your pyjamas?'

Simon sank heavily on the bed, next to his laid-out clothes. How did Gloria know things like that? Was there some kind of long-distance telescope on the Surrey Hills Death Star? Or could she hear the sound of the flannelette fibres as they snuggled against each other?

'Because Tansy works very hard and the last thing she needs is some deadweight of a husband,' Gloria said. 'Are you addicted to porn?'

'What? No!'

'Are you depressed?'

'Me?'

'Depression is nothing to be ashamed of. Oh, sure, it used to be. I'm old enough to remember the days when we thought people with depression were just spineless, weak-willed layabouts who needed a swift kick up the arse. Lazy. Bums. But times have changed. These days, it's considered a medical condition. You can't call depressed people names anymore, so I've been told.'

Simon couldn't help but wonder who had been the brave, late-lamented person who'd told her that.

'The bankruptcy, losing your former business, losing the house,' Gloria continued. 'The kids having to change schools. Tansy having to be the breadwinner, working such long hours for those horrid real estate people. Women cope much better with these kinds of things. For men, it hits them right in the ego and the self-worth. They feel like failures. It'd be considered strange if you weren't depressed, considering everything.'

The longer Gloria went on, the more depressed Simon felt.

'I'm fine, thanks for asking,' he said. Or he would be fine, as soon as he ended this conversation, showered and changed and drove across town for his coffee with Flora, who would treat him with the respect and dignity he deserved. He looked at the shirt on the bed beside him. Was that a stain on the front, between the buttons? Or was that part of the pattern? He scratched it with his fingernail. It was hard to tell.

'Viagra,' said Gloria.

Simon almost choked on his own tongue. 'I beg your pardon?'

'Perhaps you should get your hearing checked as well. Viagra, I said. What is the point of living in the twenty-twenties if you don't avail yourself of some pharmaceutical assistance now and then? I'm thinking of Tansy, and you should be also. Stress can take its toll on a man your age.'

'I am not having this conversation with you,' he managed.

'All right, all right. I can take a hint,' said Gloria, who most assuredly could not take a hint. 'Never let it be said that I'm not sensitive to other people and their little moods. Far be it from me to cast aspersions on anyone's natural sloth-like inclination. Just be yourself, Simon, that's always been my perspective. Regardless of who you are. Anyway. I've decided on a stretch limo for the memorial service – can you take care of that? Not a Hummer, nothing vulgar. Something very tasteful. Sunroof optional. There's . . . let's see . . . five of us, and the kids. Seven in total.'

'Eight,' Simon said, because he was relieved that Gloria had moved on from her free character assessment of him and he was distracting himself from the extreme awkwardness he felt by thinking about how long it had been since he wore this shirt. The last time he took Tansy out for dinner the first lockdown was only days away, though they hadn't known it. Back then, he and Tansy tried to have a date night once a month. *Tried* to. What with the long hours he worked and the networking required to run a successful business, they didn't manage every month. Or even every second month. But sometimes Tansy would insist so he would come home from work early and Kylie or Nick would babysit. The kids looked forward to it also – a night of takeaway pizza and age-appropriate science experiments (Kylie) or age-inappropriate movies (Nick). On the night of their last dinner out, he and Tansy dressed up and went to a small Italian wine bar not far from their old house. Nothing fancy. Tansy ordered spaghetti with clams, he remembered. He had ravioli, the pasta soft as butter, and a lovely Sangiovese. Tansy wore a plain black skirt and her gold-coloured silky blouse, the one that looked like liquid when the light caught it just so.

A simple dinner with your wife was the kind of ritual that was easy to take for granted, once upon a time. When all that stopped – first, because of the lockdowns and then because they didn't have money to spare – only then did he miss it.

'No wonder you went bankrupt, if that's your skill in maths,' said Gloria. 'Me, Nick, Tansy, Kylie, you, and Mia and Lachie. That's seven.'

Mon, of course, could still go out for dinner whenever she wanted. Every night, if she liked. She could come home anytime she wanted. She didn't pay rent; instead she could have spaghetti with clams. She could have a bowl of clams without the bulking carbs that made the dish affordable. She could have oysters. Caviar. Not that Simon wanted to have caviar; he'd never really understood the appeal – it was like slimy fishy popping candy, and probably a swindle perpetrated by Big Fish – but still. She could have as many bottles of Sangiovese as she liked.

'And Mon,' Simon said automatically.

'Who?' said Gloria.

Chapter 21

Simon had once watched a documentary on SBS on a Sunday night about the nature of time, but he hadn't actually understood it. Did time have something to do with string theory? Black holes? Einstein? How would Stephen Hawking explain, for example, the fact that time stopped as soon as Gloria said the word '*who*'? Yet simultaneously, time also sped up – because now it was apparently the middle of July. Simon could tell it was July because a deep and pervasive cold settled in the marrow of his bones.

'Simon,' said Gloria. 'Simon, Simon, Simon.'

There was a long pause, during which Simon's blood stopped pumping and began congealing in the tips of his fingers and in his eyeballs. The tapping sound of Gloria's fingernails became sharper and closer. He crossed his legs and cupped one hand around his testicles without even realising it. He squeezed his eyes shut.

'I asked you a question, Simon. Who is this Mon person, and why is she coming with us to the memorial?' she said.

He cleared his throat and blinked his eyes open. 'Um. Mon. Monica. Is David's daughter?' he said. 'From his second marriage?'

'Is that a question? Are you asking me, or telling me?' said Gloria.

'Um. Telling you?' said Simon.

Silence again. It was the kind of silence that enabled Simon to hear the concrete underneath the carpet on the floor expanding and contracting with the rotation of the earth.

'I see. You know this Mon person. Somehow she has entered into your orbit. Tansy, I'm assuming, also knows this Mon person. How about Kylie and Nick? Have they met her also?'

'Um. Yes?'

'I see. I see. Possibly everyone knows her except for me.'

'It just kind of happened . . .' he said.

'Simon. I'm going to ask you a very simple question, and I want you to concentrate. Where is Tansy now?' said Gloria.

'She wasn't in the office half an hour ago,' Simon said. 'I rang. That's what they said.'

'Simon. Think carefully. Did I ask you where she *wasn't*?'

'No. I don't know.'

Gloria's talons went *rat a tat tat, rat a tat tat*. Simon could hear a muffled noise, which he assumed was the strangled Death Star employee being released from their midair hover and hitting the ground. WorkCover would have an absolute field day with that.

'This isn't over,' Gloria said. 'You can tell Tansy that from me.'

———

As soon as Simon hung up from Gloria, he made a cup of tea and composed himself. Then he texted Tansy to say that he *might possibly* have let something slip, and that there was a small but not insignificant chance that Gloria knew that they were in contact with Mon, and there was a *teeny* possibility that Gloria would be not thrilled with that development.

There was no reply.

He was now running late for his coffee with Flora. The bathroom door was still closed, Mon's shower still running. He sniffed under his armpits, applied deodorant he found in Tansy's gym bag, changed and drove across town. When he arrived at the cafe, he parked around the corner.

Not that he was ashamed of Flora noticing he no longer had his SUV and instead drove an old ute belonging to some friend of Nick's.

Nothing like that.

He just wasn't in the mood for angle parking, that was all. Besides, someone disabled or old or pregnant might need the closer space. It would be irresponsible to park out the front. Which was fine. He was in the mood for a leisurely, spacious park halfway down the side street and a gentle stroll to the front of the cafe.

Outside the cafe, he checked his phone again. Still no text from Tansy.

It wasn't the kind of cafe he would have chosen. Inside, everything was a dusky pink: the terrazzo floor, the panelled walls, the marble tabletops, the velvet banquette seating. For a moment, he wondered if something was wrong with his vision. But no, someone had done this deliberately.

He scanned the room and saw Flora at the back in a long booth for six. She was sitting between two young men.

He walked over.

'Simon!' Flora said. 'Great to see you, man.'

The three of them stood, or stood as much as possible while remaining in the booth. Flora looked even younger than she did two years ago. Her hair, once straight and geometric, was now a nest of curls and she was wearing heavy-framed black glasses that made her face look tiny. Simon would have liked to give her a hug but she was wedged in the middle seat. She thrust her hand out. Shaking Flora's hand seemed too formal to Simon; he'd known her since she was fourteen. Still, he shook it.

'It's good of you to come,' Flora said. 'Please, sit. Can we get you a single-origin? A vegan donut? This is Lars, and this is Milo.'

They grow up so fast! Oh, she was adorable, offering him a drink and introducing him to her friends! It reminded Simon of sitting on the floor with Mia when she was a toddler, watching her pour imaginary tea for him and her teddies. In that moment, Simon was so happy to be there with Flora, happy to do anything he could to help. It was all he could manage not to reach over and pinch her cheeks.

'It's my pleasure,' he said firmly. Regardless of his private thoughts, Flora was a grown woman. He needed to treat her like one. He had another memory of Mia pretending to be the teacher of a classroom of dolls wearing Tansy's old reading glasses, which were similar in shape to Flora's. He thought of how angry he'd be if Mia was patronised by an older male when she was Flora's age. He adjusted his smile.

'We are totally stoked you're here, man. Very excited.' This from Lars, who wore a plaid shirt unbuttoned over a white V-neck tee and, for some reason, a beanie.

Milo also shook Simon's hand. He wore a denim shirt buttoned up to his neck, with the top of a tattoo sticking up under the collar on one side. He had an enormous beard like Alfred Deakin and Simon could see his scalp through his buzz cut, which reminded him of Monica's. Why did young men cut their hair that short? Simon had never understood it. Did they not grasp the dreadful impending baldness that was lurking in their future? *Wait until you turn forty*, Simon wanted to say, *no need to rush it.*

'Great to meet you,' said Simon, who had no idea who these people were or why they were here. Surely he wasn't meant to role-play a job interview for the three of them?

'Flora's told us so much about you,' said Lars. 'She said you are the absolute bomb.'

'Awesome, that's what she said,' said Milo.

'Legendary,' said Lars.

'It's true. Simon taught me everything I know,' said Flora.

'Not even close,' said Simon, though he was beaming. 'Flora was always gifted. I was the lucky one. I got far more from our relationship than she did.'

'What are you working on right now?' said Lars.

Simon thought of Naveen's place. 'It's a multi-use hub. Suburban.'

'Family-friendly?' said Flora.

'Very,' Simon said.

'Green?'

'Could literally not be greener,' said Simon.

'It sounds aligned with what we're doing, which is excellent,' said Milo. 'Can we get you a cold brew?'

'Yes,' Simon answered, even when he realised Milo meant a coffee. 'A latte?' He turned down the donut.

'They only make black coffee here, unfortunately,' said Lars. 'Milk interferes with the crema.'

They ordered from a passing waitress and while they were waiting, the three of them pushed business cards across the table towards him. Identical dusky pink cards that matched the cafe, Simon realised, all of which said their names with the word 'Director' underneath. *SLTY Architecture*. Each of them had identical leather journals in front of them, and iMacs, and fountain pens in different colours in their hands. All at once, he noticed how shiny everything was. How new, how expensive.

'We met at uni, then we stayed in touch,' said Flora. 'The three of us. We started SLTY over a year ago, just after I finished up with you.'

'Salty?' said Simon.

'No "a", man,' said Lars.

It was Simon's turn to say something. That was how conversations worked. The other person says something, then you say something. *Go on, brain,* he thought. *Say something.*

'You have a company now,' Simon said, in a voice that sounded almost like his own. 'Congratulations, Flora. I'm so happy for you.'

'Thanks, man,' said Lars. 'It's been a pretty steep learning curve. We worked from home at the beginning –'

'Everyone worked from home back then,' said Milo.

'– but now we have offices in a converted warehouse in Prahran,' Lars continued.

'When we first started, we did cafe and bar refits and focused on Pinterest and Houzz and Insta,' Flora continued. 'But lately, we've pivoted towards bigger projects.'

'This space was one of our first gigs,' said Lars, sweeping his hand around to indicate the cafe. 'I don't want to brag, but we were one of the originators of millennial pink in the inner north.'

'You don't say,' said Simon. In that moment, they didn't seem so cute anymore.

'As a colour, it really sums up our world view,' Milo said. 'It's inherently political due to the overdue feminist reclamation, but also new-fashioned and functional. That's us, in a nutshell.'

'We see ourselves as a traditional architectural practice, with a difference,' said Flora.

'The difference is that we prioritise a rich digital ecosystem,' Lars said. 'The conversation between the channels where we source inspiration and those where we showcase our content and provide discoverable visual-oriented branding is continually in flux.'

'Conversation in flux,' said Simon. 'Cool. Cool, cool, cool.'

'Emerging technology is the way we infuse our practice with an experiential aspect,' Milo said. 'VR, mobile-responsive 3D – they've been game-changers for us. And design-wise, cutting the time between some Pantone colour popping up in an influencer's feed to seeing it everywhere is crucial. Our projects look like now, like, yesterday. Fresh, that's what we're after. Though we style it as Frsh.'

'Frsh?' said Simon. It sounded like Milo had spontaneously developed a Kiwi accent.

'That's fresh, but without the "e",' said Flora.

'Vowels can be extremely dictatorial,' said Lars.

'Obviously,' said Milo.

The coffees came, all identical, in heavy glasses. The waitress took some time to sort out the bourbon-washed (Milo's and Simon's) from the cold drip (Flora's and Lars's).

'Sustainability is key,' said Flora, cupping her coffee in both small hands. 'The footprint needs to be measurable but not tokenistic or altruistic. We're all about high-performing, reliable construction solutions. That's textually and subtextually all over our tenders. It's the way of the future and, frankly, firms that can't grasp that – they're dinosaurs. That said, we're aware that we're design-heavy, communications-heavy and technology-heavy, and that we're commercial construction-light, experience-wise.'

She had a new tattoo: a trail of tiny ants climbing her forearm before they disappeared under the sleeve of her shirt. The sight of them alone made Simon feel itchy.

'We want to be upfront about this,' said Milo. 'We acknowledge our strategic insufficiency with multi-storey, multi-user, multi-zoned developments, which weirdly enough is where we've been the most successful in our tenders. And we've a bit of a hole in our project-management department when the designs get off the scale.'

'We definitely have a knowledge gap,' Flora said.

'And we've got to fill it. Now we're at the pointy end of the planning phase of this one particular project, it's starting to show. To be honest, it's blue-sky thinking that got us this far. We're diving into some really challenging opportunities right now. This specific project is part replacing existing stock, part additional growth facilities, with multiple stakeholders across government, private enterprise and community,' said Lars. 'You with us so far?'

'Absolutely,' said Simon. 'Also, I've changed my mind about the donut.'

'No problem.' Lars waved the waitress over. 'Which one would you like?'

On the counter was a tower of donuts in various shades of pink.

'Surprise me,' Simon said to the waitress.

'Where do you see yourself in five years' time?' said Milo when the waitress left. He then burst into laughter. 'No, seriously, man, we're not that square. I'm taking the piss.'

'But where *do* you see yourself?' said Lars. 'Do you have a resume on your phone, by any chance, that you could airdrop me? We want to hear all about you and your plans for the future. Obviously we don't want to bring someone in and then . . . well, hiring has substantial onboarding and training costs, as I'm sure you know.'

Hiring?

Oh my god, thought Simon. The job interview that Flora mentioned on the phone wasn't one that *she* was attending as a potential employee. *This* was the job interview. *He* was the potential employee, and Flora and her colleagues were the interviewers.

He felt a rush of heat up his neck, up his cheeks. He shut his eyes for a moment and breathed. It was as if a gaping pit had opened beneath his feet and he was falling. His head buzzed. He felt as if he were naked before them, as if everyone in the cafe and the rest of the world knew his years of success had been fluked and here was where he belonged: right here, sitting in front of three young people deciding if he was worthy of working for them or not. If he could shut his eyes and vanish and never reappear anywhere again, that would be fine with him.

'What Lars is saying,' said Milo, 'is that we don't want to employ someone, and then find that they want to – I don't know, I'm just spitballing ideas here, plucking stuff out of the air – retire.'

The shock pulled Simon back to the world. He gasped. 'Retire? How old do you think I am?'

'Guys,' said Flora, 'ageism is not cool. Besides, I think we should tell Simon about the project first. See if he's interested. He has other things on his plate; he's in demand.'

'Sure, of course.' Lars pulled a series of plans from his folder and spread them out, facing Simon.

The best approach, Simon decided, was to go through the motions. That way everyone's dignity remained intact. Simon leaned forward. It had been almost two years since he'd looked at plans in a professional capacity and even then, it had been a house extension for a young family with new unexpected twins. The plans in front of him showed an enormous development with multiple buildings and new roads and trees, and what looked like a park with an amphitheatre. It was the blueprint for a massive community precinct.

'The Child and Family Centre will go here, and here will be a cafe and bookstore,' said Flora, pointing. 'The main building will be here – it will also have youth facilities – and the retirement units go here. The aged-care centre will be in phase two.'

'And which building are you doing?' said Simon.

'All of them,' said Flora.

'*All of them?*' Simon blinked. 'You're doing . . . all this? This is enormous.'

'Thirty million dollars, give or take,' said Lars.

'What? You've been going for less than two years, and you're working on a project worth thirty million dollars?' Simon took a bite out of a ruby-pink donut that had miraculously appeared in front of him. Then he spat the mouthful back on to the plate. 'Jesus, what the fuck is that?'

'Mango and coconut,' said Lars. 'Oh, you mean the glaze? It's sriracha.'

'When we do a restaurant fitout, we supply a complete turnkey solution to the client, vis-a-vis staff uniforms, menus, and of course the visuals of the food itself,' said Milo. 'Everything is Insta-ready. Sriracha is the only thing we could find that gave the exact shade of pink we were looking for.'

I deserved that, Simon thought, staring resentfully at the donut. *Consider me surprised.*

'Here's our problem. We have draft subdivision plans, elevations, traffic control, shadow plans and environmental impact studies,' said Flora. 'But none of them are finalised.

We also need some decisions, asap. Does the playground go on the left of the amphitheatre, or the right? Where should the trees be relocated to? We need a workflow and spec spreadsheets. Land-clearing and demolition are about to start. We're a little under the pump.'

'What we need, like, yesterday, is a project manager on the ground to finalise the documents and the DA, and to manage the drafters and coordinate with the engineers and builders,' said Lars. 'And if that someone was a bit . . . more experienced . . . with a bit of gravitas. Someone older . . . that'd be good. The whole precinct needs to be family-friendly. Someone at your . . . stage of life would be perfect.'

At his *stage of life*? Which stage of life is that? The parenting stage, because these infants were looking for someone to take care of them in their little 'business'? Someone to hold their hand and check their work. Simon was definitely at the parenting stage of life, which involved watching *Frozen* twenty-seven times, but he was determined to keep that for his actual children. One's parenting and one's professional life need to be completely separate. Simon had learned that through bitter experience. Only a few months ago, before he'd let his membership lapse, he'd leaned across to the man sitting on his left at an Institute of Architects dinner and absentmindedly cut his chicken for him while continuing his conversation with a woman sitting on his right. Was that the kind of staffer these *children* were wanting to hire? Someone to cut their metaphorical chicken? Parenting was exhausting; he wasn't doing it during the day as well. This 'interview' had gone far enough.

'To be completely honest,' said Simon, 'I'm not really a good fit. I work mainly with residential projects. I don't have much experience with commercial buildings or with precincts this size.'

This was almost accurate, considering he didn't have *any* experience with such things at all.

'Not important. It's about the pivot,' Flora said.

'Pivot, pivot,' said Lars. 'What did we know about donuts at the beginning? Nothing. We don't even eat them. We're gluten-free.'

'We always envisaged not being strong at the delivery end. We don't have to be; it's the age of the gig economy. We just need someone to take charge,' said Milo. 'We can outsource a quantity surveyor, a building engineer, electrical engineer – contract them from agencies, short-term. We can't be expected to have every single skill set in-house. I mean, we have over thirty staff now—'

'Jesus Christ, you have thirty people working for you?' said Simon. 'Get the fuck out of town.'

'That's across all the projects,' said Flora. 'We'll need to double that soon, obviously, particularly when the big one in Western Sydney comes online, but it's not easy to find the right associates. We've been taking our time to ensure a strong cultural fit.'

'How are you feeling about all this, opportunity-wise?' said Milo.

How was Simon feeling? Dizzy, that's how he was feeling – or that might have been the mouthful of surprise sriracha. He had run his own company for almost a decade, he'd been successful for a time. He'd even won a couple of architecture awards, back in the day. And these three – *children* – were asking him to work for *them*? To report to *them*, to be under *them* in a chain of command, when Flora was once his work-experience kid? He'd worked on more projects than they'd had hot dinners. Smaller projects, but still. When he had his own business, he was in charge, he was the one determining his direction in life.

Now he felt like he was in a reality television show and that Flora, Lars and Milo were the stars and he'd been brought in for a walk-on part. Here, in this meeting, he felt like a minor character in his own life.

'Let me get this straight,' said Simon. 'You're offering me a job?'

'We need someone mature and smart,' said Milo. 'Someone we can trust. Flora says that's you.'

'This is what we were thinking, vis-a-vis the package.' Lars wrote a figure on a piece of paper and slipped it across the table to Simon.

And what's more, where did they get this idea – that you meet someone in a *cafe* and write a figure on a piece of paper and slip it across the table in a job interview? From some American web series, probably. Simon had hired dozens of people over the years and this was not how you did it. You were supposed to hire people while sitting in your own office, while wearing a tie, and the size of the package should be detailed in an email.

Simon opened the folded paper. 'Fucking hell,' he muttered.

The figure Lars had written down was enough to upgrade Tansy's car straight away, and in a little while, after they'd saved a deposit, they could apply for another mortgage and buy another house. A new family home, where his children could have their own rooms and space to play. And a new fridge. It was enough money for everything in Simon's life to be perfect again.

'Super is on top of that, naturally,' said Lars. 'And we provide your laptop, phone and car. And we have a small profit-share scheme for key personnel.'

Simon felt himself swallow. 'That's certainly ballpark,' he said. He took another bite of the sriracha donut.

'We're thinking it'll take about two years on-site to get this project over the line,' Flora said. 'But we're trying to think further ahead than that. We'll need a dedicated GM by then. Things would have to work out, naturally. There'd be a three-month trial period, but we want you to know that we're thinking long-term. The right candidate would have an MBA, we think, but you'd be able to do that on weekends.'

'There's not a lot of nightlife up there,' said Lars. 'It's buckets of fun during the day, if you're the outdoors type – fishing, jetskiing, sailing, camping, hiking. You'll be flat out working though. It's a big job, we have to be upfront about that. Long hours. Not a lot of downtime.'

'Up where?' said Simon.

'The development is on the outskirts of Gladstone,' said Flora. 'Did we not mention that?'

'Gladstone?' said Simon. 'Is that near Pakenham? Or the other way? Past Caroline Springs?'

'It's in central Queensland. It's about six hours' drive from Brisbane, give or take,' said Flora.

'*Central* Queensland?' said Simon. 'As in, the middle of Queensland?'

'We'd need you on-site 24/7,' said Lars. 'It's a bit of a pain to get to – two flights, and the ones out of Brisbane aren't very regular. And there are bound to be weekend commitments because we're a wee bit behind with the dates. Where you spend your annual leave is up to you, of course. But we need you to put in a full year before you take leave. We figure you'd come back to Melbourne – oh, around once a quarter, for the weekend?'

'That's four times a year,' said Simon. 'I'd only be back here every twelve and a bit weeks?'

'Bingo,' said Lars. 'Accommodation is included, of course. Motel-style, close to the site. What do you say?'

Simon had absolutely no idea what to say. It was as if his brain had been emptied of possible words. He needed to think, that's what he told them.

He could tell from their faces they were disappointed. They were like teenagers who'd given their father the most wonderful present they could imagine and had received an underwhelming reaction in return. They didn't live in a world where spouses needed to be consulted or children to be considered. They could pack a bag, hop a flight, crash in a motel. At their *stage of life*, decisions were quick and easy.

'No problem,' said Flora. 'Though if we do need to widen our search – which we don't want to, let me stress, we want you in the role – we'd need to have all the documents ready for the employment agency by first thing Monday morning. Today's Wednesday – we'd need your final answer by Saturday at the latest.'

No problem. Simon told them they'd have it.

Chapter 22

Alone in his ute driving to Naveen's place, Simon would have liked to make fun of them. The omnipresent pink, the sriracha donut. The trouble was, he couldn't bring himself to be even a little snide.

Those young people were the future. They were idealistic and naive and entirely pure of heart. And yes, he couldn't see how vowels could be dictatorial, but they were asking themselves the most important question anyone can ask: *How do I live ethically in the world?* Simon had long ago ceased to ask himself this question. The question he asked himself now was more like: *How can I get through one more day?* His moral priorities were simple – he would do whatever was best for Tansy and his children. Flora and her colleagues had a broader view of the point of their existence. The more he thought about their energy and diligence and drive, the more he saw this lack of comprehension of their priorities as his problem rather than theirs.

When he was their age, his own father couldn't grasp his urge to make something beautiful, or even grasp what beautiful was. It wasn't that his father had different subjective tastes from

Simon – he would have understood had his father genuinely admired shag carpets or velvet paintings or non-ironic ducks on a wall. It wasn't that Simon's father was unmoved by things around him. A lovely set of teeth, especially in a child or an old person, made his father happy. He enjoyed bird-watching; the sight of a rare plumed something-or-other made his heart soar – but that was only because of its rarity.

The problem was this: the very question of what was aesthetically pleasing never occurred to his father. To Simon's father, one shirt, for example, was the same as any other – provided it wasn't obviously too tight or loose, and was wash-and-wear. His father simply didn't notice whether an object was attractive or not. In furniture, and in art also, design and colour and pattern and texture were as immaterial as the day of the week the thing was manufactured.

In a similar way, the gap between Simon's understanding of Flora's priorities didn't meant she was wrong. Just because Simon couldn't delineate the political nature of varying shades of pink didn't mean it didn't exist. It meant instead that time was passing and Simon wasn't growing with it. Simon was staying still.

Of course, it was impossible to accept their offer. Of course. To see Mia and Lachie four or five times a year? Think about how much of their precious childhood he'd miss – not to mention Tansy! Life without Tansy would be like living with a hole in his heart. And to leave her to effectively be a single parent? That wasn't fair. Why had he asked for time to think about their offer? He should have declined it straight away. No amount of money would compensate for what he'd be giving up.

For a moment, though, he imagined himself striding across a huge building site, work boots and hard hat on, plans in hand, negotiating with engineers and buildings and council inspectors, serious people asking him serious questions and nodding with admiration at his decisions. He certainly had the skills to run a growing, cutting-edge company. He could understand Flora approaching him. It was quite a logical progression, really. He was only forty-two! That wasn't old. He could adapt.

Why was he even thinking about his father, and his father's tastes? He certainly wasn't old enough to be Flora's father. He was more like a groovy older brother. He saw himself in a plaid shirt, beanie optional, with a small tasteful tattoo on the inside of his wrist. Something styled around his kids' birthdays or something. In his vision, he didn't carry a briefcase the way he used to – instead, a Crumpler messenger bag was slung across his chest, which somehow seemed broader, and less man-booby. He saw his business card: dusky pink. *Simon Larsen*, it said. *General Manager*. That would shut his father and Gloria up. Actually, it probably wouldn't shut Gloria up. He could imagine her coming over with an expensive bottle of champagne to celebrate his new job, and the champagne lolling him into a false sense of security before she toasted him, saying, 'Good work, Tori Spelling. I guess it's who you know. Wonders will never cease.'

Waiting at a traffic light, he caught sight of his reflection in the window of an empty shop: a tired man on the cusp of middle age with his arm out the window of a second-hand ute. He didn't look like the kind of man whose best was good enough for anyone, much less Mia and Lachie.

—

Bugger, Simon thought when he saw Naveen's car in the driveway. Naveen was usually at work at the chicken shop by now, and wouldn't have known how late Simon was arriving. Again. He shut the door of the ute as quietly as he could and snuck in through the side gate, which he lifted as he opened to stop it squeaking. Simon saw that the pavers were stacked against the side of the house. That must have taken Naveen ages.

At the back of the house, the blinds were up and the floor-to-ceiling sliding doors were closed. Simon cupped his hands around his eyes and pressed them against the glass. Inside, the lights were off and it was messy – dirty dishes on the dining table and the kitchen bench; clothes on the floor. The house seemed deserted. Perhaps Naveen had car trouble and had ridden his bike to work and would never find out about Simon's sleep-in this morning. At last, something was going right.

Simon decided against starting on the courtyard. He wanted a full day for that, so he could make sure the pavers were perfect and level, and so any overnight rain wouldn't get beneath the grout. Instead he started cutting timber with the electric saw. In the next few days, he would dig out the lantana and crabgrass with a pick in preparation for the new turf. All the scrappy trees at the back of the block would go – some to be replanted in line with the new scheme and others to be given away. It was peaceful in the garden. He had to acknowledge that. He liked the way the shape of the yard changed in line with his intentions. It reminded him of everything he'd loved about architecture back when he was starting his practice. Simon was still convinced that the design of a man-made space – its light and flow and elegance and utility – influenced the way humans feel when they're in that space. He believed that people could think and behave and interact better when surrounded by a space that was uplifting and true – and he believed the converse, that people were more likely to behave in ugly ways when their surroundings were ugly.

Simon worked solidly and only stopped after an hour for a drink from the outside tap. And then an hour after that, to google *distance from Melbourne to Gladstone* on his phone.

It was 2000 kilometres, give or take.

Then he googled *average temperature Gladstone winter*. It said 14–23 degrees.

Bloody hell. That was t-shirt weather, in the middle of July. It was unnatural. What species of human lived like that? Those poor, sorry bastards – to never know what they were capable of. It takes reserves of will to wake in the dark to chip ice off your windscreen before leaving in the morning. It takes strength of character to normalise the shoulder pain caused by continually hunching to avoid the icy blast of drizzle, like pins and needles in your face. Oh yes, it's easy to have a happy and fulfilling life while golden sunlight caresses you from a sky of iridescent blue. Anyone could feel relaxed when they're a short drive from a world-heritage-listed reef, with thrilling water sports and white sand for miles. Simon could only imagine what these Gladstonians must look like. Their necks would stick up vertically instead of arching forward in a hump, and their eyes would look straight ahead instead of down at the ground.

Freaks.

And yet. What a wonderful design challenge that would be, to grapple with wide verandahs and glass louvres and think about passive solar design and different varieties of trees. And what a privilege it would be to make something uplifting and useful for a whole community, to improve the lives of real people on a grand scale.

Then Simon was startled by a yelping sound. When he lifted his head, he saw Naveen through the sliding glass doors, standing near the dining table with his furry chest visible under a loosely tied dressing-gown, and a broken coffee cup at his feet.

Simon headed towards the sliding door. Naveen gingerly did the same, opening the door a couple of inches and leaning into the gap so it was blocked by his body.

'Simon!' Naveen called out. 'Hi! I wasn't expecting you today. I thought you'd taken the day off, when you didn't show up, I mean. How are you, Simon?'

'Yeah, I'm good,' said Simon. 'I thought you'd be at work by now.'

'Right,' said Naveen. 'I'm not at work, Simon. I'm here.'

'Right,' said Simon. 'I can see that. Mate, are you okay?'

'No. Actually. To tell you the truth, I'm not feeling great.' Naveen rubbed his head with one hand, pulling his dressing-gown closed with the other. 'The . . . er . . . new casual is getting the chickens on. I'm going in a little later.' He was gripping the door, his body still leaning against the gap.

'New casual? I didn't know you'd taken someone on – that's excellent.' And astonishing. Naveen had overcommitted when he bought the chicken shop after his divorce, according to Tansy. He'd been working ridiculous hours, managing everything by himself. Simon gestured to the broken mug, then to his own boots. 'Can I give you a hand with that? You're in bare feet.'

'No, no, no,' Naveen said. 'No need. I'll be fine, no problem.'

'Um, okay. Don't cut yourself,' said Simon.

They each stood there.

'Is there something else?' said Naveen.

'Can I use the loo?' said Simon.

Naveen's eyes opened wide. He didn't move from his spot in the gap between the door. 'Actually, you know what? I've got a bit of gastro. Contagious, probably. Can't be too careful. Might be best if you head down to McDonald's.'

'Oh, sure,' said Simon as he took a few steps back as unobtrusively as possible. 'No worries. But if you're sick, you shouldn't go into the shop. You know that, right?'

'Great, okay,' said Naveen. 'See you later.' He slammed the glass door closed, and drew the blinds.

Chapter 23

'Kids!' Tansy called out, as she and Simon were leaning on opposite sides of the front doorjamb, waiting to head out to the Chees'. 'We're leaving in four minutes! Don't bring too much stuff.'

'But I want to show Lily my new pens,' Mia called out from the bedroom.

'Mum, Mum, where's my other shoe?' said Lachie.

'Can't you show her at school?' Tansy called back. 'And did you look behind the TV?'

'No!' said Mia. 'I'm not taking my good pens to school! Anything could happen to them.'

'And I want to show Tyler my rocks,' said Lachie, as he hopped across the lounge room.

Somewhere in Simon and Tansy's past, they had friends who were not the parents of Mia and Lachie's friends. They must have known childless people when they were themselves childless; they invited guests to their wedding! But these days, the concept of socialising with people who didn't have children the same age as their own seemed ridiculous. What would they talk about? And how would they manage *to* talk, if the children didn't distract each other? And what would be their shared excuse for drinking too much? They had met the Chees because Mia was friends with their Lily. It was counterintuitive, but the Chees preferred socialising on school nights – Saturday and Sunday mornings were even more hectic than weekdays, what with Mandarin classes and soccer and ballet and violin and visits to the grandparents. Simon knew they were deeply in entertaining-debt to the Chees but it couldn't be helped. The Chee kids each had their own room. The Chees had a big backyard, with barbecue. And a cupboard under the stairs just for wine.

'I'm boiling! Do I have to wear pants?' yelled Lachie.

'Yes!' yelled Simon. Then, under his breath, 'If I have to wear pants, everyone has to wear pants.'

'Can I bring my lizard?' yelled Lachie.

'No. Three minutes,' Simon yelled back.

Before Simon had children, he hadn't realised how a conversation could become randomised, as though each participant's lines were written on a piece of paper and thrown into the air before being read aloud in no particular order. How he longed to have a conversation where he said one thing, and Tansy said another thing that followed logically from his thing, and they just went on like that, alternating sentences, like people on television. It seemed impossible to imagine.

'I almost forgot to ask,' Tansy said. 'How was your coffee with Flora?'

'Yeah, good,' said Simon. 'Wait, since when does Lachie have a lizard?'

Tansy stared at him. 'I was just about to ask you that.'

Some things are better left for the weekend. Simon took a deep breath in, and let it out. 'Did you speak with Naveen today?' he said.

'I found it!' yelled Lachie. 'It was in my backpack with the rocks.'

Simon was alarmed for a moment, before he realised Lachie meant the shoe, not the lizard.

'Good work, Lachs!' Tansy yelled. 'Why do you ask?'

'He was acting weird when I saw him this afternoon.' Simon proceeded to tell her that Naveen was planning to head to work despite feeling unwell. Who on earth did that? And Monica was out when he'd arrived home. Why was everyone around him so unreliable? 'Two minutes!' he yelled.

He also hadn't realised how important both yelling and countdowns are in the lives of parents. Yelling, countdowns, wondering why the electricity bill was so high and spending all weekend driving children with social lives like Kardashians to parties and sporting events were the four common denominators of parenthood. Simon rarely left the house with his children without yelling a countdown, and lately he counted down even when he was alone. Being a parent was like living inside Mission Control at NASA, if it was entirely populated by the hard-of-hearing.

Tansy leaned against the doorframe. 'I can't deal with Naveen's problems right now,' she said, almost whispering. 'I'm so tired. People are exhausting. Even my own children are exhausting. Parenting was so much easier before I had children and I only had to pass judgement on other people's parenting. Remember how I was so superior around other people's revolting children? Because I knew our children would be perfect?'

'They are perfect,' Simon said. 'Besides, that's how the human race continues – everyone thinks they can be a better parent than everyone else.' Then he called out, 'One minute!'

—

On the walk down the street to the Chees', Tansy turned to him.

'Okay?'

It occurred to Simon that she'd been speaking for some time. 'Yep, fine,' he said.

She narrowed her eyes. 'What did I just say?'

He searched his mind. 'About not drinking too much?'

'Good guess, but no. God, you're so preoccupied. What is it?'

The reason he hadn't heard her at first was this: he was thinking about all the things he should have been talking to her about, but wasn't. Flora's job offer, for a start. Tansy had asked directly, to his face, how his coffee with Flora went. And what did he say? *Good.* What kind of an answer was that?

Simon thought of how the conversation should have gone: *You'll never guess, she offered me a job! I said no, though, because it was too far away and I'd miss you all too much.* See? What was so difficult about that? Why couldn't he talk to his own wife?

'Nothing,' he said.

Chapter 24

Then he realised: he was trying to spare her. That was it! The thought of turning down that much money – and he would turn it down, obviously – was agonising. Why should he put Tansy through that kind of anguish? The buck stops here. Keeping such a painful dilemma to himself was actually his duty. Flora's job offer would remain his secret. Then, when he turned it down, Tansy wouldn't feel conflicted.

Okay, he'd relieved himself of the pressure of one outstanding conversation. But that wasn't the only thing they ought to have been discussing. Why hadn't he asked her whether she'd spoken to Gloria? And if she had, how much psychological pain was Tansy in? And if not, was there still time for the four of them to organise new passports under assumed names and fake their own deaths in a boating accident so the conversation with Gloria need never occur? He should bring it up, definitely. After all, he was the one who'd spilled the beans about Mon. It was his responsibility.

He was still thinking about his communication failures as they knocked and Sonny Chee opened the door holding a tall glass of transparent liquid crammed with ice cubes and slices of lime.

'Honestly,' Simon said, and then hoped it sounded like part of a conversation he'd been having with Tansy before they arrived instead of what it actually was, which was exasperation at the sight of Sonny. Despite having three children, being at least ten years older than Simon and working long hours as a physiotherapist in the business that he and Edwina ran together, Sonny always looked fit and vital, freshly pressed and smelling faintly of vanilla, like a distinguished male model in a river cruise advertisement.

'The Larsens are in the house!' Sonny said, doing an embarrassing dad-version of a rapper hand gesture. 'Come in, come in. I just got home from the gym. Leg day! Don't skip it, am I right? White? Red? I'm having a vodka and soda because I'm back on keto. Happy to make you one if you'd rather. Eddie's in the backyard. Hi Mia, Lachie! The kids are in their rooms.'

'Red,' said Simon and Tansy together, as Simon handed Sonny the bottle they'd brought. Mia and Lachie said hello and disappeared upstairs with their backpacks full of pens and rocks.

'Is that Simon and Tansy?' yelled Edwina from the backyard. 'I sat down for a minute and now I can't get up. Pretend I came to the door to greet you.'

The Chees' house wasn't large, it only seemed that way. Despite having three children, they had chosen – deliberately – a white kitchen and concrete floors and somehow enforced knick-knack-free surfaces and a strict one-painting-per-child policy for the fridge. Where did the Chees put all their crap? There were no ceramic figurines of goose girls with said geese which had been Christmas presents from great aunts; no manky carved elephants with mother-of-pearl eyes they'd bought on holiday in Thailand, and no sets of Japanese dolls won in school raffles. There were no old food magazines, no bottles of vitamins past the expiry date, no assorted working and non-working pens. Where did the Chees put their keys, their coins, their odd buttons and dead batteries? Their weird screws that could sit there for months until the day you threw them out, at which time it became apparent that they were vital for some appliance or furnishing and now you had to go down to Bunnings and buy several new sets of screws in various sizes to find an exact replacement? And most importantly, what did the Chees do with all the free time they saved from not spending hours searching for things?

Out the back, the Chees' yard was green with a manicured lawn and a border of magnolias. It was an oasis of tranquillity, although Simon would have planted Lily turf underneath so it all looked a little less stiff. Edwina was lying on a banana lounge on the deck with a glass of white wine in her hand and a platter of cheese and biscuits beside her. She was tiny, almost elfin, and always wore red lipstick and earrings of differing shapes and textures, but always red.

'It's so lovely of you to have us, Eddie,' said Tansy as she and Simon made their way through the house.

'It's my pleasure,' said Edwina. 'Especially since Sonny's doing everything and I'm doing nothing.'

'She's had a hard day,' said Sonny as he delivered glasses of red to Tansy and Simon and filled up Edwina's glass from a bottle of white in a cooler beside the banana lounge. They pulled out chairs. Sonny did lunges on the lawn with his vodka in one hand. Sonny was congenitally unable to relax. Edwina often said that when he died, she'd need to arrange a deeper coffin than usual so he could do crunches while decomposing.

'What happened?' said Simon.

'I don't want to talk about it,' said Edwina. She pursed her red lips in an exaggerated fashion.

'You don't have to talk about it,' said Tansy. 'Let's talk about something else.'

'Maybe we should go,' said Simon. 'If you've had a bad day, we don't want to be an imposition.'

'Don't be silly,' Edwina said. 'If you weren't here, tonight would disappear into that never-ending blur of dishes and home-work and I'd have nothing to do but drink carbs by myself and keep obsessing over my tale of woe to Sonny.'

'And I've already heard it twice,' Sonny said, mid-lunge.

'Instead I get to drink carbs with my friends and dream of the day I retire,' said Edwina.

'It wasn't her fault,' said Sonny. 'It was an accident. Could have happened to anyone.' He stopped lunging and started squatting.

'I said I don't want to talk about it,' said Edwina.

'Fair enough. What have you been streaming?' said Tansy. 'Anything good? And what are you reading for book club?'

'So this is what happened,' said Edwina. 'I've been seeing this patient for a while, right? Lower back. A shooting pain that goes right up her spine. She played a lot of golf, too much. Never did any stretching or weights. So anyway, we agreed she should take a break from golf while we work on it. She was completely on board, this patient. So she's taken three months off, no golf, and she's really improving.'

'I've never understood golf,' said Simon. 'The kind of people who play golf really love playing golf, but the point of golf is to play the least amount of golf possible, right?'

'That's perilously close to being a dad joke,' Tansy said. 'We had a deal: dad jokes are only to be told to the children, never to adults.'

'You love my jokes,' Simon said, and kissed her on the cheek.

'You're making dinner, aren't you, Sonny?' Edwina continued. 'The pasta salad and a green salad are in the fridge. Just barbecue the steak for us and the sausages for the kids. They're veggie sausages because Lily isn't eating meat right now and kids can't tell the difference anyway. I'm not moving.'

Steak! Midweek! For no discernible reason at all! Simon shook his head.

'On it,' said Sonny. 'The meat's out of the fridge, just heating the barbie. Anyway, the whole thing was blown way out of proportion.'

'I don't want to talk about it,' said Edwina. 'I'm too upset.'

'This red is delicious,' said Simon. 'I might just have a top-up.'

'Anyway,' said Edwina, 'last week, this new patient came in. Male, late forties, kind of jowly with tiny teeth in a not-unattractive way, if you like that look. A little bit Blake Shelton, a little bit early Matthew Crawley from *Downton Abbey* before he went to Hollywood and got a chin.'

'I don't know who either of those people are,' said Simon.

'No one does. Only women know stuff like that,' said Sonny.

'Anyway,' continued Edwina, 'he tells me that his wife is a patient of mine – the golf lady.'

'He – the husband – has some ankle issues,' said Sonny.

'You're telling it wrong,' said Edwina. 'He – the husband – has some ankle issues. She – Golf Lady – doesn't know her husband has come to see me. He didn't tell her. He just wakes up one day and decides, "I'm completely sick of this ankle. My wife is happy with her physio so I'll go and see them as well, and I won't mention it to the wife because it just slips my mind", or something.'

'Them being Edwina,' said Sonny.

Just then, there was a thundering down the stairs, like a herd of tiny cattle: Lily Chee and Mia, followed by the twins, Tyler and Ruby, followed by Lachie.

'Mum, Mum, Mum,' said Ruby. 'You should see Lachie's rocks.'

'Is there any snacks?' said Tyler.

'Are,' said Edwina. 'Are there any snacks.'

'I don't know,' said Tyler. 'That's why I'm asking.'

Edwina sighed heavily. 'Daddy will get you some snacks.'

'On it,' said Sonny as he sprinted towards the kitchen.

'And I need a throw rug,' Edwina called after him. 'A soft, fluffy one.'

'It's not cold though,' Sonny called back.

'I. Want. A. Throw. Rug,' said Edwina, kicking her legs. 'I've had a hard day.'

'Roger that,' Sonny said. 'One throw rug, coming up. Now kids, who wants carrot sticks?'

'NOT ME!' shouted all five children in unison.

'Ah, you must want celery then.'

'NO!'

'Where did I go wrong?' moaned Sonny. 'How about some pizza Shapes?'

'Now you're talking,' said Lachie.

'Where does Sonny get his energy from?' said Tansy.

Edwina blinked so slowly that for a moment it seemed she'd fallen asleep. 'When I first met him, I thought he was on speed. That's why I dated him, to be honest. He must have a really good supply of speed, maybe he'll get me some. That was my rationale. Now I know it's just the way he is. It's exhausting just watching him. He can't sleep in. He's physically incapable of it. He's on his bike by 5 am, all lycraed up. Do you know how relaxing it is, to be married to that? Not. At. All. The first sight that greets me when I open my eyes in the morning is my husband, squeezed into an enormous black condom, doing lunges beside the bed. Meat and two veg, right at eye level. It's confronting.'

'Maybe you should get one of those vaporisers,' Tansy said. 'Maybe get some calming essential oils. Chamomile or patchouli.'

'Or chloroform. Not a bad idea,' said Edwina. 'I'll look into it. So anyway, back to the story. So I said to Jowly Ankle Man, your wife's lower back is really improving now that she's not playing golf anymore.'

'Oh no,' said Tansy.

'Oh yes,' said Edwina.

Tansy cupped her ears with her hands, grimacing; Edwina covered her eyes with her palms. See no evil, hear no evil. But one of them had better speak soon, because Simon had no idea what was going on.

Chapter 25

'Oh no, what?' said Simon. 'How can you tell where this story is going? There has been insufficient information to deduce what's going to happen next.'

'It's obvious,' said Tansy, ears uncovered.

'Yep, it's the oldest story in the world. The saucy minx has still been leaving home twice a week in her golf gear with her clubs in the back of the Passat,' said Edwina. '"Bye, darling," she says to Jowly Ankle Man as she leaves. "I'm just off to play golf in a completely normal manner, which is my usual routine and utterly unsuspicious! See you soon!" Well, not exactly that, but you get the drift. Anyway, after our appointment, Jowly Ankle Man – who isn't as dumb as he looks – follows her on her next alleged golf day. Turns out she's been shagging her remedial massage therapist on the sly.'

'Oh no,' said Simon.

'Oh yes,' said Edwina. 'No wonder she was feeling better.'

'Sex instead of golf. Insert joke about balls, shafts and strokes here,' said Sonny, who had reappeared after giving the children their pizza Shapes.

'So then my client, Golf Lady, rings me up. She's furious. She says her husband is divorcing her and it's all my fault.'

'The cheek!' said Tansy.

'I know, right?' said Edwina. 'I said there was an outside chance that it was *her* fault, on account of her extramarital shagging. And do you know what she said then? That she's going to report me to the Health Complaints Commission for breaching client confidentiality. I told her, if I go down, I'm taking the massage therapist with me.'

'She won't take it any further, trust me,' said Sonny as he refilled everyone's drinks. 'People don't divorce over things like that anymore. No one can afford it. The more fuss she makes, the more of a big deal it becomes. She'll come to her senses. She needs to sort it out at home and put it behind her, rather than have even *more* people involved.'

'That must have been a terrible shock to her husband,' said Simon.

'It just goes to show,' says Tansy, 'you never really know anyone.'

—

Simon was a self-identified Australian male (he/him), so it was legislated that he should stand beside Sonny while he was cooking meat on the barbecue. The leave-the-steak-alone-and-only-turn-it-once method had been passed down from Simon's grandfather to Simon's father to Simon himself as though it were a Stradivarius, but Sonny had no respect for tradition or Simon's Larsen pride. It was passé to cook a steak that way, according to Sonny, who explained what was happening inside the steak with hand gestures, as if he were delivering a TED talk. This was a new development. Even since their last barbecue, the world of back-yard grilling had moved on. Everyone used the flip-continually method now, which was guaranteed to something something something. (Simon lost concentration in the middle of Sonny's explanation.)

The steaks were magnificent. The kids were happy, sitting on the grass in a circle, eating sausages wrapped in white bread and dripping sauce, and giggling. Edwina had been coaxed off the banana lounge and sat with the rest of them at the outside table with the throw rug around her shoulders as if she were an invalid. No pasta salad for Sonny of course, but Simon was starving and helped himself to seconds.

'So what's happening with your new sister, the influencer?' Edwina asked.

It wasn't a surprise that Edwina already knew the details of Mon's arrival. Tansy was never too busy to chat with friends – even if most of the actual information seemed to be exchanged via mental telepathy.

'She's not a patch on Tansy,' said Simon. 'In the daughter stakes.'

'That's sweet, but it's not a competition,' said Tansy.

'Of course it is!' said Edwina. 'And you are killing it. Let's look at this scientifically. You, Nick, Kylie: well-adjusted, happy, engaged members of society, who all grew up without a father. Your sister: social media influencer with failure-to-launch syndrome, who grew up with said father.'

'She's young, she's still finding her way!' said Tansy. 'Give her a chance.'

'We're not judging her,' said Edwina. 'We're just feeling defensive for you, that's all.'

'Hang on,' said Simon. 'Are you suggesting that it's an *advantage* to grow up with an absent parent?'

'Not in every case, obviously,' said Sonny. 'It would depend on the quality of the parent. Children copy behaviour, after all.

That's the way they learn how to talk and walk, and it's how they learn how to live, to contribute to the world, to have successful relationships.'

'It's better to have a missing parent than one who's a terrible role model,' said Edwina. She looked at Simon, then down at her drink. 'I don't mean unemployment. Unemployment clearly doesn't count. Kids don't model that. At all.'

'Anyway,' said Tansy. 'Monica's fine, but today we had a teensy possible problem involving my mother.' She proceeded to tell Sonny and Edwina about Gloria's premature discovery of Mon's inveigling herself into all their lives, and about Gloria not being thrilled about the whole arrangement (though Tansy chivalrously left out the culpable blabber, i.e. Simon).

'Oh no,' said Edwina.

'Oh yes,' said Tansy. 'She left me a voice message, like it's 1993. She's probably waiting right now for me to call her back.'

'That is absolutely terrifying,' said Sonny, who had met Gloria more than once and was not an idiot. 'What are you going to tell her? You must be shitting yourself.'

'Sonny, please,' Tansy said. 'This is my *mother* we're talking about. The woman who gave birth to me. She's not a monster. She's a reasonable, intelligent, loving person who just needs things explained to her in a logical way. I am absolutely confident that once she has time and space to process the idea of Mon becoming part of our lives, she will be absolutely fine.'

'Wow,' said Edwina. 'You're going to get Nick to do it.'

'Of course I'm going to get Nick to do it,' Tansy said. 'I don't have a death wish. There are a million downsides to having a former teenage football star, golden boy baby brother who's Mum's favourite and who's been spoiled his whole life, but there is one big upside. He can be the one to have conversations like this.'

'But will he do it? I mean, Nick can be . . . difficult to motivate,' said Edwina, who had met Nick more than once and was also not an idiot.

'Oh, he'll do it. He's probably doing it right now,' said Tansy. 'Kylie and I know exactly how to *motivate* Nick. He wants to hit Mum up for another loan. One thing about Mum is that she's very transparent about the money stuff. She wants to treat us all absolutely equally, financially at least. If Kylie and I both object, Nick won't get his loan.'

—

It was getting late for a school night, so after a couple more wines for Simon, they began to say their goodbyes. The kids were finished eating and had disappeared back upstairs by then, so while Tansy was helping Sonny clear the plates, Simon headed up to get them.

There's a special joy in listening to young children playing. As Simon approached Lily's room, he could hear the five of them involved in some kind of complicated game spread out on the floor, revving toy cars and trucks and a fire engine, and walking Barbies around and talking for them like they were ventriloquists' dummies. He paused just outside the door so he could listen to their glorious imagination. Childhood was a magical time, full of joy and innocence. Had he ever been so carefree?

'You weren't born then,' said a voice he knew to be Lily Chee's. She was nine, a year older than Mia although in the same grade, so was the natural leader when all the kids got together. 'Only me and Mia were born then. You were still in your daddy's balls.'

Okay. Possibly childhood was a little less innocent than Simon recalled.

'I was never in Daddy's balls!' said Lachie.

'You were,' said Lily. 'You and Tyler and Ruby are too little. You don't know about anything. Me and Mia know important things, because we're queens and we're bigger than you and that means that we're in charge.'

'We're not little! We know important things,' said Ruby.

'Oh yeah?' said Lily. 'Do you know where babies come from? Do you know how cats talk to each other? Do you know about stranger danger?'

'My mummy talks to strangers all the time,' said Lachie. 'That's her job.'

'It's different for grown-ups,' said Mia.

'Yeah,' said Lily. 'Say you're waiting outside school, right? And a man comes up to you. And he's a stranger, right? And he says, "I'm a friend of your daddy's and he said I'm picking you up and come and get in the car, and I have a puppy." Would you go with him?'

'No!' said Lachie. 'Of course not. That would be stupid.'

Simon felt a rush of pride. Of course Lachie wouldn't go with some strange man who'd stopped outside the school, puppy or no puppy. It was ridiculous to even think so. Not only were both his children unusually intelligent, they had been well brought up. Although he himself couldn't recall teaching them about stranger danger himself. Tansy had, he was sure of that.

Then Lachie went on. 'Because that man is telling a big fib. My daddy doesn't have any friends.'

Oh.

That was suboptimal, Simon thought. That was a suboptimal thing for one's child to say about oneself.

Lachie had said it in a *gotcha* tone. Simon couldn't see from where he stood outside the door, but he pictured Lachie folding his arms and lifting his chin in satisfaction, the last speaker in a debate who'd nailed his rebuttal.

Simon waited for Mia to correct him. *That's not true, Lachs,* she would say, any moment. *Daddy has lots of friends. Or he did, until the time pressures of parenthood and earning a living made him lose contact with the people he'd formerly been close to. It's quite normal and unremarkable to drift apart from your friends when you face the kind of financial challenges that Daddy has. It happens every day.*

But Simon didn't hear Mia say anything, which was in itself a type of agreement. The children went on squabbling until Simon interrupted to tell them to pack their pens and rocks.

My daddy doesn't have any friends.

Overhearing that had been suboptimal, Simon thought again on the walk home. And he was unemployed, which, according to Edwina, they could well grow up to model. Also suboptimal. Could his children really grow up to be unemployable, friendless bankrupts?

Quick, thought Simon. *Think of something else.* The rest of the week would be very busy; think about that. And Saturday was Tansy's father's memorial service, where a range of people would no doubt sum up David's life. Think about memorials instead.

THURSDAY

Chapter 26

The next morning, Simon was at work in Naveen's backyard as the sun was rising. He'd found it easy to get up early because, again, he'd barely slept. He'd heard Mon as she tiptoed through the door in the early hours, but it wasn't thoughts of her that kept him awake as they had the night before. All through the small hours as he lay beside a sleeping Tansy and stared at the stained ceiling of that cruddy flat, various versions of Simon's own future funeral unfolded before him.

It wasn't death itself that occupied his mind. It was the ceremony, the formality, the ritual that kept him tossing and turning. It wasn't the cheeriest night of his life.

In one of his imaginary renditions, his final farewell took place in a church. Simon wasn't a churchgoer, so this was a surprise – he hoped whoever had chosen the persuasion favoured good music, female clergy, gay parishioners and a belief in science. Other imaginary funerals took place in the non-denominational chapels of various undertakers; sometimes these were modern spaces with walls of copper-look sheeting, occasionally gothic ones with ornate carved pews and soaring rafters and one that seemed stuck in the seventies, all unstained pine and groovy glass bricks and a bearded solo guitarist who looked like a young Dylan.

After he had imagined those to completion, he next visualised a ceremony held around the graveside, with everyone wearing sunglasses and holding black umbrellas like a scene from a mafia movie, and after that, he saw his mourners huddled around a bar in an atmospheric pub speaking in Irish accents. In one particularly romantic requiem, grieving people in moody cloaks and hoods swayed on the deck of an olde-worlde sailing ship, timber creaking underfoot while he, a lumpen shape sewn into bleached calico, was tipped into the waves, accompanied by a twenty-one gun salute and a touching obituary given by Russell Crowe dressed as the captain from *Master and Commander*. (What did Simon think he became in his twilight years, a pirate?) In some of his imaginary funerals, he was present – bodily at least – in a respectful but not ostentatious coffin. Sometimes he wasn't there at all. He imagined all variations of flowers and music and candles, but he knew that none of those things really mattered.

What mattered, of course, were the *people* present to see him off. Simon had spent the bulk of the night imagining who his inevitable mourners would be.

His kids would be there, of course. They had both taken urgent compassionate leave and flown in from the United Nations (Mia) and the set of his latest film (Lachie). He could picture them sitting in the pew (or standing under a tree, or leaning on the railings on deck), hale and hearty with linen handkerchiefs in their hands, smiling through their inconsolable tears. Their own lovely families would be beside them, also sobbing. Simon couldn't picture his future children-in-law and grandchildren – they were too distant, considering Mia and Lachie's ages.

(Though their marriages and possible children were closer than his funeral, surely?) Tansy would be in the front pew – she was old but still hot, like a curvy, shorter Helen Mirren. Kylie and Nick would be there, he was sure of that. Despite Kylie's advanced years, she would likely be mistaken for one of the undertakers. Nick would have a much younger woman on his arm and wouldn't have aged a bit – a combination of exercise, good diet and the kind of luck that made normal people hate the naturally beautiful.

His own parents would be understandably absent. They would have predeceased him, considering Simon's demise was some decades away. Gloria was of the same vintage as his parents so should by rights have passed away also, but Simon couldn't imagine her being successfully excluded. She'd be there – she was one of the undead, after all. The Chees would be there, and Naveen and Lexie. Flora? Some of his other employees, who he hadn't seen in months? Some of his old buddies from uni? His cousins from Brisbane? He hadn't seen Brock for years; they'd drifted apart when he became a youth pastor. And his friends, of whom he had lots. Lots. He just didn't see them anymore; everyone was so busy. When he had his business, he was forever socialising with builders and tradies and sales reps for suppliers. He went out with them at least one night a week, maybe two. And the lunches! So many lunches. And football on Saturdays, fishing on Sundays. They were mostly divorced, with lots of free time. Great mates. Dazza and Thommo and Stavros, for a start. True, he hadn't seen any of them for a while. Since the business closed, if he was being entirely honest. But that was on him. He could have phoned them, seen what they were up to. He hadn't. He didn't want to tell them about the flat, Tansy's job, the kids' school. He didn't want to have that conversation.

If he died, who would tell them?

That's why Dazza and Thommo and Stavros weren't at his imaginary funeral – they wouldn't have realised he was imaginarily dead.

He tried to put his funeral out of his mind. He was alive, now, working in Naveen's garden, on time. That was good news. Finally, he could make real progress, get this done and put it behind him.

It was cooler, and the clouds were back. Simon couldn't deny that it was pleasant being outside so early in the morning. In his architectural practice, he'd leaned towards working later at night because that was generally when his residential clients were available. So in his former life, Simon hadn't often experienced the sunrise. Or the sunset, actually, considering the hours he used to work.

Those were the good old days: at his desk, so enthralled by a project that he hadn't realised time was passing until Tansy phoned to ask if he was coming home for dinner. How many nights a week did he stay late and have pizza delivered to the office then arrive home when everyone was asleep? How many weekends did he work? He thought of all the mornings he'd missed out on. How had he not realised how beautiful mornings were? The day looked different at this hour. The grass was still tipped with moisture and the air was calm and clean. It seemed as though everything was fresh and new, as though Simon a chance to start again from scratch. He could almost believe that redemption was possible, every sunrise.

His phone beeped with a text:

Simon, mate! How is Naveen's backyard coming? Mum is out of control. You'll be finished on time, yeah? Nick

Bloody hell, thought Simon. It was like trying to pee in front of a packed Ponsford stand. *It'll be finished when it's finished,* he thought. He replied:

> *Hi mate! Good to hear from you, hope you're well. Everything's fine here. If Gloria is worried, perhaps ask Kylie to slip her some drugs. Best, Simon.*

Inside, the house was still. Perhaps Naveen was still sick. Or sleeping in, which he often did when Lexie was at her mother's. Simon imagined getting a teenager like Lexie off to school. She'd be a handful, probably worse than Lachie. Though it was unfair to compare either of them to Mia. She was always on time, with her bag packed and her uniform laid out the night before. He frowned, thinking again about Lachie. *My daddy doesn't have any friends.* Mia would never say anything like that. Mia understood the concept of loyalty. She was Daddy's little girl, always on his side.

After a couple of productive hours, he took a break and sat on the side of the garden bed with his thermos and a cheese and devon sandwich he'd brought from home. His muscles had warmed up; he stretched his shoulders and calves, felt that delicious tingle. Then his mobile rang. It was an unfamiliar number, so it wasn't Gloria or Nick. He answered.

'Simon, good morning,' the voice said. 'It's Khadisha Das from Fairbank Primary.'

Simon's blood ran cold. Principals never called parents during school hours to congratulate them on how happy and well-adjusted their children were. Images of broken arms, bleeding noses and violent gastrointestinal illnesses flashed through his mind.

'Of course, hi,' he said. 'Are the kids okay?'

'Everyone's fine and well,' she said. 'There hasn't been an accident, nothing like that.'

'Great, good,' he said. 'Phew.'

'But there is something we need to discuss in person. Is there any chance you can drop in to the school at, say, 11 am? In my office? I've just got off the phone from Tansy; that's when she's free. I'd prefer to speak to you both together.'

So much for his long-awaited full day in the backyard. He had finished cutting the stack of recycled timber, but not much more than that.

'Yep, sure,' he said. 'What is it about, exactly?'

'It's a disciplinary matter,' Khadisha said, 'and I'm sorry to tell you that it's serious enough to warrant action on behalf of the school. I'd rather not get into it over the phone.'

A disciplinary matter! What could it possibly be? Not bullying, he hoped to god. Fighting, which was acceptable if it stemmed from standing up for someone else? A little boundary-pushing rabble-rousing, which was a stage many children go through, especially children who go on to live long, law-abiding lives? Or was it something to do with the lizard? It was on him, whatever it was. How many times had he known he should be dealing with Lachie and his issues, but hadn't? Simon always had some excuse: it was too late, he was too tired. A father's job wasn't to be his son's best friend. It was to be a parent, and that meant loving but firm correction from time to time.

'Okay, sure,' Simon said. 'But look, Lachie's a good kid with good intentions. He just has some impulse-control issues. Whatever it is, I'm sure he didn't mean any harm by it.'

'The issue's not with Lachie,' Khadisha said. 'The issue is Mia.'

Chapter 27

When Mia was just born and wrapped and placed in Simon's arms, he had started crying. There had been nothing sad about that moment, his eyes had simply become incontinent. Tansy was exhausted and pale and bathed in sweat but well, and Mia was healthy. Simon knew himself to be the luckiest man alive. He was aware that tears were a wholly inappropriate reaction but was unable to stop them overflowing from his eyeballs. Yet at the same time, he started laughing. The nurses were greatly amused by Simon, laughing and crying. Tansy was fractionally alarmed.

What had happened, Simon realised, was that the layer of skin that protected him from the world had become thinner. He felt more joy and also more sorrow. He cared more than he did yesterday, about everything. Because Mia existed, he wanted the world to be a better place. He wanted for her never to see anything ugly or cruel, he wanted nothing but joy and peace for her, forever. He remembered looking down at her pure perfection and thinking that he would give his life for her, right now.

Lachie's birth, on the other hand – well, he couldn't exactly remember much. Everything seemed so much harder the second time around: the low-level exhaustion and runaway train of tasks that is caring for a toddler, Tansy's extended morning sickness, the long hours he was working to secure their future and pay the mortgage. Then the day itself and its intensity, the way the atmosphere in the delivery room went from casual chatting to focused intervention in a matter of seconds, then Tansy was under general anaesthetic and surrounded by beeping equipment that came from nowhere and the doctors and nurses were blood-streaked and grim-faced and he was ushered to the side and hurriedly gowned before entering the surgical suite. His memories were jostled and confused, to be honest.

And it wasn't just the birth that was a blur. During Lachie's first few months, Simon was working even harder and longer. It was difficult to rationally explain the rising terror that struck him in the middle of the night, now there was another mouth to feed. Having one child – there was a happy-go-lucky aspect to that. One child could be a hippy-esque accident; they could be a young couple with a baby in a sling, on pushbikes, buying vegetables from the organic co-op.

Two children were another matter altogether. A second baby spoke to a level of stability and suburban values. It placed him squarely in middle Australia. It was time to sell the bikes and buy an SUV and start a savings account to pay for university. His long hours at work made no difference to Tansy, Simon was sure. She was always so much more competent at housework and child-rearing than he was; him flapping uselessly around would only get in her way. Families have to be efficient, and it was simply more efficient to have Tansy do the domestic and child-related tasks. Mind you, he wasn't one of those husbands who didn't help! Of course he helped, he was always happy to help whenever Tansy asked. And he mowed the lawn. And besides, Simon always made sure he made it up to Lachie. Whenever he was home, he made sure Lachie got as much of his attention as was possible. Continual positive affirmations, praise and love.

And Mia? She'd been the centre of attention for close to three years before Lachie arrived. She was the light of Simon's life, she knew that. She exceeded all her milestones, she didn't give them a moment's trouble. She was in no need of parental over-compensation. Lachie, on the other hand? As soon as he could toddle, they had to watch him. Once he disappeared at Coles and Tansy had been frantic before finding him wedged inside the upright freezer, surrounded by plastic tubs with the lids peeled off, shovelling ice cream into his mouth with frostbitten little hands.

Could it be that they'd taken Mia's good behaviour for granted and instead devoted a disproportionate amount of time and energy on Lachie? And could this have reinforced Lachie's cheeky demeanour and, let's be honest, poor-ish grades and tendency to act the class clown? Could Simon have fallen for a gendered parenting trap, where girls were expected to display ladylike composure and perfect grades while boys were rewarded for poor behaviour? Was he guilty of the same sexist thinking Gloria had shown when raising Kylie, Tansy and Nick, the lingering effects of which could still be seen in Kylie stiff perfectionism, Tansy's sense of sacrifice and Nick's charm and happy-go-lucky, unearned confidence? Was this the way archaic gender roles and expectations passed down through families?

Certainly not.

Besides, this was quite obviously some kind of mistake. Simon knew his own flesh and blood. Mia – *his* Mia – was the perfect child. Everyone said so. Every report card, every parent, every teacher said she was smart and kind and respectful. This so-called *principal* clearly had some kind of agenda! She was a poor administrator who couldn't keep control so had decided to make her most exemplary student a scapegoat for her own incompetence.

Khadisha Das wants to discipline my little girl? Simon rolled up his sleeves. *Bring it on.*

—

When Khadisha Das's assistant showed Simon in to her office, Tansy was already there in her business suit with her bag on her lap, switching off her mobile phone. She smiled glumly at him.

The principal's office was in the original building, not the seventies building or the nineties building or the modern one. The school was a warren of classrooms with no aesthetic or functional connections, having mushroomed as enrolments grew. It was a spatial nightmare that depressed Simon by its very existence. Out the bank of windows, a scrappy strip of grass seemed to yellow as he watched.

Khadisha Das was a bustling woman who smelled of rose petals and wore a garish floral blouse over black pants, and a head scarf. She had two desks so she could work at the computer from the one behind her and intimidate defenceless students and parents across the other, and three visitor chairs. Stacks of papers were piled against the walls and statues of Disney princesses and stuffed toys were lined up on the bookcase. Evidence of the latest fundraising endeavour – a book-club drive to increase new volumes in the library and purchase sets of take-home readers for each class – was strewn everywhere: posters for car washes and lamington sales, and a pile of certificates to local butchers, bakers and greengrocers to thank them for their donations to last month's sausage sizzle.

'Sorry,' Khadisha said. 'These days, I'm part-principal, part-fundraiser.' She cleared the clutter from her desk and plonked it on the floor.

Tansy smiled and muttered something sympathetic. Simon did not. The visitor chairs were too narrow and too low to the ground for adults. The whole office made him feel queasy and his heart was racing as though he were the eight-year-old sitting in front of Mr Lee, answering questions about the broken window in the school library, which was not Simon's fault.

I am a grown-up, he kept telling himself. *I'm not the one in trouble.*

'Thank you both for coming at such short notice,' Khadisha said. 'Mia's in class right now. Erica, her teacher, won't be joining us – she's in class too, and I'm trying to disrupt everyone as little as possible. She asked me to stress to you both that Mia is a joy overall.'

'Of course she is,' said Simon. 'No surprise there.'

'That said, I'd like to talk to you both first before deciding what action we should take.'

'Perhaps you could tell us what she's done,' said Tansy.

'If anything,' said Simon.

Mia's last school – the private school – had its own pool. It had a Maths Olympiad and Italian classes and an orchestra and on-site psychologist and an oval you could land a plane on. He was sure the principal there – what was her name again? He couldn't recall ever having met her, but he was sure she'd never complained about Mia. *This* school – the *government* school – had a principal with a plastic Princess Jasmine doll and a dubious understanding of the criminal justice system. Tansy had always liked Khadisha. She considered her a plucky soldier on the side of underfunded public schools, tirelessly striving to work miracles with few resources. Tansy was wrong. Simon saw her for what she really was: the warden from *Shawshank Redemption*, but shorter and with better teeth.

'I want to say again that everyone thinks Mia is a delight.'

'Is. That. So,' said Simon. He crossed his arms and leaned back in his chair. 'It makes me wonder what we're doing here.'

Tansy laid her hand on his knee.

This *person* didn't even know Mia. Mia wasn't one of those kids who only ate white food (chicken nuggets, noodles) or soft foods (crustless sandwiches, crustless pizza) like Lachie. Mia ate olives and spinach and anchovies on a pizza, no complaints. She wore her bike helmet without being asked. She hummed 'You've Got a Friend in Me' from *Toy Story* while brushing her teeth because it's exactly two minutes long, and the dentist had told her that was the optimum time for optimum plaque removal. When Lachie was a newborn, they would catch her sitting next to his cot, talking in a soft voice about all the things he'd get to see as soon as he got bigger – kittens and the iPad and scooters and sneakers with lights and wheels on the sole – and there was nothing to be frightened of, and that she was his big sister and she would always look after him. Did Khadisha Das know any of that? Did she care?

'Before we get into the specifics, I want to assure you that we're only talking about a single incident,' Khadisha said. 'Mia's behaviour overall is exemplary. My goal here is to act decisively now, to make sure she gets back on track.'

'We understand,' said Tansy. 'Don't we, Simon?'

'Not really.' He uncrossed his arms just so he could cross them again the other way.

'Her teacher drew this to my attention. It's her homework from last week.' Khadisha passed a sheet of A4 paper across her desk towards them. 'It's a take-home spelling test. They get a lot of these.'

Printed on the page was a series of twenty-five simple illustrations of objects in two columns: everyday things like a hamburger, a purse, a church, a tub of yoghurt, a giraffe, a swimming pool. Next to each word was its first letter – an *h* next to the drawing of a hamburger – and a series of dashes to indicate where the student should spell the corresponding word correctly in the space. Mia's sheet was marked as twenty-four correct from a possible twenty-five. Simon looked closer. Next to the image of a pair of scissors was Mia's confident: *skissors*.

'So she missed one, big deal,' Simon said, flicking the sheet back on the desk. 'She's eight.'

'And here is the homework belonging to the rest of her class.' Khadisha spread out a series of similar sheets, each with a different child's name – Oliver, Amina, Suhaan, Jess, et cetera – across the top. The scores were spread from thirteen to twenty-three – there were *hambergers* and *humburglers* and *cherches* and *geeraffs* and the occasional *yogerts*. All the children had passed but Mia had topped the class with her single error, which was unsurprising.

At first glance, there was nothing similar at all about the sheets.

Except for one thing. Every single sheet contained the word *skissors*. Every single child had spelled scissors the way Mia did, with a *k*.

Chapter 28

That's quite a coincidence, thought Simon.

'That's clearly not a coincidence,' said Tansy.

'Normally, it would be unusual that every single child passed the test, but this is an extremely bright cohort,' Khadisha said. 'So the results itself aren't surprising. But look at all the handwriting.'

Simon examined the sheets. Every one, including the child's name, was completed in a different colour – pinks, reds, blues, greens – or type of pen – ballpoint, fat felt tip, or thin. A couple were in different coloured pencils. The handwriting on some was a block print; others were cursive; some were completed with letters that leaned to the left while others tilted to the right.

'That's the first thing that made Erica suspicious when she was marking them – the different pens. That beggars belief. Look, here: Oliver's is written in mauve. Oliver is not the kind of boy who owns a mauve pen. Ravi's is in aqua. That just wouldn't happen. The boys usually use what's to hand, which is usually a black or blue ballpoint or a plain pencil.'

'Because boys have no appreciation of colour or design?' Simon said.

Khadisha shifted her gaze to Tansy. 'It's my suspicion, and Erica agrees, that the same person filled out all these tests.'

Tansy bent her neck to look closer and rubbed her forehead with her fingertips. 'Someone who has a collection of different coloured pens and pencils, and who spent hours with an incredible amount of diligence making sure the handwriting looks different on every sheet,' she said, examining each one. 'Someone who can spell every word on this test except for scissors.'

The very idea was so impossible that it took Simon a few moments to work out what they were implying.

'You don't mean Mia,' he said. 'You can't think she did all these. Our Mia.'

'That's my suspicion, yes,' said Khadisha. 'Scissors is a diffi-cult word for Year 3, but it's not impossible. I'd certainly expect at least a couple of other children in the class would be able to spell it, even if they weren't as strong as Mia overall.'

'That's . . . ridiculous,' said Simon. 'She's a little girl, not a criminal mastermind.'

'There will have to be ramifications, there's no way around that,' Khadisha said. 'The school has a clear policy. I just can't overlook cheating.'

'Even if this is true, which I'm not conceding . . . it seems to me that *the other kids* are the ones doing the cheating, and Mia is the scapegoat doing all the work,' Simon said. 'You're telling me that she's doing . . .' – he skimmed his hands over the pages – '. . . fifteen, twenty times more homework than she needs to, and you're going to punish her?'

'If I punish the whole class, then I have to tell all the parents why. Mia becomes known as the person behind all this.'

Khadisha tucked a stray hair into her scarf. 'As I said, she's settled in so well. You can never tell how the other parents will react, and her classmates might blame her for getting caught. It might well affect her socialisation and ability to make friends.'

'Mia is extremely good at making friends. She has lots of friends,' Simon said. 'As do I.'

Khadisha and Tansy both looked at him.

'I don't doubt it,' Khadisha said, blinking, 'but once a child has a reputation as a troublemaker, it can be hard to shift.'

Tansy said, 'I don't know what to say. I can't imagine why Mia would have done this.'

'That's what concerns me the most, her reasons,' Khadisha continued. 'As I said, this is an extremely bright class. Everyone would have passed the test, no problem, so why has she intervened? She's gone to an extraordinary amount of effort. Was it peer pressure? I'm relieved that she's cheated for the entire class, to tell you the truth. If it was just one or two children, I'd worry she was being bullied. Or blackmailed. We had an incident among the Year Sixes last year – one of the boys was threatening to distribute a . . . compromising photo that one of the girls had sent him if she didn't do his homework. Text it to all his friends. A nude.'

'Jesus Christ,' Simon said. He felt a rush of nausea.

'Year Sixes are eleven or twelve years old,' said Tansy.

Khadisha shrugged. 'It's not the same world as we grew up in. We talk to them about cybersecurity and the dangers of social media and what privacy means, but I don't know how much they absorb. But you shouldn't be overly concerned – something like that is unlikely in this case.'

'Maybe we should ask her,' said Simon.

'Quite right.' Khadisha picked up the phone on her desk. 'Peter? Can you have Mia Larsen brought over from 3B?'

If there had ever been a more awkward ten minutes in Simon's life, he couldn't recall it. Outside the window on the yellowing grass, a group of three girls, smaller than Mia, appeared with clipboards and proceeded to sketch the pattern on the trunk of a small paperback gum on the fence line. They were innocent children, whose parents were at work instead of squirming on short chairs in the principal's office. Tansy was gamely chatting away; she and Khadisha talked about the football for a while, and the traffic. Khadisha asked about the general rental market because her eldest son was leaving home to move in with some friends and they'd just started looking for a flat. Tansy was busy. Khadisha was also busy. That's all people seemed to say to each other these days, how busy they were and how quickly schedules had refilled after the lockdowns lifted. Some people even looked back on lockdowns fondly, to Simon's extreme annoyance. *It was okay for them,* he thought, *but not all lives had resumed normal programming. And now they were complaining about being busy!* He almost chimed in with how lucky Khadisha was because teachers have so many school holidays, but he'd once said that to a primary teacher who Nick had briefly dated. He wasn't making that mistake again.

At last, Mia appeared at the door. It seemed as though she'd shrunk since he saw her last night. Had she always been this pale, this thin? He could circle her wrist with his thumb and forefinger. It was all Simon could manage not to pick her up, pop her in his pocket and bolt for the door.

'Hi, darling,' said Tansy.

'Hello, Mimzi,' said Simon. His lips formed themselves into an upside-down smile.

Khadisha Das asked Mia to sit.

'Am I in trouble?' she said. She was biting her lower lip and wringing the edge of her skirt with both hands.

'Mia.' Khadisha Das spread the homework sheets over the desk. 'I have a question to ask you, and it's very important that you answer honestly. Is this your handwriting? Did you do everyone's spelling homework for them?'

Mia would deny this ridiculous charge any second. Any second now, the word *no* would come out of her mouth. *I am innocent of all charges*, she would say. *I refute all allegations.* Mia was Dreyfus. She was Doctor Richard Kimble. By his reaction, Mia would know that her parents had her back, that they would never believe such a terrible thing about her. It would be a deliberate, measured speech, but he reserved the right to end it with *Suck it, Khadisha!* and a mic drop. He was prepared to jump to his feet the moment Mia said no.

'It was the pens, wasn't it?' said Mia. 'I used too many pens.'

Simon's breath caught in his chest and he let it out in a series of tiny puffs, as if he was in a Lamaze class. The speech he'd planned shrivelled on his tongue; he was so overwhelmed with a cyclone of feelings that he hardly trusted himself to open his mouth.

'We need to hear it in your own words,' Khadisha said.

'Yes, I did everyone's homework.' Mia's voice was small but she was strangely composed. Simon felt closer to tears than she was.

'Oh honey,' said Tansy.

'Thank you for your honesty,' said Khadisha. 'This is cheating, you understand? Cheating is strictly against the school rules.'

Simon wasn't sure what he was hoping Mia would say next. Was he expecting her to be *surprised* that it was against the rules? *I hadn't realised*, was that what he wanted her to say?

I was only trying to help all the other kids because they're not as smart as me and I am so incredibly kind? Would that make him feel better?

Did he really believe that his child would be calculating enough to fill out each sheet in a different coloured pen but too stupid to know what cheating was?

Instead she nodded. 'I guess,' she said.

'You're doing very well so far. I'd like you to continue being honest with me, Mia. Help me understand how this happened. Why did you fill out all these sheets?'

Mia shrugged and looked down at the mottled grey carpet of indeterminate vintage.

'Did someone force you into it?' Khadisha said.

'No,' she said to the carpet. 'I was only trying to help.'

'Trying to help your classmates is a good thing, Mia, but sometimes other things are going on behind the scenes. I'd like to understand what happened.'

Khadisha was very calm and non-accusatory as she ran through some of the reasons someone might do the whole class's homework, hypothetically. Children withheld invitations to parties or outings, or threatened theft or violence. Friendships were conditional upon certain favours. Sometimes they had photos that should be kept private. The way Khadisha spoke, childhood was like an episode of *Wentworth*.

'Did any of this happen to you, Mia?' she said.

Mia shook her head.

'You can tell us, honey,' said Tansy. 'We're not angry, we're just worried.'

Mia started to blink faster, and the skin around her lips turned white. 'No,' she said.

'I think that's probably enough.' Khadisha showed Mia outside, gently, and she and Simon's heart waited in a chair on the other side of the closed door.

'In normal circumstances, I'd give a week's detention for cheating,' Khadisha said when they were alone again, 'but I can't see how Mia has benefited. That worries me.'

'It doesn't make any sense,' Simon said. 'She's so diligent and hardworking.'

'I could give her two days' detention – this afternoon, and Friday lunchtime,' Khadisha continued, 'but again, everyone is going to see her and wonder why. The whole class should be in detention really, but I'm worried that could backfire on Mia. If she's seen as the ringleader there are some parents who'll be unhappy about their kids associating with her. I certainly don't want her labelled as a cheat, especially not after one incident that could well have been an act of kindness from her perspective.'

'Kindness!' Simon said. 'That could be it. She's incredibly kind.'

'We could keep her at home for a couple of days,' Tansy said. 'We still haven't had the full story. Perhaps if we give her some space, we can get a bit closer to figuring out what's going on.'

Khadisha thought for a moment. 'This wouldn't be a suspension,' she said. 'Suspensions carry legal and administrative obligations. They're kept strictly for health and safety reasons or repeat problems around lack of respect, and they must be detailed on her file. I'd like to keep this whole incident *out* of her file.'

'Not a suspension, we understand,' said Tansy.

'If she stays home for the rest of the week, it can't be a holiday. It's a parentally driven time-out. It has to be clear to her that she's being punished and that she needs to use this time to think about her motives. She won't be able to miss any work. In fact, I'd like her to write a letter apologising to her teacher.'

'A letter, no problem. We appreciate this, Khadisha,' said Tansy.

'It wouldn't be a holiday. She hates missing school,' Simon said. 'That's the kind of fantastic kid she is.'

'I'm allowing this because it's the first time she's ever been in trouble,' Khadisha said. 'It's an aberration to her usually excellent behaviour. If we see any recurrence, I'll have to re-evaluate my decision.'

So it was decided. Next week, every teacher in every class would deliver a lesson on the evils of cheating and the ethics around homework so that a consistent message was communicated across the school and Mia's class wouldn't be obviously singled out. This afternoon, Mia's teacher would email through some additional work and Mia would take the next two days off to think about her actions. Khadisha arranged for Mia's bag and books to be brought over from her classroom, and she brought Mia into her office again and explained what was happening, and the letter she had to write.

'Do you understand why you're being sent home, Mia?' Khadisha said.

'Because it's not allowed. Everyone's supposed to do their own homework,' Mia said. She twisted her arms together behind her back.

'And what are you going to do with all those pens of yours, from now on?'

Mia shrugged. 'Draw things, I guess.'

'You're a clever girl with a great deal of potential,' Khadisha Das told her. 'From now on, I want to hear only good things about you, Mia.'

Mia nodded and kept her gaze to the floor.

Tansy thanked Khadisha, and Simon tried to. As they left, Simon felt the narrow stare of Khadisha's assistant assessing his parenting; he felt every single adult and every single student they passed judging his child, judging him. Even though he had no reason to suspect that anyone else knew anything about Mia's trouble, his face burned.

Together, Tansy and Simon and Mia walked out of the school in silence, Simon carrying Mia's bag, nobody saying anything.

Chapter 29

His darling, angel girl. He wanted to pick her up right now. He wanted her never to grow up. At this age, he could still protect her. He could make everything right. Simon didn't care about Naveen's garden anymore, or about anything else. He felt guilty, as though he'd been the one copying homework. He'd been negligent somehow but he wasn't quite sure what he'd done or what he should do differently. He looked down at Mia. She was blinking and sniffing. Simon felt such fury towards . . . he didn't know exactly what or who he was angry at. But as soon as he worked it out, that person was going to cop it.

He reached for Mia's hand and held it as they walked.

'I'll take the rest of the day off,' he said to Tansy, when they were outside the school gates. 'And tomorrow. Naveen's backyard doesn't matter, not compared to this.'

Tansy stopped walking and turned to him. 'Ah, no. You need to finish the backyard, for all the reasons we've previously discussed.'

She was right. It was, however, a truth universally acknowledged that two working parents unexpectedly in possession of a child for the day must be in want of a non-working relative.

Children can't be at school every single weekday. Children get sick. They have school holidays. So, so many holidays. Not every parent can work from home, and not every child was self-sufficient enough to enable their parent to be productive when said child was present.

This would seem an insurmountable problem except that it was surmounted by parents worldwide, every day. Simon and Tansy were not without resources. Nick was unavailable today, because he was a teacher himself. Kylie was also a scratching – she sometimes worked weekends and so had a weekday off, but never a Thursday or Friday. Under normal circumstances, Mia could have come with Simon and written her letter, but Naveen wasn't well, so that was out. Yulia from downstairs was happy to sit on their couch and watch Russian soap operas on DVD, but Tansy preferred to keep her for emergencies.

'Mia,' said Tansy, 'you're going to stay with Nana for the rest of the day.'

It was the logical solution. Gloria had a big house with a large garden and space for a child to play. She worked, yes; she was always lunching with friends or playing tennis or having her hair done. And there was this tennis club fundraiser that seemed to be taking a lot of her time. *All of these things could easily be postponed,* Simon thought. Gloria's first priority would be her granddaughter.

The downside of having Gloria look after Mia was that she'd want to know *why* Mia wasn't at school.

Oh god. Simon dreaded the thought of Gloria's frank assessment of his parenting skills, now that his child had been sent home for cheating. And on top of her odds-on already-seething fury about Mon? Simon wasn't sure he was psychologically prepared for that. If fact, he was positive he wasn't prepared for it. Going anywhere near Gloria right now was out of the question.

'When you see her, say hi from me,' Simon said to Tansy.

Tansy turned to Simon. 'Where's the ute?' she said.

He nodded a little way down the street. 'But I thought you might drop her, if that's okay?' he said. 'I haven't slept well for the last two nights, and as you said, I really should get back to Naveen's place. I'm a little behind schedule.'

Tansy stopped. 'You're behind? Is that what you're saying? That it won't be finished on time?'

'No. No. Not at all. I'll catch up, no problem,' Simon heard himself say.

'Phew,' said Tansy. She took Mia's bag from the crook of Simon's arm, then walked down to the ute and waited for Simon to open the door. Mia followed. 'We love you very much,' Tansy said to Mia as she settled her into the passenger seat and did up her seatbelt before kissing her on the forehead. 'But there are things we need to talk about when we get home tonight. You can start work on your letter, like Ms Das asked. Be good for Nana.' Then she shut the car door and turned to Simon. 'I'm flat out today. I'll be home late. I'll ring Mum and let her know you're on your way.'

It has to be clear to her that she's being punished, Khadisha had said. As he started the car and headed towards Gloria's, it was clear to Simon that Mia wasn't the only one.

———

If Lachie were sitting beside Simon in the ute, he had no doubt how they would have filled the drive. They'd be playing 'Bottoms', a game of Lachie's devising in which each participant counted the number of protruding bottoms visible from their side of the car, the winner being the player who spotted the most bottoms over the course of the drive. For the purposes of the game, a valid bottom was one in protuberance. Certified protruding bottoms included those of parents lifting children from strollers or groceries from the back seat of cars; gardeners bending to pull weeds; and joggers with one leg straight and the other bent, stretching their hamstrings. Each individual bottom spotted was marked by a loud, forceful cry of 'Bottom!' (After an unfortunate incident at Target, Tansy had instituted a strict rule that this game must only be played while in a car with all the windows up.) It never failed to astonish Simon how many bottoms Lachie could spot on the shortest of drives. It was as though he had some special kind of bum radar.

Instead, Simon was in the car with Mia.

Every day this week, it seemed he'd been lost in a different foreign country. The arrival of Mon, Flora's job offer, and now this! He could not speak the language here. He did not know which way was east. His child was sitting beside him and she was miserable and there was nothing he could do to help. His own father would have said and done the perfect thing, and his father before him. Simon looked down to the backs of his hands on the wheel. They were his father's hands – Simon had so obviously inherited them, they may as well be branded with a tattoo that said *Property of Larsen male*. But what good did they do him? You had no say in the things that were passed down to you. It's galling to realise that the things you've inherited are not the things that really matter.

Snap out of it, Simon told himself. *This isn't about you. It's about Mia.*

When Simon was Mia's age, grown-ups used to talk about their midlife crises, make jokes about sports cars and toupees.

He never heard anyone say that anymore. In the nineties, the focus moved to a third-life crisis, then in the 2010s, a quarter-life. Children matured faster these days, that's all. This was probably Mia's tenth-life crisis. This could well prove to be her single act of defiance, a passing display of anti-authoritarianism that was now out of her system. Probably her teenage years would be a breeze.

'You know that I love you very much and that you can tell me anything, right?' he said as he drove. He faced the road ahead, his gaze darting over to the passenger seat. He'd read somewhere that difficult conversations were easier in a moving car with both participants facing forward: cars provide for fewer distractions and no inhibiting, embarrassing eye contact. That shared feeling of forward momentum stimulated confidences that wouldn't otherwise be offered. This was called the *Carpool Karaoke* principle of communication.

Mia nodded. She had one ankle on top of the other knee, and was focused on picking small stones out of the rubber sole of her shoe.

'Anything at all,' Simon said.

She gazed out of the window. 'Yeah.'

'Because there's nothing you can ever say to me, ever, that'll stop me loving you.'

'I know.'

On the other hand . . . perhaps this incident wasn't a deviation, but the beginning of a long-term pattern. Take Gloria. She did not respect any kind of regulation or authority or social more. She refused to be told what to do by anyone. Simon had long suspected some kind of oppositional defiant disorder by the way she ignored even the gentlest and most helpful instructions or advice. Perhaps Gloria's behaviour was genetic, and had skipped Tansy and been passed straight to Mia? Perhaps Mia was doomed to resist everything, forever? He thought of the other cars he passed on the road: registered cars with licensed drivers wearing seatbelts, all following the road rules. What if Mia grew up to be the kind of person who didn't believe in community: an anti-vaxxing, driveway-blocking libertarian who didn't recycle and hoarded toilet paper?

'I got in trouble at primary school once.' If it was an aberration for him, it could also be an aberration for Mia.

She looked over at him, interested. 'What for?'

'I was about your age,' Simon said. 'There was a broken window in the library and I was the only one there at the time. I got called to the principal's office.'

She turned towards him in her seat. 'Were you scared?'

'Terrified. I don't think I'd ever been so scared in my life. I could hardly speak. I think I cried.'

'Did Grandma and Grandpa come, and did you have to go home and write a letter?' Mia said.

'Er, no. Dad didn't find out. The headmaster eventually realised it was broken from the outside, not from where I was. It was pretty obvious, in retrospect. The broken glass was inside. I was so relieved, I can't tell you.'

Mia folded her arms and turned away again. 'It's different. You didn't do it. I did.'

Simon swallowed. This would be so much easier if they could only scan the streets for bottoms. 'Nana's going to look after you for the afternoon, and me or Mum will come and get you later on.'

Mia didn't reply. She leaned her head against the window, wrapped her arms across her chest and hugged herself.

Everything that came out of his mouth was utterly inadequate. He wished again that Tansy was driving Mia instead of him;

she'd say the right thing, he knew it. Maybe he was allowing himself to be distracted by worrying about Gloria. She had been the parent of young children herself once. She'd probably be much more understanding than he expected.

—

When they pulled up in Gloria's driveway, she was in the front yard. She wore a tight pair of black and white checked pants that finished at her mid-calf, a black fluffy sweater, flat shoes and cat's eye sunglasses, like she was a retired go-go dancer from an Elvis movie. In her gloved hands were a huge pair of hedge shears. Gloria had gardeners come in for the 'menial' work, as she called it, like mowing and fertilising. She did the pruning herself but refused to use an electric trimmer. Instead she owned a large range of tools that she kept surgically sharp, and a long spirit level. Her yard was bordered by a hedge so flat, with sides so vertical, that it looked like a piece of green cubist street furniture, as though it would support your weight if you sat on it. Other shrubs were tortured into perfect balls, cones and spirals. For a normal person, this would mean constant maintenance. Gloria, Simon suspected, had her plants so terrified that they didn't dare put a leaf wrong.

She lay the shears down on the verandah and pulled off her gloves deliberately, finger by finger. Then she walked around the front of the ute, ignoring Simon, opened the passenger door and scooped Mia out.

'My darling girl,' she said, holding Mia's face to her breasts. 'You know this absolutely isn't your fault, right? It can all be traced back to the parenting.' She narrowed her eyes at Simon.

Simon leaned across the front seat on one forearm. 'Thanks for this, Gloria,' he said. 'It's very good of you. I hope we haven't put you out.'

'Anything for my Mia.' She kissed her on the top of her head and gave her a beatific smile. 'You pop inside, darling, while I have a little chat with Daddy, and then I'll order something nice in for lunch. And don't worry about Mummy, you can have as much ice cream as you like.'

Simon could hear himself swallow. *Pick your battles*, he thought. 'Remember what Ms Das said,' he called to Mia through the still-open door. 'It's not a holiday. You can get started on your letter. Or maybe draw something.'

Mia nodded. She kept her gaze low as she waved goodbye and disappeared inside.

As soon as Mia was out of sight, Gloria's smile shrivelled. She slammed the passenger door and raised her sunglasses to sit on her head. Then she looked across the bonnet of the ute through the windscreen, right into Simon's eyes. The paint of the bonnet started to bubble and the windscreen glass began to soften and melt.

'Wind. Down. Your. Window,' Gloria said. 'So we can have a little chat.'

Chapter 30

Simon was a grown man with free will. Strong, independent, the master of his domain. No one could tell him what to do. He could definitely fake a sudden urgent phone call, or pretend he hadn't heard anything Gloria had said through the closed windows. At any moment he could lift his hand, turn the key in the ute, put the shift in reverse and burn out of the driveway.

But there was something mesmerising about Gloria's gaze. She swayed her head and shoulders from side to side as though she was a cobra rising from a bulbous woven basket, accompanied by a dancing flute. Simon could not resist. He felt his arm move of its own accord and press the button to wind down the window.

Gloria walked around the front of the ute to the driver's side and looked down at him. She smiled as though she was a cop who'd just pulled him over in a random traffic stop and had seen, in full view on the front seat, a bag of meth.

'Simon, Simon, Simon,' Gloria said. 'As you know, I'm a humble person.'

'Gloria,' he said, 'actually I'm a little under the pump right now.'

'I rarely focus on myself,' she continued, 'but at this juncture, I'd like to share with you something about me. Something personal.'

'Oh god,' said Simon. 'Must you?'

Gloria's eyes seemed to glow. 'It's this: I've come to the realisation that I've spent my whole life thinking about the needs of other people. Example: I'm organising a fundraiser for the tennis club. That speaks to my sense of sacrifice. I'm always putting myself last. Trying to be the bigger woman.'

Simon's left knee began to shake. 'Of course you do.'

'I could have reacted badly to the arrival of this Mon person and the coordinated tactic of my children in withholding information from me. But I did not.'

'Er, good on you?'

'When Nick explained it all to me yesterday, I made a decision to be calm. To be strategic. I did not overreact, or take my feelings of betrayal out on poor Nick, who was merely the messenger for what, I gather, was a group decision by my children and you, my only son-in-law, who were all jointly complicit in the callous breaking of their mother's – and mother-in-law's – heart. I will manage that issue in my own way.'

'I'm glad to hear it,' Simon said. 'Anyway, I'd better be—'

'Which is my usual approach to life. Live and let live has always been my motto.'

'Of course it has,' said Simon. He held his trembling knee with both hands.

'But "live and let live" is not the way I'm feeling right now. This . . . incident with Mia . . . this behoves a level of intervention on my behalf. I am the matriarch of this family. That burdens me with certain responsibilities. This is a situation I cannot overlook.'

'You don't have to worry about Mia,' Simon said. 'Everything's under control. Look, I'm really behind with Naveen's backyard—'

'You're behind with the backyard? How is that possible? You specifically told Nick this morning that you were on schedule.'

'No. No, no. I'm not *behind*. I didn't say that. I said, I'd better get going because I don't *want to* fall behind. Not behind now, no, not at all.'

'Well that's a relief, at least.'

Gloria did not look relieved to Simon.

She continued. 'Let me ask you this: do you know how many people Tansy dated when she was in her twenties?'

Simon hoped to god that that was a rhetorical question.

'A lot.' Gloria, with more enthusiasm than seemed warranted, began counting on her fingers. 'Karl, the German exchange student. Jeff, who's a stockbroker now . . .'

'Considering Jeff's father owns his own stockbroking firm, that's not a surprise,' Simon said. 'I could have my own dentistry practice by now if I'd followed in my father's footsteps. And as it happens, I dated a lot of people in my twenties as well. I remember—'

'Axel, the Swedish exchange student. Paul, the hockey player. Raoul, the Brazilian exchange student . . .'

Paul? Paul Nguyen from uni who, yes, played club hockey and who Simon had taken that skiing holiday with? Tansy had never mentioned . . . Simon gave his head a little shake. 'Your point, Gloria?'

'Jamie with the red hair, who became a dermatologist. Think of the free procedures! Laser resurfacing and whatnot. Mohanaraj – oh he was a brilliant boy, I knew he'd go far. And look where he is now. A consultant, with a PhD. Then there was Katie. Then Will, who wanted to buy a campervan and drive around the country with her. Very romantic, all sunsets and flowers and the great outdoors. He was an electrician, which is even handier than a dermatologist and almost as handy as a plumber. If Tansy had ever dated a plumber, I would have proposed to him myself. Then after Will there was Wal, the Fijian exchange student. He was studying filmmaking. The shoulders on that boy, I cannot tell you.'

Wait, what? 'Katie? Who was Katie?'

'For a long time, I thought she'd end up with Naveen, considering they've been best friends since they were children. But not to be. In the end, none of those people matter. Do you know why, Simon?'

He shook his head.

Gloria all at once smacked both palms on the side of the ute, causing Simon to jump as though electrocuted. 'Because they're all in the past.'

'The past, yes,' he managed.

Gloria leaned down towards him, a geriatric Olivia Benson, determined to force a confession from an offender. 'Because you're the one she married. You're the one she had children with. Two beautiful children, the loves of my life – and, to be frank, probably the only grandchildren I'm going to get, the way Nick is dawdling. We can rule out Kylie. That girl has always taken after her father but there's a big difference between men and women in that regard. David had a baby in his forties, yes, but just because you can doesn't mean you should. No one wants to be Rupert Murdoch, with a head like a single scrotum by the time your children are out of nappies. Scrota? Anyway. Kylie's out. That means all my grandchild eggs are in one basket, Simon. Your basket.'

'There's no problem with my basket, my basket is fine,' he said. 'Mia's had a little issue at school, that's all. These things happen.'

Gloria's nostrils flared. She came even closer and rested her forearms on the side of the ute. 'Simon, Simon, Simon. Let me take you back in time. When Tansy first told me that you were the one she wanted to marry, I won't lie to you, Simon –'

Lie to me, Simon thought. *Please.*

'– I was surprised. Shocked, in fact. Tansy had to pour me a glass of riesling before I felt sufficiently revived to discuss it. I remember it precisely. It was from the Adelaide Hills – bone-dry and sharp, with just a tiny floral note. Now, Simon, I'm not a shallow person. I don't think even my worst enemy could say that. I have no interest in how someone dresses or if they trim their eyebrows or not; I'm completely non-judgemental in that way. If someone chooses to de-prioritise their physical appearance, more power to them. We never would have cured cholera if John Snow had been messing about with his hair.'

'Cholera? I'm not sure I follow—'

'The point is this: on that fateful day when Tansy announced she was marrying you, she gave me every opportunity to express my feelings. And do you know what I told her, Simon?'

He shook his head and shut his eyes. This would be something he could never unhear.

'I told her that if you made her happy, nothing else mattered,' Gloria said.

He opened one eye with the confidence of a man cowering in a trench who heard a shell whistling towards him but hadn't yet heard it land. 'Was that all?'

Gloria shrugged. 'I might have said one or two other things in the heat of the moment, but that's water under the bridge. I'm far too big a person to indulge in "I told you so's". The gist of my comments was this: I would do anything to support my daughter's happiness and she, for some reason, thought that marrying you would make her happy. It didn't matter whether I agreed with her decision or not. That was irrelevant. If you were the one she wanted, then I was entirely in favour of Tansy marrying you.'

'Um . . . thanks?'

'You're welcome.' Gloria gave her impression of a smile and regally dipped her head. 'And while you continue to make my little girl happy, Simon, and to give my grandchildren the best possible start in life, you will continue to have my full support. Do I make myself clear?'

Simon nodded.

Gloria leaned closer down towards Simon's face and began tapping her nails menacingly on the ute. 'Good. Don't make me regret it,' she said.

—

Digging, planting, paving. His hands in soil, fresh and loamy and alive. His body awake with sweat and strain. No one nagging him. Simon laboured in Naveen's backyard for the rest of the day. Gardens were often overlooked in architectural plans for renovations and new buildings. He understood why. The responsibilities of the architect were wide and deep: client relations and structural issues; the exact shade of the bathroom tiles and intricate schematics of wiring and plumbing. There was simply too many building-related things to consider, and the aesthetics of the garden was one burden too many. He'd been guilty of it himself – spending dozens of hours planning every aspect of a building then, at the last moment, drawing a series of vague circles on the blueprints to represent generic trees, or having Flora make models out of grated kitchen sponge dyed green and glued to twisted wire. As though one tree were as good as another; as though much of the atmosphere and liveability and humanity of a home didn't come from its garden.

Tansy did work late, so Lachie went home with the Chee kids after school and Kylie volunteered to pick up Mia from Gloria's and drop her home. Which meant he might be forced to speak with Kylie this afternoon. He stood, stretched his back and plucked a distorted leaf from a cumquat in a huge green-bronze pot. Between his fingers, the leaf felt smooth and supple and if he hadn't seen the twisted deformation with his own eyes, he might have thought that it was whole and healthy. That nothing at all was wrong.

Chapter 31

It was past six when Simon arrived home from Naveen's. Kylie and Mia were sitting on the short brick fence at the front of the flats, chatting. He said hello to them both.

'Nice to see you off the couch, Lebowski,' said Kylie.

Simon narrowed his eyes at her. 'Did you have fun with Nana?' he said to Mia.

'I guess,' Mia said. 'I wish she had a cat.'

'I think you'll find it's called a "familiar",' Simon said. 'So what did you get up to?'

Mia picked at her laces. 'She's organising this fundraiser thing and working out how many people don't eat chicken. Vegetarians and vegans and people who just don't feel like it. So she has to make sure there's enough of the eggplant.'

As if Mia wasn't being punished enough! Listening to Gloria bang on about catering would be at the very bottom of things Simon would choose to do – and that included hearing about it second-hand, via Mia. He gave her the keys to the flat and told her to go ahead and let herself in.

'Thanks for dropping her off,' he said to Kylie.

'It's always a pleasure to spend time with my niece,' she said.

'Tansy's working late. Won't be home for hours.'

Kylie nodded, but she didn't move from her spot on the fence. Surely *Thanks for dropping her off* meant *You can go now*?

'So I'll see you on Saturday, at the memorial?'

'Yep.' She jangled her keys in her hand.

'And . . . everything's under control? Gloria won't want to speak, will she? Because that would not be good.'

'All taken care of,' said Kylie. 'I've seen the order of service. No Gloria. Plus Nick has stressed that the best revenge is to act completely classy in front of all David's friends and relations so that everyone thinks he was mad to leave her.'

'Good plan.' She still wasn't moving. 'Um, is there anything I can get for you?'

Kylie climbed off the fence and dusted down her black pants. 'What's our new sister like?'

Sweet and a little naive, was Simon's first instinctive answer, but somehow that seemed disloyal. To who, he couldn't say. 'She's fine,' he said. 'I can't believe I was ever that young.'

'She'll need a bulletproof vest for when she meets Mum on Saturday.'

'"Life wasn't meant to be easy."'

'Isn't that the truth.' Kylie flicked her keys around in her hand again and started towards her car. 'I don't envy her. I wouldn't be a young person today for anything, with the world in this state.'

'At least she grew up with a father, which is more than the three of you did.'

'I'm not sure that matters in the long run.' Kylie held up a hand to shield her eyes from the last of the sun. 'Parents are like friends and chocolate. Quality beats quantity every time.'

—

Lachie was too small to sit in the front seat of the ute, so Tansy had arranged for Edwina Chee to drop him off on her way to pick up Lily from her after-school coding class and – perfect timing – there he was, getting out of the Chees' car when Kylie drove off. Edwina and the Chee kids waved out the windows. Simon said a silent thankyou for their friends.

'Dad, Dad,' said Lachie as Simon finally collapsed on the couch. 'I had dinner at Lily's place. They eat so many vegetables! So many. Broccoli, which tastes like a pea that farted.'

'You are gross,' said Mia.

'Vegetables are gross. Lily should be green like the Hulk. But we had ice cream, which they don't normally have because it's a sometimes food but because I was there, it was sometimes. Because I'm not there all the time.'

'Me and Nana had fish tacos,' said Mia. 'A man brought it on a motorbike.'

Simon managed to tune out most of the ensuing conversation between his children, debating the merits of fish tacos (Lachie: 'Puke!') and the superiority of fish fingers (obvious to all). Then he sat on the couch and ate his microwaved two-minute noodles. Mia was quiet. Lachie was never quiet but even he seemed to sense that something was up with Mia. He lay on her bed on his stomach, playing Minecraft on the iPad. Mia sat on the rug in the corner of the lounge with all her pens laid out in rows, drawing, her back to Simon. He peered over her shoulder and saw her page was covered in sketches of shoes of different colours with complicated straps and buckles. He poured himself a glass of red and hopped on his laptop to work through the plans and final budget for Naveen's garden, and double-check the spacing and fertilising requirements for the plants. And yes, occasionally keep an eye on his Facebook feed, and fill up his glass.

Just a little while later, Lachie said he was hungry.

'*Starving*,' he said. 'My tummy is *grumbling*. I had to eat *vegetables* at the Chees. I'm going to *die of malnutrition*.'

'I thought you were full,' Simon said without looking up.

'That was my *dinner* stomach,' said Lachie. 'I still have plenty of room in my *dessert* stomach.'

'Okay,' Simon said. 'What would Mummy give you for an after-dinner snack?'

'How about a fruit roll-up?' said Lachie. 'Fruit is good for kids. And some hazelnut spread?'

'Fruit, nuts. Sounds fine to me. You're a good boy to ask for something so healthy.' *Who knew there was so many videos of animals riding Roombas?* he thought. *How do they get the cats to sit so still? Perhaps they're more trainable than I thought. And what is that? An opossum? Cute.*

'And some biscuits? To put the nut spread on?' said Lachie.

Simon wasn't born yesterday. 'Biscuits are processed. I'm sure your mother wouldn't like you to eat that before bed.' He thought for a moment; he remembered something about brown foods being better for you than white. Brown rice, brown bread, wholemeal pasta. 'What colour is the nut spread?' he said.

'Brown?' said Lachie. 'Dark brown.'

'OK. Better eat it straight off a spoon. And only one spoonful. One. Mia, can you give your brother a hand with the fruit and nuts?'

She sighed dramatically and stomped to the kitchen. Lachie followed. *Another parenting crisis averted,* thought Simon, which deserved another glass of red. Fruit and nuts were an excellent idea. If he'd let Lachie have a sugary snack at this time of night, he'd never get to sleep. Tansy would be furious.

What seemed like a couple of minutes after that, he heard Tansy's key in the lock. She looked like she'd gone ten rounds with Kostya Tszyu: her makeup was smudged, her suit was crushed and her hair was flat. She smelled weird also. *Have you been dragged backwards through a fryer?* was on the tip of his tongue. Luckily for him, he didn't say it.

'Hi,' he said. 'I thought you were working late?'

'I did. It's almost ten,' she said. 'I thought you might be in bed as well, seeing as you didn't sleep well.'

He looked down at his phone. Was that really the time?

'Mummy!' Lachie screamed when he saw her, and hit Tansy at speed. She staggered back a step. 'Mummy, you smell yummy, like chips!'

'Do I, darling? They were eating some in the office. They're far too greasy for me.'

Mia said hello in a quiet voice and waved weakly to her from where she sat, now at the kitchen bench. How on earth did she get up there?

'Hey, it's way past both your bedtimes.' Tansy kissed Mia on the forehead. 'You're not even in your jammies. Daddy should have tucked you in by now.' She looked at Simon meaningfully. 'And why are you so jumpy?' she said to Lachie, who was bouncing up and down beside her. 'After dinner is quiet time, you know that.'

'I'm quiet, Mummy,' said Mia.

'Of course you are, my good girl.' Tansy kissed her on the forehead.

'I wanted to see you, Mummy,' said Lachie, too loudly and at too high a pitch. 'Daddy forgot all about bedtime. It's *awesome.*'

He did a lap around the lounge room with his arms spread wide, aeroplane-style.

'Way to dob someone in, mate,' Simon said, and he stopped Lachie mid-flight and directed him back to Mia's room. Then he took Tansy's bag. She kissed Simon, and her hair brushed the side of his face. Lachie was right, Tansy did smell like chips. Like chicken and chips. She smelled spicy and a little greasy, and Simon realised he was hungry. 'Come here, soldier,' he said to her. 'Do you fancy some two-minute noodles?'

'You didn't make dinner?' Tansy said.

'Um. I've been flat out with the kids.'

'What did the kids eat . . . Never mind,' Tansy said. 'I'll have an apple.' She walked into the kitchen and took one from the fruit bowl. 'What's this doing here on the bench?' She held up one of their large stainless steel serving spoons by the handle. The huge one, the size of a ladle. It was smeary, as though it had been licked all over.

'No idea,' said Simon.

Tansy put the serving spoon in the sink and sat beside Simon on the couch. 'Landlords, oh my god. There are some good ones but the majority are shockers. Why is it so hard for them to grasp that their tenants are their clients? Clients who have a massive lifetime value and who are literally living inside their biggest asset? A little goodwill would go a long way. Also, my head is killing me.' She glanced towards the dining room. 'Where's Mon?'

'No idea,' he said.

'But we have to do this' – she jerked her head towards Mia – 'then we can put them to bed.'

'We don't have to do it now,' Simon said. 'We can leave it for the weekend.'

Tansy shook her head. 'This is important and besides, it'll only take ten minutes. Just let me get changed.'

So despite the hour, Lachie was rewarded with bonus screen time. He sat in front of the iPad in Mia's bedroom, headphones on, watching *Frozen* and twitching like a junkie, while Simon and Tansy sat on the couch with Mia between them.

Chapter 32

This conversation would have been so much easier if they still had their old couch. Other than the house itself and their cars, the couch had been the most expensive thing they'd ever bought – they chose it from one of those minimalist stores too posh to display prices. Simon loved that couch. It was an heirloom in the making.

This couch, the one he and Mia were sitting on now, he'd bought off Gumtree and picked up in a ute hired from the service station. It had cat scratches up its vinyl back and one of the faux-timber legs had been gnawed, possibly by a beaver. The fabric on the seats was flasher-raincoat grey with baby-poo and bile stripes, and it was pilling and bobbled, as though someone had attacked it with a stainless steel barbecue brush.

How could a good outcome possibly come from a conversation on a couch like this? Simon felt doomed before they even began.

'Sweetheart . . .' Tansy held Mia's hand. 'We need to talk about what happened at school today.'

Mia nodded glumly. She was idly picking some of the pilling balls off the fabric.

'Do you understand that doing everyone's homework was wrong?' Tansy said.

'I guess,' said Mia.

'Then why did you do it?'

She covered her face in her hands. 'I don't want to talk about it.'

'Honey,' Tansy said, 'I know you don't. But it's our job to teach you to make good decisions. So when you make a decision that isn't a good one –'

'Which everyone does, at some point,' said Simon. 'No biggie.'

'– we want to understand what you're thinking.'

'I told you already, I was trying to help,' said Mia, through her hands.

'But it *doesn't* actually help, do you see that?' said Tansy. 'If kids don't do their own homework, then they're not learning. And if they're not learning in Year 3, then Year 4 will be harder for them, and Year 5 will be harder still. If you do their homework for them, you're not actually helping them at all.'

'Der,' she said. 'I know all that.'

Tansy looked at Simon expectantly.

'Mia,' he said, 'that is not an appropriate response. This is very serious.'

Mia said nothing. Oh, words came out of her mouth all right. *I know. I guess.* She nodded several times. Simon wasn't sure what he was hoping for – some kind of insight? A blinding flash of contrition? But she said nothing that gave Tansy and Simon any more idea of why she'd cheated. Eventually Tansy was dead on her feet. She needed to shower, to sleep, they needed to wrestle Lachie into bed. They decided to try talking to Mia again over the weekend.

Bedtime at the Larsen residence was rarely easy but for some reason Lachie was bouncing off the walls tonight like he'd skolled a Red Bull: trampolining on Mia's bed then jumping around the lounge as though he were a frog. This was ridiculous. Simon and Tansy were both exhausted, and now this? Lachie was nonstop. And when they finally had him tucked in next to Mia, he kept wriggling and talking. *I need a drink of water. Mummy needs to read us a story. I need it. Another story? Dad has to tell us a joke. Can I have a tissue? Where's B1? No, that's B2. Dad can't tell B1 from B2!*

That was deeply unfair, thought Simon. *They are literally the same banana. Their own mother couldn't tell them apart.*

'Mum, wanna see something cool?' said Lachie, wriggling down the bed.

'Sleep, Lachie,' said Tansy.

'If you give me a snack, I'll go to sleep,' said Lachie. 'Pleeeeeese?'

'Be quiet,' Mia said. 'Mum, make him be quiet.'

'No, *you* be quiet,' Lachie said, and he thrashed until he kicked the covers off.

'No, *you* be quiet,' said Mia.

'I want a snack,' said Lachie.

Anything for a bit of peace. Simon had been on the verge of saying yes when Tansy said, 'No way.'

'Please?' said Lachie. 'How about a banana?'

'No,' said Tansy. 'I do not negotiate with terrorists.'

'When I'm big, I'm going to live *by myself.* And *you* will get invited, never ever ever!'

'You can live with me when I grow up, Mum,' said Mia.

'That's lovely,' Tansy said, 'but your husband might not be too happy about that.'

'If he's going to be a bumhead,' Mia said, 'I'll marry someone else.'

'You're the meanest mum *in the whole world,*' said Lachie.

'Oh, my darling boy,' Tansy said. Simon could hear the smile in her voice as she kissed Lachie on the forehead and ruffled his hair. 'If you get a better offer, take it.'

After what seemed like days, both Lachie and Mia were asleep. It was almost midnight.

'I thought today would never end,' said Tansy when they were finally in bed themselves. 'I have to work late again tomorrow night, but what if we watch a movie on DVD after the kids are in bed? A James Bond, if you want? If you're not feeling too emotional already?'

'I'm not too emotional for James Bond. I cried one time,' said Simon.

'I know,' said Tansy, snuggling him from behind.

'It's just that he's an orphan, that's why he's so devoted to Judi Dench.' Tansy's hair still smelled like hot chips, warm and comforting.

'Tomorrow night, then. If we get the kids to bed at a decent hour. Lachie will be impossible to wake in the morning. What on earth did they feed him at the Chees'? They're usually so responsible,' Tansy said. 'I'm going to ring Edwina and ask her. He might have an allergy.'

Simon agreed, and shook his head in exasperation. *Absolutely typical. You ask someone to look after your kid, and look what happens! It just goes to show, you can't trust anyone.*

—

Simon's last thought before drifting off to sleep was this: *I'm drifting off to sleep!*

When a day was as long and difficult as this one, was there any better feeling in the world than sinking into oblivion as consciousness drained away? No one wants to undergo surgery, god forbid, but those final few seconds as the cold anaesthetic creeps up your arm was one of life's most heavenly experiences. Finally tonight, after two sleepless nights, Simon felt himself relaxing and becoming lost in precious slumber.

It was 2.30 am when he woke, groggy and reeling, conscious of one patch of skin near his knuckles feeling different from the rest. Had he been bitten by something in the night? Or had something else disturbed him? A noise? He listened: everything was dark and quiet. Was Tansy there? He stretched out towards her in the dark: she was a warm mound under the covers beside him, rising and falling. Then he realised there was a small shape standing beside the bed, staring down at him like a ghost.

'Daddy,' it whispered.

'Jesus Christ, Mia?' he said, jerking to a half-sit. 'Are you sick? Is Lachie?' He forced his eyes to blink and screwed up his face and leaned up on one elbow. His brain was full of stuffing, as though he'd taken one of those excellent antihistamines that knock you out.

'What is it, honey?' he said.

'What should I do with the money?' Mia said.

What? That made no sense whatsoever. Perhaps he was still asleep and this was a dream. He lay back down again and closed his eyes for a moment to investigate this possibility further.

'Dad!' Mia whispered again. She scratched his hand again.

He blinked. 'Right, sorry. What money?'

'The money from the homework.'

His brain wasn't working properly, that was clear. He didn't want to wake Tansy, snoring softly after her hard day, so he lumbered to a hunch then swung his feet down and pushed them into his slippers. He took Mia by the hand and led her to the dreaded couch, closing the bedroom door behind him. As his eyes adjusted to the light, he saw that the curtain to Mon's room was open and her bed was empty. Where did that woman get to? Their home was not a hotel.

Simon couldn't worry about that now. Now he needed to focus on Mia. She was wearing soft grey pyjamas covered in tiny smiling clouds and her hair was tousled. He sat heavily on the couch and Mia crawled onto his lap, all elbows and knees. He cradled her in his arms as though she were a baby. He grimaced. In the light from the window, he could see she'd been crying.

'What's all this about? What money?' he managed.

Now he saw she held a small red tartan coin purse in her hand.

'The money I made from doing everyone's homework,' she said. 'Do I have to give it back? I can't but, because I can't remember how much came from who. I should have written it down. Maybe I should put it in Bitcoin.'

'What?'

'Bitcoin. It's a kind of money but not really, because it's smaller. It's just little bitty coins. So it would take up less space and I could keep it in my pocket and then I wouldn't have to worry about Lachie finding it.'

Simon was suddenly extremely awake, yet at the same time his forehead became too heavy for his neck to hold up so he rested it on his hand, its weight on his elbow.

'Mia. Are you telling me that the other kids paid you to do their homework?'

She nodded.

'How much?'

She frowned, concentrating. 'It depends. Not very much at the beginning. Maybe twenty cents each? But it was a lot of work so after a while I put the prices up.'

Now Simon felt cold, as though he were sitting on a couch at Mawson Station. He wanted a cigarette more than anything. He didn't smoke, had never smoked, but his hands were itchy, untrustworthy layabouts that desperately needed to occupy themselves. He wished he'd thought to pour himself a whiskey before he sat down. He swallowed.

'Mia,' he said, 'I want you to tell me the truth. Was this the first time you've done homework for other kids?'

'No,' she said.

'How many times have you done homework for other kids?'

'Lots of times before. Heaps and heaps.'

He felt sick, he felt the world spinning beneath him. 'Why didn't you tell us you'd done it before?'

She turned her big eyes on him. 'Because you didn't ask.'

Simon thought back through all the conversations they'd had since the beginning of this whole drama. Khadisha Das had said it first: *I want to assure you that we're only talking about a single incident.* Simon and Tansy had been operating under that assumption. Mia was right. No one had explicitly asked her whether she'd done this before. In reality, this was the first time she'd been caught.

'Okay. How long have you been doing other kids' homework?'

She rested the purse on her knee and started counting on her fingers, then gave up. 'When I first got to this school?'

'That's,' he swallowed again, 'about a year.'

'I don't do it every day because kids have to learn stuff,' she said. 'I'm not stupid. It's normally just when a kid has something fun to do after school or when the homework is really boring. I've never done the whole class at once before. That was a *big* mistake.' Her face was solemn. 'When you're running a small business, you can't take on too much.'

'Mia, honey.' He rubbed her arm. 'It's wrong to charge your friends to do things for them.'

'But why? Mummy gets paid when she does work for people.'

O . . . *kaay*. 'It's different. Mummy's a grown-up, and that's her job.' He wiped his face with both palms. This was worse than a nightmare; he had spawned a free-market capitalist, a Randian bloodsucker who saw her friends as income streams, whose angelic face hid a balance sheet for a heart. 'Mummy is going to be disappointed in you, Mia. She asked you specifically why you did it. Why didn't you tell us this before?'

'I did tell you. I said I was trying to help.'

'But that's a fib, isn't it? If you were charging your friends for doing their homework, you weren't really trying to help them.'

'Not them,' she said. Then she looked around, as though they were beset by eavesdroppers. She leaned closer and held up one cupped hand around his ear so she could whisper. 'I did it for you.'

Her breath on his ear was soft, like when she was younger and would give him butterfly kisses by brushing her eyelashes against his cheek. He pulled his head back so he could see her clearly: her small, soft face and tangled hair, the sharp angles of her elbows and knees, the sweet and sour warmth of a small child woken in the night. For a moment, Simon wasn't sure he'd heard correctly.

'Me?' he said, ageing beside her.

'You were really sad when we moved out of our house. You cried and cried and you drunk so much wine and I used to check on you in the middle of the night to make sure you were all right. Sometimes you were asleep on the couch, listening to that sad music.'

He had gone through a Leonard Cohen phase, yes. And there were some nights when he'd had perhaps one drink too many and it seemed to make more sense to sleep on the couch rather than disturb Tansy. He was being considerate, that was all. He certainly could have made it to bed, had he chosen to, had felt up to the challenge.

'Kids don't have to worry about daddies,' Simon said. 'That's not your job.'

'Mum was worried as well. She told Nana on the phone that you were sick and we should do something but you wouldn't go to the doctor and get some medicine, and she didn't know what to do. And she talked to Auntie Kylie about it, and Uncle Nick. Sasha Miles in Year 4, her father doesn't live with them anymore.'

'Honey . . .'

'I wanted to help but I didn't know how to. That's why I thought I'd make lots of money and give it to you.'

She held up the purse – it sagged as though full of coins. She unlatched and upended it, and they fell onto his cupped hands. Dollar coins, two-dollar coins, fifty-cent coins. He piled them on the coffee table.

Phew, Simon thought. Small change, which equals lots of money in kid world. That's not so bad.

Then Mia squeezed the purse as though it was a tube of toothpaste. Notes appeared. Lots of notes. So many notes. Small notes, fives and tens, but a great wad of them, fell into Simon's hands.

'That's . . . that's a lot of money,' he said, spreading the notes out like a deck of cards.

'Seven hundred and twenty-two dollars and fifty-five cents,' Mia said.

Simon stared at her. '*How* much?'

She said it again.

'Get the fuck out of town.'

'Some kids get five dollars a week pocket money,' Mia said, with a narrowing of her eyes. 'Some kids get ten. Ten whole dollars. Marcy Doria gets as much as she wants, she just has to ask and her mum gives her money. It's *outrageous*.' Her small hands pressed his big ones closed around the cash. 'You can buy us a new house, then you'll be happy again.'

—

After Simon put Mia back to bed and went back to bed himself, he lay still for a long time. Next to him, Tansy was warm and soft and Simon was petrified and brittle. He felt his muscles and tissues turning to rock, weighing down on the mattress. Through the rest of that long night of broken sleep, Simon dreamed and imagined twisted things creeping from the walls and floors and threading up through his fingers and toes and winding their way into his heart where each pulse sent them further around his body, making it heavier and heavier. Some of these twisted things were words, like Edwina's talk of children modelling their parents, and Kylie's *I think we did better without him*, and some of them were physical things, like the cramped and horrid rooms of this rented flat, and some of them were things impossible to label, like the look in Tansy's eyes when they sold the house and the feeling of being offered a job by Flora. He woke with a start many times, gasping for air as though he was sinking through the floorboards, then he drifted back to the same desperate dream.

The most pressing thing, though, was everything that Mia had said. *Then you'll be happy again.*

She was right. He'd been unhappy for a long time. Longer than he thought possible. And for all those long days and nights of misery, he'd been thinking only of himself – his shame, his feelings of inadequacy – when he should have been thinking of his family. He was the kind of man whose eight-year-old felt she needed to save. He had failed as a father, and that was the only thing that mattered.

Without him around, lying on the couch, drinking too much and acting as a bad example, his children would take after Tansy and her siblings and become productive and engaged members of society. It hit him like a blow – all the times Tansy had kissed him and tried to make love to him, and he'd fobbed her off with rubbish about the children hearing when in reality he didn't want anyone to touch him, not even her. Not even Tansy. He didn't want her pity, didn't want to see the look of generosity in her eyes. He, Simon, who for years had thought that being blessed with Tansy was the single most wonderful thing that had ever happened in his life. It was as if his own body had known long before his brain that he had nothing to offer her.

This feeling of heaviness; it wasn't a dream or a weird imagining. It was crushing him from the outside, grinding the bones of his family to dust. He remembered reading something about correct procedures when saving someone from drowning: throw a rope or anything that floats, the article had said. Avoid at all costs diving into deep water to help, no matter how good your intentions. Drowning people panic. They struggle and they writhe and they drag their rescuers under the surface when they sink.

FRIDAY

Chapter 33

Across the broad and vital city, dawn was breaking. People were rising, dressing, making breakfast, sitting in front of their screens. They were taking the train and the tram, picking up coffee, checking their phones and arriving at their desks thinking of ways to avoid the morning meeting. On building sites, mostly men climbed towers and drove cranes and mostly women held *Stop/Slow* signs. There were children to be cared for, and the elderly, and the ill and injured. Everywhere was industry and energy and commitment.

Except for Simon. At that moment, he lived in another city, a different place altogether. He took no pleasure from the cotton of his pyjamas against his skin or from the softness of his pillow, or from the noises of his wife and children moving through the house because soon they would no longer be *his* wife and *his* children, and every time he thought of that, he could barely breathe, knowing what was coming, what needed to be done to free his family from the weight of him. He wanted to sleep forever. When a sound or a thought disturbed him, he felt himself rising to consciousness as if he were a scuba diver drifting to the surface of a cold black sea but every time he became aware of the density of his sleep thinning, he turned on his somnolent heels and kicked his legs and swam deeper, deliberately forced himself down, down, down to the quiet, murky depths. He knew what he needed to do, if only he could bring himself to do it. He must have courage.

Hours passed. His hands were clenched. He lay very still, foxing, when he felt a weight on his side of the mattress. He opened one eyelid: Mia was in her school uniform, her hair in lopsided pigtails. She'd done them herself.

'Hi, Daddy,' she said.

'Good morning, sweetheart.' His voice seemed overly cheery. He forced his mouth up at the edges and himself up on one elbow.

'Mum's at work and Lachie's at school and I finished my letter. It's morning-tea time. Are you still tired?'

'No, no,' he managed. His breathing was so shallow, it was miracle he could generate speech. 'I'm feeling much better. But you're not going to school today. You don't have to wear your uniform.'

She sniffed. 'That's no reason to let yourself go.'

His phone rang on the bedside table. He turned: it was Flora. 'Is it Mum?'

No, he told her. He stared at the screen until it stopped ringing and a moment later, a text came through:

TBF we need a decision ADN latest TMRW IYKWIM. LMK if you need any further info or F2F. BFN

He would accept the job, of course he would. It was predestined – why hadn't he realised that? But not now, in front of Mia. Besides, he had no idea what the text was saying.

Mia went back to the lounge and after that, Simon was fully occupied sitting on the edge of the bed with his head in his hands. The garden must be finished this afternoon in time for the memorial tomorrow, he knew that. But somehow he couldn't bring himself to shower, to dress, to go anywhere. He felt the same as he had for all those months when they first moved here – as though the air was sticky around his limbs, as though the thought of fighting the weight of suspended molecules was beyond the strength of his muscles or the will of his nerves.

From his side of the bed, he could see the dirty laundry again taking over a corner of the bathroom. How long since their sheets had been changed? He must have done it last week but he couldn't recall. He could do some loads right now. That would be something he could manage. He hauled himself to his feet.

Mia was colouring at the coffee table. She looked up. 'Are you okay, Daddy?' she said.

He swallowed. 'Never better, pumpkin.'

Mon's room was again empty. Why did she want to stay with them when she was hardly ever here? He stripped her bed anyway and dumped the sheets on the bathroom floor. Then he did the same with his and Tansy's then the kids', which were already showing icky evidence of four nights of two small people sharing. He emptied the laundry basket into the pile. He looked hard for stains and sprayed them; he began sorting lights from coloureds. It was repetitive, soothing work. It suited his mood just fine.

The first load was already on when he found the sock.

Chapter 34

It was patterned in a similar way to the kids'. He processed it quickly, threw it on the pile with the other coloureds, didn't even register what it was or who it belonged to. It took almost a minute for him to stop dead, right there in the bathroom. Something was wrong. In the corner of his mind there was a little sign flashing: *Unexpected item in the bagging area.*

He hunted back through the pile until he found it. He held it up in the light, as though he were a scientist with a test tube in a stock image. The sock was bright red with little hamburgers on it.

'Have you ever seen this sock before?' He held it so Mia could see it.

She shook her head. 'It's not mine or Lachie's. It's too big.'

She was right. It was too big to be a child's sock. It was a man's sock, but it wasn't his. It didn't belong here.

Then, all at once, he knew. He had a clear memory of being in Naveen's house on Monday, talking about Lexie's influence on his fashion choices. *She's bought me a pair with little hamburgers on them ... I honestly don't think women find that kind of thing attractive.*

What was Naveen's sock doing in his sheets?

There was something about this he wasn't understanding. It was something to do with Naveen being sick and not letting him in the door and hiring casuals despite his money troubles, as though he needed more free time all of a sudden. Something related to Tansy working late all week without saying why. Also Tansy hadn't wanted any more tacos because she was on a diet for some reason, when she hadn't thought about her weight for years – yet when she walked in last night she smelled salty and greasy, like chips. Not like Macca's chips. Like chips that one would buy from, say, a takeaway chicken shop. Simon thought back: it wasn't Tansy's breath that smelled like that, which would be expected if she'd eaten them. The smell was in her hair. As though she'd recently spent time in a place where chips were cooked.

Something was nagging at the corner of his brain, an important detail he'd forgotten, like when you wake from a vivid dream and somehow as the seconds passed, what was so clear just moments before became impossible to recall.

He went out to the lounge room.

'Has Naveen been over to visit Mummy this week, do you know?' he said to Mia.

'Dunno.' She went back to drawing. 'Not while we've been here.'

It was a stupid question. Even if Naveen had been over, under what circumstances would he have taken off his socks? Had he sprained his ankle on the way up the stairs and removed his footwear to allow for swelling? Had he practised yoga in their lounge, bare toes gripping the carpet in his Downward Dog? Was his shower broken? If Naveen was showering here, someone would have mentioned it.

This proved all too much for Simon's brain, so it sat down in the bony chair of his skull and drafted a symbolic letter of resignation, which was instantly accepted. Simon's body took over. Simon's body developed a plan. It didn't care that he'd decided to leave Tansy and move to Gladstone. Simon didn't have a thought in his head yet he somehow found himself walking over to Tansy's cardboard box/bedside table, which was piled with library books, a lamp with a wobbly shade and a dusty old-fashioned digital clock radio. Under the bed was another box, and inside it were headache pills, a collection of bookmarks made from the kids' drawings, old batteries, a lip balm, a Liane Moriarty paperback, a tube of lube and one of Deep Heat. If Simon's brain were functioning, he might have thought in passing that keeping the Deep Heat next to the lube was a recipe for disaster, but not even that crossed his mind. Nothing crossed his mind.

Next, he opened her dresser drawers and went through the same process: he found undies, bras, socks, pyjamas, t-shirts, tracksuits. Nothing else.

He felt himself looking on, bemused. He didn't even know what his body was looking for.

Then he saw the handbags.

On the back of the bedroom door was a series of hooks, and hanging from these were Tansy's two spare handbags. They were her weekend bags; she'd taken her work bag to the office. Simon's body was driving every action, reasoning in ways he couldn't explain. His hands took each handbag from its hook and started rifling through them.

The bag on the top hook was a black vinyl backpack. Inside, he found a half-empty pocket-sized packet of tissues, a small bottle of hand sanitiser and a pen. And a ponytail elastic, matted with hair. And a half-eaten crumbling muesli bar, a pink My Little Pony with a long tangled mane, a leaking tube of lavender hand cream, a re-useable coffee mug, a glue stick without a lid, a crumpled-up disposable mask and a small handful of squished receipts from Coles and the butcher and the greengrocer.

On the lower hook was a brown leather slouchy type of handbag. He emptied it onto the floor. It held the same brand of tissues and sanitiser and pen, but also half a packet of chewing gum, four crayons, seven rocks, the curling peel from at least two mandarins, four bandaids, three tiny sachets of tomato sauce, two tampons, a flattened origami crane, a Monica McInerney paperback and the same loose, twisted receipts from the usual suspects.

There was also an odd swelling in the lining. This bag had an unreasonable number of zips, and in one pocket on the side, he found a wad of folded papers.

He unfolded them.

These were also shopping receipts, but not from grocery stores. They had been kept aside deliberately and treated with more reverence than the others. One was from a garden chain: it was for plants and pots that he recognised from their descriptions. Another was from a turf supplier and another was from a supplier of garden pavers. He recognised these also: grey honed granite. He should recognise them, because they were Naveen's garden pavers. Except on the receipt, in the space for 'purchaser', it didn't say Naveen. It said Tansy Larsen, and underneath, the address of this flat.

So that was why the pavers had been delivered here instead of Naveen's place. Tansy had given her own address when she bought the garden pavers.

When she bought the garden pavers.

When his wife of twelve years, Tansy Larsen, who was the mother of his two children, bought her childhood best friend's garden pavers, along with all the other supplies for his renovation, for him. Naveen.

He sat down on the bedroom floor. His body noted a bead of sweat running down between his shoulder blades.

Why did Tansy buy all this for Naveen's garden? Naveen should have bought his own pavers, surely? Or his previous landscape designers, the ones who went broke, should have bought them for him.

And how was Tansy paying for all this? She didn't have any money. *They* didn't have any money. Simon would have noticed if those purchases had appeared on their credit card statement.

Tansy couldn't possibly have a separate bank account, one that he didn't know about. Could she? Tansy loved him. They told each other everything.

'I've finished my letter on cheating,' Mia stuck her head around the bedroom door. 'Do you want to see it?'

Time began to warp. The space between the molecules of air in the room grew bigger, and Simon was amazed to find that he could see straight through them.

'Not right now,' said Simon's mouth.

'What are you doing?'

He looked up at her small face, her bright eyes. 'I'm looking for something,' he said. 'Something I lost.'

Mia squatted on her haunches next to him. She patted him on the arm. 'Do you want to come and do drawing with me?'

He shook his head again and instead, walked towards the front door. He took his keys from the bowl and, still in his pyjamas, opened it, leaving Mia open-mouthed on the bedroom floor behind him. On his way down the stairs, he passed Yulia coming back from her walk. She spoke to him, but whatever she said didn't register.

He lifted the garage door. To the right of the tins of unopened paint, next to the stack of timber and behind the grow-your-own mushrooms kit was the stack of their lovely mid-century dining chairs that didn't fit in what was Lachie's bedroom. Simon wriggled one free and brought it upstairs.

'What are you doing now?' asked Mia as he kicked the front door closed again, chair in his hands.

'Daddy has misplaced something,' Simon said. 'Silly Daddy.'

'Right.' Mia blinked. 'What's for lunch?'

'Take ten dollars from my wallet and go down to the milk bar,' said Simon. 'You can have anything you want.'

Her eyes widened, but she didn't say anything.

Simon turned his attention back to the bedroom. Like every house across the country, above the built-in wardrobe in their bedroom were a row of hard-to-reach cupboards filled with decades of both his and Tansy's lives.

His body knew what it had to do. If there was any evidence to be found, that's where it would be. He stood on the chair and pulled the doors open. He rolled up his sleeves.

—

An hour later, he sat on their bed. Every box from the cupboard above the wardrobe had been opened and its contents spread across the room from corner to corner, as though the result of a cyclone or a small localised explosion.

There were old family photographs going back generations, and Tansy's school reports and uni exams. There was stuff belonging to Simon also: decades of tax returns, loan documents, wages forms and equipment receipts from his ex-business and all the papers relating to his bankruptcy. There were his and Tansy's and the kids' medical files and everything from Lachie's birth and Lachie's tonsillectomy. There was a box of Christmas baubles packed into egg cartons and a tangle of lights and a faded plastic tree, shedding green spikes everywhere. There were three boxes of Tansy's paperbacks that couldn't fit in their tiny bookcase. In a cardboard file box marked *Personal*, Simon found a stack of letters from Tansy's father, David, that dated from her teenage years, and decades of her childhood birthday cards from people he'd never heard of. He found travel journals from Tansy's overseas trip, and he found an unaddressed envelope bearing the logo of a lawyer. A family lawyer.

He opened it.

—

Before he opened the envelope, he didn't stop to think that he was snooping. Had a hypothetical person asked him at a hypothetical time what he thought of husbands going through their wives' possessions, he would have said that violating one's partner's privacy was unacceptable under any circumstances. Right now though, he didn't think at all. These fingers weren't his.

Inside the envelope was an invoice for an initial consultation with said family lawyer attached to a receipt and a few pages of handwriting. The handwriting consisted of dot points of advice about the family law act, as though an unspecified hypothetical married person was sitting in a meeting with a family lawyer and, fearful of forgetting something important, made a series of hurried notes for posterity.

These notes were short, impersonal, entirely logical jottings about the mechanics of divorcing one's spouse.

Simon would have liked to read each one carefully but found his eyes losing the ability to distinguish one word from another. Some random phrases jumped out though. He saw *mutual agreement best re prop. settlement*. He saw ... *formalised by court*, and *most resolved without court hearing*. There was *Advice Line* followed by a phone number, and *obtain estimate of costs at each stage* and *likely outcomes*. There was *parenting plan* and *separation for one year before divorce application*. At the bottom it said, *Simon likely blindsided*.

Simon.

Likely.

Blindsided.

There was no possible misunderstanding. All these were in Tansy's handwriting. The receipt, marked with the fancy logo of the law firm, said *Initial Consultation*. It was made out to Tansy Larsen.

And with that, the earth stopped turning.

Chapter 35

'Mum's going to be so mad,' said Mia from the hallway.

Simon looked up, startled. He'd forgotten about Mia for a moment, as though nothing of the last twelve years was real and she and Lachie no longer existed. He wiped his nose on the back of his hand and folded up the lawyer's envelope again and again until it was a small square, then he reached for his phone and tucked the folded envelope inside the case. He felt a terrible pain. He hadn't known that kind of pain existed. 'I suppose she is.'

All at once, he noticed the floor of their bedroom. Where had all that mess come from?

Mia picked her way across the floor and squatted down beside him. 'If I put all this back in the boxes, you can put the boxes up there again. Okay?'

He stood up on the chair and watched her scoop handfuls of papers and books and folders and fill boxes at random then slide them across the carpet towards him. Nothing was in the right place, he was sure of that, but somehow it didn't matter. After a surprisingly short amount of time and only a little swearing and wedging of boxes that no longer fit, it was all put away. Inside the boxes everything was jumbled but the bedroom looked the same as it did before, as though nothing in Simon's life had changed.

When they finished, Simon sat on the couch. Mia put on her shoes and stood at the door with her pink plastic shoulder bag over one arm.

'Okay, well,' she said. 'I'm going to the shops now. All by myself.'

'Fine.'

'What should I buy, do you think?'

'Whatever you want.'

'Cheezels? And cheese sticks? And snakes? And hundreds and thousands? And white fluffy bread to make sandwiches?'

'Go for it.'

She folded her arms. 'Is this a test? Are you going to tell Mum if I don't get something healthy?'

'Not a test. You're a very sensible girl.'

Still she hesitated. 'You're going to be here when I get back, right?'

'Right.'

She nodded, then she opened the front door. Then she shut it again and turned around to face him.

'Are you sure I'm allowed to go to the shop by myself?' said Mia. 'Because Mum doesn't let me.'

'Mia, what did I just say?'

'Okay, fine,' she said. 'Just checking. Do you want anything?'

Simon had disliked this flat from their first inspection. He disliked the cruddy carpet that never seemed clean, even after Tansy hired the machine from Woolies and went over every inch, and he disliked the small windows that only existed to throw sunlight on the pasty, snot-green walls and the water-stained ceiling. How many people had stood under that smeared skylight and washed their crevices and sprayed their bodily fluids in that damp and mouldy bathroom? How many strangers had fried eggs and opened tins of tuna and exhaled their sour breath in that kitchen? And who built that kitchen anyway? Someone who'd never cooked anything in their life, that was clear. A labrador with an allen key.

Now he didn't merely dislike this flat, he loathed it. He was infected by it, as though it was the source of all his troubles. Their old house smelled of nothing. If not for this flat, he would never have found the sock and had he never found the sock, he never would have found the receipts for the pavers, and so on, back to the notes from the family lawyer. This flat was responsible. Well, the virus, but ultimately the flat. Simon had a sudden desire for light, for space, for other humans, the way everyone did at the end of the each lockdown. Also he was starving beyond reason and he knew without looking that there was nothing to eat here at home. There was never anything to eat here.

Do you want anything?

This was what he wanted, in this moment. He wanted to not exist. He was once the luckiest man alive and he hadn't even realised it. This was how poisonous he was. Tansy was the best person he'd ever known and he had driven her to this. He'd thought the last two years were bad. Things were about to get much, much worse. He wanted to leave before he ruined anything else, but at the same time, he saw Mia in front of him, hands on her hips. Soon, in a matter of days, the solid foundation of her life would fracture and crack. This week may be the pivotal time in her life, the one she recalled in her memories in twenty, thirty, forty years' time. Life before her father left, life afterwards, like Tansy and her siblings. He wanted to give Mia some kind of memory to sustain them both in the years ahead.

He would not allow her last memories of living with him to be eating Cheezels for lunch in this flat.

'Change of plan,' he said. 'We're going to the mall.'

—

The small girl strapped in the seat beside him had Tansy's eyes and nose, and her chin and cheeks and smile were clearly Simon's – yet somehow Mia was completely herself. For someone so small, she had a big presence. His part in her existence had been long ago and infinitesimally tiny. He remembered from Tansy's birthing classes that 400 sperm could fit on the head of a pin. His minuscule seed could hardly account for Mia, could it?

His phone was in the centre console of the ute next to his wallet, and it throbbed with the radioactivity of the lawyer's envelope folded inside its case. The aura it emitted was so pervasive he couldn't have spoken to Mia even if he wanted to. Tansy was a stranger to him. He didn't know his wife at all.

A wave of nausea swept across him. Was it all a lie, him and Tansy? All of it? He thought back to the beginning of their relationship; did they ever really talk about what made a good life and how to build one? Or had he simply assumed that Tansy wanted the same things he did: to be settled and successful with children, a nice house, a European car and an overseas holiday every couple of years? Had she wanted more? Something different? Had he bullied her, taken her agreement for granted? Had he failed her even worse than he'd known?

At a red light, his foot felt weird on the brake. He glanced down: he was wearing Tansy's old slippers, the purple fluffy ones they kept outside the front door for traipsing down to the clothes line. Mia noticed him looking at his feet and she peered down towards the pedals.

'We can go back, if you want,' she said.

He shrugged. What he wore on his feet was irrelevant. Let's face it – like Tansy, Mia was also a stranger, with her own thoughts and schemes. She'd told no one else about the money. If Lachie had known, he would have blabbed immediately, and Tansy hadn't a clue or she would have fixed it. Simon knew he should tell her but couldn't, at least not until he had a plan. He'd asked Mia to keep it between them for now. If anyone could keep a secret, it was Mia.

'You're pretty big now, aren't you,' he asked her. 'What are you? Six one? Six two?'

She stared at him. 'I don't know what that means.'

No, Mia wasn't *only* herself. She reminded him of Tansy: the shape of her face, her upper lip. Was there a gene for being unflustered? Would he remind her of Tansy forever? Would he be unable to look at his daughter or even hear her voice for the rest of time without seeing Tansy in her? Tansy, Tansy everywhere. Would this be his life?

•

The food court was brighter than a thousand suns so he kept his sunglasses on. Mia was in her school uniform, skipping to keep up with Simon even in the purple slippers. He'd pulled tracksuit pants and a hoodie from the dirty clothes pile. His hands were deep in his pockets, the left one closed tight around his fat phone case, bloated with the lawyer's envelope.

Simon hadn't been at the mall in the middle of a weekday for months. Where did all these people come from? There were old people, and parents with babies, sure, but there were also adults who should be at work and kids who should be at school. An older woman with a deep red mask and blue hair, pushing a trolley filled with craft supplies, gave him the side-eye as they passed, as though he was a homeless man in fluffy purple slippers who'd kidnapped a schoolgirl.

'This is the funnest thing ever. We haven't been here for ages,' Mia said. 'Remember when we used to come sometimes, for pancakes? I used to have a short stack, and Mum let me put the syrup on myself.'

'I don't remember that,' he said.

'Oh, that's right. You weren't here. You were working.' Then she took his hand and came closer. 'Is being here allowed? Because Ms Das said it wasn't a holiday.'

'It's a holiday if I say it is.'

She didn't look convinced. 'Will I get into trouble if someone sees me?'

'Who's going to see you?'

'Some kid's mum? Or one of the teachers, having a day off? Maybe there are spies. Or maybe Ms Das comes herself, to find kids that are supposed to be at school.'

'I'm the boss,' he said, 'not Ms Das. We're having a daddy–daughter lunch date.'

'Or we could be on our way to the dentist, couldn't we, Dad? I mean, we're not, but they don't know that, right? Maybe we should just drop in to the dentist, just in case.'

It was a different world here; it was glossy and new and fresh, and it smelled like 60-day free credit and free wi-fi and freedom. Over the last two years, Simon had forgotten about so many things he used to take for granted. He'd forgotten about shopping malls, their marble and gleaming steel and mirrors, and their window displays of shiny laptops and sparkling headphones in pristine white boxes. He'd forgotten the smell of new leather.

Look at all these people, walking around with their shopping bags and trolleys – they still had money. None of these people rented disgusting flats with intruder socks. None of them were scrimping and saving.

Then, out of nowhere, the food court vanished around him and he was cast back to a family holiday they'd had when he was eight, his parents and him on the Gold Coast. He shut his eyes and he was there: hotter than he'd ever been in his life, the sand grainy on the arch of his feet, the distant rumbling of a crowd. What had possessed his parents to choose something so patently frivolous and out of character he'd never know. They'd stayed in a high-rise, right on the beach. He remembered being convinced that Surfers Paradise was another word for heaven. He was obsessed with the lift, pleading with his mother to let him push the buttons and he could feel those buttons now – cold steel under the pads of his fingers, lighting up from within. He could not believe room service was a thing, that all his father had to do was pick up the phone and someone would bring him a cheeseburger and chips. The agony and delight of those final moments, waiting as the man with the tray came inside their room and rested it on the small round table in the corner and lifted the silver cover. And the ocean! How could one substance be so many different shades of blue at once? Then they spent a day at Sea World. His parents, so sanguine, as though they did this every day at home. Simon, eyes bulging, almost brought to tears by the exquisite waterskiing girls in bikinis and the dolphins jumping in formation. When you're a child, the world is full of wonders. Even now he could taste the salt on his lips, feel the spray on his face.

'Dad? Are you okay?'

He nodded.

'Are we having lunch here?' said Mia. 'Or are we buying stuff to take home?'

He rubbed his hand over his beard. 'Both.'

Chapter 36

He bought a pulled-pork burger with melted cheese and hot chips and onion rings and a thickshake for himself, then he gave Mia a twenty from his wallet so she could choose her own lunch. She joined him at his table with a salmon sushi pack and a lemonade.

'I told you, pick anything you want,' he said. 'Ice cream? Cake? Today there are no rules.'

'I like sushi.' She squeezed soy from the little plastic fish to make a puddle on the flip side of the tray and mixed in the knob of wasabi using the tip of a chopstick.

'That's not avocado. That green stuff's hot.'

She rolled her eyes like they'd come loose from their sockets. 'I know what wasabi is.'

Who was this child, eating sushi of her own volition? At her age, he wouldn't have eaten raw fish if his life depended on it.

His burger, on the other hand, was the best thing he'd ever tasted in his life. The juice dripped down over the bun and the yellow cheese oozed over the side. With every bite, he felt a new layer of fat coat the inside of his cheeks. It was magnificent. While he ate, he opened his phone case that bulged on one side from the lawyer's envelope and began deleting apps from his phone, leaving greasy thumbprints on the screen. The meditation one was the first to go. Wanky bullshit. The very sight of that golden bowl annoyed him. Apps for learning foreign languages? Why on earth did he have those? Delete, delete. Next, his weather apps. Delete. Who cares what the humidity is? What difference could it possibly make to know in advance if it will rain this afternoon, tomorrow, on the weekend? For all Simon cared, it could rain for the rest of time.

He'd finished his burger and Mia was halfway through her sushi when a shadow fell across their table.

'Simon?' a voice said. 'Simon Larsen, is that you, old mate?'

He raised his sunglasses and turned a bleary gaze to one side.

'Mate, it's me, Dazza!' the man said. He was tall and bald and solidly built, with wraparound sunglasses perched on his scalp and tiny dark eyes much too small for his soft, fleshy face.

Simon blinked. It *was* Dazza, the sales rep from the huge building firm that Simon had used for several dozen extensions. Dazza, who was Simon's mate, together with Thommo from the lighting wholesaler and Bazza from the timber and building materials supplier and Stavros from the kitchen manufacturer. He could picture their faces before him; he remembered everything. Those were the days! The football, the pub, restaurants with famous chefs and overpriced steaks; Simon's life, when he was an architect. Before the virus, when he was flying high and the world was a better place.

He wished Lachie were here. No friends, heh? Who's this then?

'It's been ages. Darl, this is my old friend Simon, I've told you about him.'

Standing beside Dazza was a woman in a white floral dress that looked like a meadow and a black cowboy hat made from felt. She was young, in her early thirties. Dazza was in chinos and a patterned blue business shirt. They both smelled insistent, like they worked at Lush. Beside them was a gangly, zitty teenage boy in a purple striped tie and dark blazer with an oversized gold crest on the pocket.

The woman nodded abstractly.

'Shiraz Simon? The architect. Before your time, but I definitely mentioned him. You remember, the guy with the great taste in wine? So generous with his expense account back in the day. God, the fun we used to have. Remember when we went paintballing? You shot Stavros right in the dick? Classic.'

'*This* is Shiraz Simon?' said the woman. At least a dozen bracelets and bangles slid up and down her forearm as she moved it, tinkling. A great many golden rings jostled on each finger like splints; it was a wonder she could bend them. Her earrings, blue and gold feathers, fluttered around her cheeks when she spoke. She looked down at Simon's slippers. He tucked his feet under the seat.

'Mate, where did you get to? It was like you disappeared into a black hole. My girlfriend, Kimberley. And my boy, Oliver,' Dazza said.

Simon nodded to them both. He used his sleeve to wipe the pulled-pork juice off his face.

'And who's this little munchkin?' Kimberley said, bending forward with her hands on her knees.

'I'm Mia,' she said. Her lopsided pigtails made her face seem like it tilted to one side even though it didn't. *Diagonal Child with Sushi*, by Picasso.

'Aren't you adorable? Are you the baby of the family?' said Kimberley.

'No.' Mia placed her salmon sushi down, right side up, and laid the chopsticks beside it. 'I'm in the middle.'

Simon frowned. 'No you're not. You're the eldest.'

Mia shook her head. 'No, I'm the middle child. Lachie's the baby and Dad's the eldest. I heard Nana say that once.' Then she grinned. 'It's a joke. Dads aren't kids, they're dads.'

Dazza and Kimberley both laughed as though it was hilarious. Simon felt a dull ache in his chest which must, he thought, be a preview of tonight's indigestion.

'Shouldn't you be in school?' Kimberley said.

Mia glared at Simon, as if to say, *See? Spies.*

'We're having a daddy–daughter lunch date,' said Mia.

'Flexible custody arrangements.' Dazza nodded sagely. 'It's great if it works. If I tried to take any of my kids out of school for lunch, the ex would hit the roof. We're on our way to the orthodontist.'

'She's a psycho,' said Kimberley from behind her hand. Her nails were long and the softest pink, and each had a tiny rhinestone sparkling on one side.

'Dad, can I have one of those after?' Oliver said, his eyes on Simon's empty burger box. His eyes were the colour of Kimberley's blue feather earrings, and his mouth was a nest of silver braces. Perhaps he'd grow hefty like Dazza but now, in mid-adolescence, there wasn't a muscle on him.

'Not on your life,' said Kimberley. 'You can have a Buddha bowl, if you must. Otherwise all those retinoids are going to waste.'

'Anyway, so good to see you back on your feet, mate!' Dazza said, and he patted Simon on his shoulder blade. 'We were all worried about you, after . . . well, you know. After it all went down. I said to the boys a dozen times, I hope Simon's all right. You were in our thoughts, all right.'

'All right,' Simon said.

'The lads are good. You won't believe it – Stavros bought a boat, the bastard! Might as well pile up your money in the backyard and set fire to it, am I right? Took us out on the bay last weekend. Caught nothing. Not a nibble. And Thommo's new missus popped out twins! Let's see him get out of changing nappies this time around, hey? Anyway, you should have phoned me, buddy! Followed me up. I spent a few sleepless nights thinking of you, I'm not ashamed to admit it. What are you up to now?'

'This and that,' said Simon.

'Great to hear it,' said Dazza. 'I knew you'd land on your feet eventually.'

'Darl,' said Kimberley, 'we've got to get going. Don't want to be late for my pedicure.'

It was that kind of mall; upstairs in the shiny professional offices were all kinds of dentists and orthodontists and chiropractors and browologists and tattoo removalists and a medical aesthetician with a reputation for liberating women of all ages from the shame of thin lips.

'Yep, busy-busy,' said Dazza. 'It's a big day for the boy – braces are coming off. Of course, his mother couldn't be arsed applying for leave, so I had to rearrange my schedule to take him. I mean, hello? That's basically what mothers are for.'

'Poor Darren has to pay the bill as well,' said Kimberley, and she giggled. 'I'm just along for the ride. I can't say no to a trip to Chaddy.'

'Congratulations,' said Simon to Oliver, who replied with a shiny grin.

'They cost as much as a holiday in Palm Cove, braces,' said Kimberley. 'Beachfront.' She raised her arm so her bag fell into the crook of her elbow. The bag was white leather and covered with blue feathers to match her earrings.

'Still, they're an investment for the young fella. You can't get ahead in business without a winning smile.' Dazza nodded at Mia. 'Wait till this one's a teenager, you'll see.'

'Good on your little one for having the sushi. Omega-3, it's essential. Junk food causes so many problems.' Kimberley blinked slowly, flared her nostrils and turned to Oliver. 'For the skin as well as the teeth.'

'So anyway, we better get moving.' Then Dazza paused, as though a thought had just occurred to him. 'Listen, we should catch up for a coffee sometime. I'll give you a tingle.'

'That'd be great,' Simon said. 'Don't be a stranger.'

They said goodbye and he watched the three of them walk across the food court.

'Who was that man?' said Mia.

Simon wondered how much Dazza had earned in bonuses over the years from bringing in Simon's business. Enough for a holiday to Palm Cove, certainly. Enough for braces and a divorce and a new girlfriend.

'I thought I knew,' he said. 'But now I'm not so sure.'

Chapter 37

Simon's local Coles had the atmosphere of a mausoleum. Here in the marketplace, the noise – background muzak and announcements of licence plates parked in loading zones, the occasional squawks of babies and the shouts about the raspberries on special if you hurry – was disorientating. Glass and chrome cabinetry glistened and gleamed, shielding mounds of glossy luscious fish and vibrant bloody meat, manned by smiling teenagers in white aprons. Each piece of fruit looked hand polished. Different cheeses reclined in their temperature- and humidity-controlled compartment beside rosy-pink salamis the size of small dachshunds.

He and Mia waited next to elegant women with bulging trolleys and bought free-range bacon and marinated olives and orange juice squeezed to order by a machine and sourdough that smelled like Prague, or how he imagined it. They bought four white peaches and a ripe blue cheese and asparagus and scotch fillet steaks and baby tomatoes on a vine and a tub of Greek yoghurt and an avocado and a big block of dark chocolate dotted with salted caramel. He picked up a bottle of pinot from the Yarra Valley that cost more than three of his usual shiraz, then put it down again because this was not about him. He did not buy the raspberries because he would suffer no discounts, not today. Instead, he bought a bag of dry-roasted cashews. A large bag. And a small bunch of purple flowers for Mia, because he couldn't remember ever having bought her flowers before. He tried to pay with his library card at first – he still felt a little discombobulated. The deli attendant frowned as though he'd never seen one of those before.

'Are you sure this is allowed?' Mia said, brushing the flowers over her cheek. 'Mum usually goes through the catalogue on her phone before she makes the shopping list. So she can find the specials. And we never buy any of that.'

'Well, today is all about treats,' he said, digging through his wallet looking for his credit card with the emergency buffer. 'We're making memories, that's all that matters.'

Mia looked at the blue cheese, unconvinced.

—

By the time they were in the car, he felt a little queasy. The burger was lodged somewhere under his rib cage, a knotty reminder that he was too old to scoff half a pig and a week's worth of calories in twenty minutes. Tansy usually kept an eye on things like that.

'Dad, you're all sweaty on your face,' said Mia.

'That's completely normal.' He twisted around his hood and used it to mop his cheeks, then wound down the window for some air.

He'd never noticed before, but her voice was exactly like Tansy's. There was no way to be in the company of his child without imagining his wife. He could never move on while Mia was around. After a divorce, every time he saw his child, he would feel as though a filleting knife was working its way around the bony barrel of his chest.

'Are you really okay?' Mia said. 'That was a funny noise.'

'Never better.' Breathing through his mouth was a slight improvement.

They pulled up outside the flats, in front of the pathetic lawn where, only three days ago, he was relaxing, eating tacos, thinking everything was fine. Last week, everything *was* fine.

They both got out of the ute and closed the doors. Simon, exhausted, leaned against the side of the ute as he locked it. Across the road was a removal van, and he watched two men in blue singlets and inappropriate shorts carrying an old-fashioned dressing table down the driveway of a single-storey weatherboard. The mirror attached to the dressing table was in three parts and had silver scalloped edges and it wobbled from side to side with every step the removalists made but even that didn't slow them down. They were practically daring the mirror to topple off and smash on the driveway. *No care, no responsibility*, Simon thought. These days, people just do what they want, regardless of the repercussions.

Mia noticed his gaze. 'That's Binh and Cathy. They're moving back to Queensland because Cathy's mum's getting old and they have to be closer.'

Did Tansy know the private business of everyone in the entire street?

Just then, a pink ice-cream van with a giant plastic cone on its roof turned into their street, music blaring.

'Would you like a soft-serve?' Simon said. 'With a flake in it?'

Mia shook her head. 'We can't. The music means they've run out. They have to go back to the ice-cream place and get more.'

Simon opened his mouth, then shut it again. *Evidence of Tansy was everywhere*, he thought.

Paper bags in both sets of arms, he and Mia made for the dark and grim common stairwell to the flats. The stairwell could have been airlifted from a Victorian-era debtors' prison. It resonated with the odour of a million cigarettes and a thousand boiled cabbages, smells impossible to remove from bricks and mortar and, in all likelihood, from the inside of his nose for the rest of his life.

Across the road, a removal van. Binh and Cathy, Mia had said. Moving. Binh and Cathy, whoever they were, were doing the right, selfless thing.

'Dad?' Mia said. 'We've got one floor to go.'

Chapter 38

He leaned against the crumbling brick wall of the stairwell because if there was one thing this hoodie was missing, it was a huge dusty mark on one sleeve. Sweeping arcs of agony radiated outwards from his chest. His whole body felt in pain, every cell, yet somehow it was familiar. Perhaps he had always been in pain and he'd never noticed it until now.

'Is anything wrong?'

He took a deep breath in and out. His abdomen involuntarily contracted. 'I'm thinking.'

'Is this an emergency?' Mia said 'Should I call Mum?'

'I'm fine, pumpkin. Nothing to worry about. Thinking is not an emergency.'

Inside the flat, the TV was on – some kind of legal drama. A courtroom scene cut to a tall woman who looked like the first mate of an intergalactic smuggling ship except instead of being in outer space with her pilot husband, she was in a glass-walled penthouse apartment. She wore a tight dress and leaned over a posh kitchen bench while she poured a glass of wine and said something devastating.

Had he left the TV on? Simon thought.

Then he saw Mon slouched on the couch with her feet on the coffee table, eating hot chips from a takeaway box balanced on her stomach. She muted the TV when they came in.

'You know what I really hate?' she said in lieu of a greeting. 'The way female characters in TV shows walk around inside their own houses in high heels. TV writer, hello? Have you ever actually *met* a woman? The very first thing a woman does when she gets home is kick her heels off, moron. The second thing she does is take off her bra. If she hasn't already taken it off in the car on the way home. While driving.'

'We only have free-to-air,' said Mia. 'We don't get this show.'

'I know, right? Inmates in maximum security have more channels than you lot. You've already used your free month, but I signed you up anyway. These are the golden years of television and you Larsens are making shadow puppets on the cave wall with your hands in front of the campfire.' She ate another chip.

'We really can't accept,' said Simon mechanically. 'The coffee machine is already too much.'

'A gift from family should not be a drama. Think of the kids. When you're a kid, your favourite TV show makes a deep impression.'

'What was your favourite show when you were a kid, Dad?' Mia said.

'Er, what?' Simon felt dizzy, and the smell of Mon's chips was making him nauseous. 'Um, when I was really little, like Lachie's age? I had two favourites. One was a comedy set in a World War II Nazi prison camp and the other was about a witch who upsets her mother when she gives up her magic powers to marry a man who works in advertising and become a housewife.'

Mon turned, blinking. 'Jesus, what? What was wrong with people back then? You should all be in therapy.' Then she clocked Simon, red, sweaty and gasping for air in his bulging, burger-juice-stained tracksuit. 'What happened to you?'

'We had lunch and bought treats,' Mia said, lifting her bag. 'Nothing yummy, only stuff for grown-ups. Dad put it on his credit card and Mum doesn't know. And we met one of Daddy's squad, from the olden days.'

'I've had quite the afternoon,' Simon said.

He was thinking about Naveen's garden, of all things, out of all his half-finished projects, out of all his responsibilities. When lined up next to – in no particular order – the laundry he'd started this morning, still wet in the machine; the welfare of his children; showering and shaving; the unthinkable issue with his wife; putting the cold stuff in the fridge; the festering mushroom boxes in the garage; Flora's pending job offer; the unfairness of Mon's optimism; his lack of *squad*; the future criminal career of his daughter; and the million other task-bubbles of modern life, it was Naveen's garden that stuck in Simon's mind.

'I'm going to say one word,' Mon said. 'Xanax. Seriously, run, don't walk. Get to the GP, like yesterday. Get a script. It'll change your life.'

'I'm going to say one word.' Simon put his groceries on the floor. 'Babysitter. I need you to look after Mia for a bit, and be here when Lachie gets home.'

'No can do. I'm just here to grab some clothes,' she said, making no attempt to shift from her sprawl on the couch. 'I'm not staying.'

'You look like you're staying,' he said.

'Well, I'm not.'

'Mon.' He sat beside her, extracted her hand from the box of chips and looked into her eyes. 'There's something I have to do. *Have* to. Right now. Yulia might be home – you can go downstairs and check – but right now, I need you to stay with the kids.'

He had made a commitment to Tansy. Tomorrow was the memorial. He had promised that the garden would be ready. If he finished the garden, he would have delivered his side of the bargain. His conscience would be clear. No one could fault him for what happened next, least of all himself. He had one chance to do one thing right.

'I have to go to Naveen's. It's an emergency,' he said to Mon.

'I knew it,' said Mia. She took a bite from one of the peaches.

—

This was how the whole garden thing happened in the first place.

After the collapse of Simon's business, he was worn out. Exhausted. Those last few sleepless months had been a blur of desperate calls to banks and credit agencies and suppliers, and making and breaking payment plans, and refinancing the house and his business loans, and negotiating with the landlord about his office, and phoning his own creditors, and putting the kayaks and the framed Bradman memorabilia he'd bought at a charity auction on eBay, and juggling accounts to pay salaries and super. He wandered the house at night. He never thought he'd be the kind of person who begged, yet there he was, pleading with securely employed arseholes for just a little more time.

He hadn't wanted to burden Tansy with any of that because he was thinking of her wellbeing. He was putting Tansy first. He was conscious of her stress levels. It was not at all related to his ego, to the embarrassment of failing in her eyes. Not at all. She asked him several times if anything was wrong; he told her *nothing*. She didn't have a clue. He wanted to manage by himself and with any luck she'd never know how close he'd come to losing her house.

—

Oh, did he not mention that before? That it was her house?

Had that one particular detail been hidden away in his unconscious mind, never to surface no matter how many times he thought about the house? Both their names were on the title, yes, but the house had been Tansy's.

Tansy had lived at home until they married. She skipped the share-house years that still gave Simon flashbacks of lentil-induced flatulence and designated fridge shelves and Tupperware with names attached on sticky labels and waking up to tousle-haired drug-addled strangers in the kitchen if your flatmate'd gotten lucky, strangers who could have stabbed you in your sleep. For some reason beyond Simon's wildest imagination, Tansy had preferred to live with Gloria.

It wasn't unusual among their friends to live at home – but why would anyone willingly live with *Gloria*? In Simon's mind, it was the equivalent of volunteering to share one's existence with an Eastern Brown.

Wait. That was probably a little harsh. To the best of Simon's knowledge, Gloria had never actually *killed* someone. It was probably fairer to say that living with Gloria was like being infested with pubic lice. You could never relax because of the ever-present irritation in the most intimate part of your being as she sucked the blood out of your body and the joy out of your life.

Yes, Gloria's house in the leafy east was spacious with every convenience. Yes, Gloria worked odd hours and had a busy social life and wasn't home all that often. All that makes living there sound like a logical choice. But other than the expected horror of seeing and hearing Gloria every day, there was one other disadvantage. From the day her children turned eighteen, Gloria had charged them one-third of their salary in rent.

This was an extremely on-brand thing for Gloria to do, and each of her children reacted differently. Kylie, the eldest, was the first to be presented with a rent bill when she found a part-time job while at uni. She moved out a week later – but that probably would have happened with or without the rent. When Nick of the charmed existence turned eighteen, he was already playing football and wouldn't have known how much money he had or didn't have – he handed Gloria cash when he was flush and never gave it another thought unless she asked for more.

In between Kylie and Nick was Tansy. For her, the rent wasn't an overwhelming amount at the beginning when she was a part-time waitress, but became substantial when she dropped out of uni and started work as a receptionist, before she went overseas. Then became more again when she arrived home and moved to business development for the real estate company.

Honestly, Gloria was making out like a bandit.

'It'd be cheaper if you moved in with me, or at least got a flat with someone,' Simon had told her after they'd been dating for a while.

Tansy looked at him. 'But Mum would be all alone!'

'You have to think about your finances,' said Simon. 'Your mother being alone is just a bonus.'

Tansy paying rent to her mother caused much tearing of hair and gnashing of teeth among their friends, who all planned to live at home for free until their late forties at least. Some of their parents still paid them pocket money.

Gloria was a single mother on a fixed income from her part-time job as a tennis coach, Tansy explained. She was trying to teach her children valuable life lessons and it was reasonable that everyone contributed to the running of the household. *No child of mine will grow up to be a freeloader*, Gloria said, often. Besides, she also said, it provided a little incentive for a reluctant fledgling to leave the nest. She could convert the spare room to a home gym.

Simon privately thought it incredibly harsh for a mother to charge their own child rent, even if Gloria honestly believed it was for Tansy's own good. Then on the morning of their wedding, before Gloria walked Tansy down the aisle, she gave Tansy an envelope.

It had a cheque in it. A huge, unexpected cheque. Tansy and Simon were both stunned. Gloria had invested every cent of Tansy's rent for the last six years, and now it was enough for a deposit on a house.

'Discipline is its own reward, never forget that,' Gloria said to Tansy when she handed her the envelope. 'But a little extra never goes astray.'

So in Simon's mind, the beautiful family home actually belonged to Tansy.

Yet when he was starting his business and asked if he could use it as collateral for his loans, she hadn't hesitated. She never hesitated. When they finally lost the house – only two days after he'd warned her that things were looking grim – he phoned her, shaking, from the bank's head office in the city. He arrived home to find her packing linen into cardboard boxes and making dinner for the kids, telling them it was all an adventure, and carrying on as though the world hadn't ended, as though he hadn't lost the only substantial asset she'd ever had.

When the bank repossesses your house, you don't even get to pick the real estate agent. It's beyond humiliating. It's like having your testicles removed.

Fast-forward to after his bankruptcy. His phone went silent. The leasing company came for both cars. They moved to Gloria's for a couple of weeks first. Then when that drained his will to live, Tansy found the flat through her old firm. Then they offered her the job in their rental division.

Then Simon got bogged.

He was mentally drained, understandably. He needed a little time to pull himself together. A few weeks. Maybe a few months. He wasn't *idle*, exactly. He was recuperating from an intensely stressful and traumatic experience and, besides, he didn't want to jump into another venture just like that. He needed time to consider his options. He didn't intend for it to happen, but time somehow ebbed away. He'd always been an active person. Now, he found it hard to move.

He applied for jobs, but he was one among thousands of unemployed. Government assistance was available, yes, but what he really wanted was a job. His wasn't the only firm to fold. Jobs in architecture were hard to find. He was alternately told that he was overqualified and that he lacked experience in the latest CAD, which seemed to change on a weekly basis. For some jobs, he was somehow both overqualified and under-experienced.

The virus had taken more than Simon's business. It had taken his confidence in the intelligence and capability of people. The virus made him realise we were living in, not the original Dark Ages – so named because of Europe's cultural and intellectual stagnation – but a new dark age. For all our modern superiority, when pitted against an enemy as old as time, we were no smarter than the Romans fighting the Antonine

Plague, no tougher than Medieval Europeans fighting the Black Death, no kinder than Edwardians fighting the Spanish Flu. When our turn came to be tested, we fell back to masks and quarantines while unbelievers stalked the streets like their pitchfork-carrying ancestors, seeking witches to burn. We thought history was in the past and woke to find we were living in it. We were nowhere near as safe as we thought we were.

Simon showered less often, he never shaved. He began to hate architecture. To loathe it. It had promised him so much. He had given it everything and now he was left with nothing. He had brought children into this world. He had made a mistake, thinking he could captain this ship. He lacked the will to force his limbs to move, and every subsequent lockdown, or mini-lockdown, or lockdown in another state, seemed to trigger a kind of PTSD in Simon, and who knew how long it would take to recover from that?

Before he knew it, he'd spent close to eighteen months on the couch.

—

Until Friday afternoon last week. He'd woke with a start to see Tansy and Gloria silhouetted against the light from the kitchen windows, looking down at him.

'Jesus Christ,' he said. 'Is it past six already? Was I supposed to pick up the kids?'

Chapter 39

'It's not even two,' Tansy said. She was in her business clothes.

'And he does this all day, does he?' Gloria was wearing her tennis whites and shoes, complete with bobble socks as though she were a teenager, and she was cleaning her sunglasses on an actual handkerchief. 'I'd be changing the locks.'

'I'm right here, you know that,' said Simon. 'I can hear you.'

'Is that . . . is he wearing pyjamas?' Gloria said.

'They're *day* pyjamas,' Simon said, who was relieved that he was at least wearing pants.

'Mum,' said Tansy, 'give him a break. He's going through something.'

'I'm telling you, this is a terrible idea. Simon's not the one to help Naveen, he can't even help himself,' Gloria said. She bent over with her hands on her knees and peered down at him, as though inspecting a small animal she'd hit with her car. 'Oh my god, is that drool? He's drooling on the couch.'

Simon sat up, wiping drool on his day-pyjamas' sleeve. 'No I'm not.'

'He can do it,' Tansy said. 'I know he can. It's what he does best.'

'Lay on the couch and scratch himself?'

'No, Mum. Make beautiful, useful spaces for people to live in.'

Gloria turned to Tansy, as though they were alone. 'Listen, my girl, Naveen is in trouble. His backyard looks like a bombsite. His landscape gardeners have done a runner. He's in desperate need of serious help. *We're* in desperate need. The memorial service is only a week away.'

'Simon worked for a landscape gardener all the way through uni. He can do it,' Tansy said. 'I know he can.'

'I can,' he said. 'I can do it.' He smoothed the hair back from his face and rubbed the sleep from his eyes. He tried to look alert, competent, conscious. He had no idea what they were talking about.

'I'm sixty-four and a half and I still work almost full-time,' Gloria said. 'Do you know how exhausting it is, being a tennis coach? And do you know how uncoordinated small children are? Half of my students couldn't hit the ball if I was holding it still in midair and they had a racket two metres wide and they were the only ones on the court. Yet I'm out there almost every day. Look at him. He should be bouncing off the walls with energy. He's only fifty!'

'I'm forty-two,' said Simon.

Gloria folded her arms. 'You're shitting me.'

Tansy sighed. She looked as though she might cry. 'You might be right,' she said.

'Hang on one minute.' *Gloria* may be right? *Gloria*? Gloria wasn't right, of that Simon was positive. He could definitely do it. Whatever it was. The thought that Tansy – his cheerleader, his number one fan – had changed her mind and now thought he couldn't do it . . . well, that was unacceptable.

'He'd need a ute,' Tansy continued, 'for picking up supplies and for getting around. I need my car during the day for work. We don't have the money for a second car.'

'A ute isn't a problem,' said Gloria. 'Nick has a friend who's going back to Oslo for a year, to help his parents on the farm. Nick was just asking me the other day: *Do you know anywhere my friend Sven can store his ute and tools for a year?* He – Nick's friend, Sven – doesn't want to sell it in case he comes back. From Oslo. Where his parents have a farm. All Simon would have to do is promise to transfer the ownership back when Sven shows up.'

'See, Tans?' Simon said. 'I can have Sven's ute.'

'I'm more worried about the design aspect,' said Gloria. 'What if Mister Day Pyjamas makes a mess of it? Naveen certainly doesn't have enough money to do it twice, and we don't have the time.'

'I won't make a mess of it,' he said. 'I'm a qualified architect with a sophisticated aesthetic sense – I can certainly handle one little backyard.'

'Tansy, listen. You need to stop this nonsense right now. What if it's hideous? Naveen is your oldest friend – how will you look him in the face? This is not a little semi we're talking about. Naveen has a big backyard. And it has to be done for Saturday.'

'Simon won't make a mess of it, Mum,' Tansy said. 'You can trust him. Simon knows how much my friendship with Naveen means to me. Simon won't let me down. If he says it'll be done by Saturday, it'll be done by Saturday.'

'You can trust me, Gloria,' he said. 'Next Saturday it is. Tans, ring Naveen right now and tell him I'm in.'

And just like that, before he'd had a chance to really think about it, Simon was committed. Before he knew it, Sven's ute appeared on the street outside the flats along with some new tools. Tansy negotiated a price with Naveen for Simon's labour and arranged for him to start work first thing Monday morning. He wasn't entirely sure how, but Simon's week as a landscape gardener had begun.

—

After he left Mia with Monica, Simon went to HireDepot and picked up a spotlight. He made a list of everything else he needed then double-checked it before heading to the hardware store before it closed. Then he went through the McDonald's drive-through and bought five long blacks and tipped them into his empty thermos. For water, he'd use Naveen's outside tap. He didn't buy any food. He could live off his front hump, chockers with pulled-pork burger. It was possible he'd never need to eat again.

Everything else Simon needed was already at Naveen's.

Naveen. So far, in his head, Simon had managed to separate the sock-owning Naveen from the man whose yard Simon was finishing. He had to keep up that pretence for a little longer. He needed to focus.

When he arrived, he was relieved to see the curtains at the back of the house drawn tight. Perhaps Naveen was at the chicken shop or perhaps his casuals were covering the Friday-night rush and Naveen was out somewhere – it didn't matter. Naveen wasn't here, that's what mattered. Life would become exponentially harder if he so much as saw Naveen, because all his calm and focus would evaporate and he would become the worst part of himself. Naveen was unrelated to this, Simon told himself. In fact, he had to finish the garden in order to finish with Naveen.

He gazed over the backyard in its current state of upheaval. It looked like a tip. This inconsequential corner of the world looked as sad as he felt – bare, exposed earth, gaping holes where shrubs should be.

It looked, he thought, *like a metaphor.*

First he set up the spotlight so it wouldn't bother any of the neighbours then he hauled all the equipment out of the ute. He sat in the front seat and pulled up the spreadsheet on his laptop. He rolled up his sleeves. It was already past four o'clock. He'd made it clear to Mon and Mia he wouldn't be home until morning.

Simon once had something good. He'd lost it. It was no one's fault but his own.

He had one chance, one night, to do something right. To salvage some tiny shred of self respect.

Three, two, one. Go.

SATURDAY

Chapter 40

When Simon was a university student, it was *de rigueur* to do as little as possible during the semester then study all night in the week leading up to the exam. And it worked: he graduated with a major in Construction of Residential Buildings and a minor in Principles and Practice of Leaving Everything until the Last Minute and then Working Flat-out While Fuelled by Pseudoephedrine, Caffeine and Sugar.

He no longer had a raging furnace behind a flat stomach that burned any old rubbish, and these days he was usually nodding on the couch by 8.30 pm after a decent morning sleep-in and a fair afternoon nap. He was also a good twenty kilos over his uni weight and, other than this week, he hadn't exercised in years.

Be honest. Decades.

When he began working in the garden that night, he started slowly, steadily. His muscles were putting up a brave front but he wasn't fooled – he'd be in agony tomorrow. Combined with the crushing chest pain he was experiencing – either severe heartburn or the early stages of cardiac arrest, maybe both – Simon had every reason to quit.

But he didn't. Somehow, he kept going.

Tansy rang at 6 pm, at 8 pm, at 10 pm, and left rambling messages about missing him and hoping he was okay. He didn't call her back.

So what kept Simon going all through that long night in Naveen's garden? The carrying, the digging – they were back-breaking. His hamstrings felt like they'd snap. His shoulders throbbed and by midnight he couldn't lift his arms above his head. This desperation to finish, to clean his slate, to free himself from this metaphorical weight around his neck – where did it come from?

For the first time in years, he was blessed with the clarity he'd experienced the first time he saw Tansy: he knew with every cell of his being that nothing in his life would ever be as important as finishing this garden and making it beautiful. That all his future happiness, all his future sense of self, relied upon it. How he knew this, he couldn't say.

—

The hours passed quickly, the way that minutes feel like seconds when you're lost in concentration doing something important or idly surfing the internet doing something that's not. Eventually, he unfurled his back, rolled down his shoulders.

It was finished.

He stepped back and looked. In front of him – the backyard.

Every part of Simon hurt. Young people can climb a moun-tain, go to a party, drink seventeen shots of tequila, get four hours sleep in a bathtub then climb back down the mountain the next day, while yodelling. At his age, if you slept without your own pillow, you'd best make an appointment with the osteo for first thing in the morning. Simon's body was ageing and the evidence was everywhere: the burning blisters where his fingers joined his palm; the creaking neck, stiffening by the minute; the stabbing pain in the small of his back that flashed down his leg like lightning every time he took a step. His arms hung loose on his shoulders and his calves twinged.

His chest, though, no longer ached. It seemed to him that his ribs moved in a wider arc with every breath. It had been a long time since his lungs were so full and then so empty.

He watered the new grass and all the plants, turned off the tap and rolled up the hose. He turned off the spotlight, packed the tools away in the ute. Naveen hadn't come home; there was no sign of life in the house.

He looked up. A softening in the air told him dawn was coming. A movement caught the corner of his eye: a pair of king parrots flying overhead. He watched them until they disappeared. Beads of dew, shiny as glycerine, glistened on the blades of grass. Simon could not resist. He took off his shoes and socks and wiggled his toes in Naveen's cool, fresh new lawn.

There was something transcendental about gardening. It's about trust. Gardeners plant seeds in deep, dark soil and after that, they are blind. There is no way to check the seed's progress; they cannot measure each tiny hair-like root. Despite this, gardeners must continue to do the work. They water and fertilise but plants can't be forced and they can't be hurried. Gardeners must believe a sprout will come.

Something else Simon noticed as he'd teased soil away from the roots of a mock orange and chosen its best side for planting: there was not one plant here that was perfect. See, this one had a twisted leaf and that one had a hole made by an insect. Flaws were part of every growing thing and were not always meant to be repaired, even if they could be. And a garden made you notice things. It hauled you kicking and screaming out of your buzzing head and into your body. Plants teach you there is no point being greedy; too much of something – water, fertiliser – is as bad as too little. And plants die! No matter how careful you are, no matter how hard you try, some are overcome by caterpillars or aphids, some turn brown for no obvious reason and shrivel back into the soil from whence they came. Some things cannot be saved. In a garden, humans reach the limit of their authority; they learn that much of life is out of their hands.

That feeling of safety in adult competence Simon had as a child? He'd held onto that too long. There is no sacred moment; you do not go to sleep one night and wake up in the morning with the uncanny ability to spot a rip off a surf beach and the knowledge of how to clean a barbecue. No one really knows what they're doing. The number of things an adult can control in this life is actually very small and almost always in the realm of their own head.

Before he knew what he was doing, he'd taken his phone out of his pocket to call Tansy, to tell her he'd finished what he'd started. There was no one else in the world he wanted to tell because he and Tansy were together in all things. It was instinct. His thumb hovered for a moment over the call button when his brain caught up with his body.

She was not his Tansy, not anymore. He was adrift in the world. The earth beneath his feet no longer solid.

He put the phone back in his pocket with a shaking hand. He felt as though the guts of him had been removed.

Then he packed up the ute as the sun was rising and, despite the whole-body exhaustion of this shell of a physical being, Simon felt like he had just woken up from years of sleep because now he *wanted* things. Was it possible to be nostalgic for something he'd never experienced himself? He longed for a simpler life, for home-delivered orange juice and tram conductors and riding his bike to school and saving up for showbags, but he couldn't remember one single incidence of a younger Simon doing any of those things. Before his bankruptcy, he'd paid someone else to mow the lawn and they'd done it badly. He knew how to look after a yard; it was burned into his brain from all those hours of part-time work for the landscaper when he was a student, yet when he was an adult with his own garden, he hadn't dug one hole, never planted one thing in it. He'd always had the ability to make a space beautiful. Even now – the flats had a backyard, a big empty one. He could have resuscitated the beds and taught his children how to grow food from the earth, a skill that would sustain them for the rest of their lives, but he had never tilled a foot of soil. Now, standing in Naveen's backyard, looking at the sky, he couldn't imagine why.

Chapter 41

He was calm as he drove home. Calm and starving. He passed a cafe with its tables already out and umbrellas up and a press of road bikes out the front, so he stopped and ordered two toasties and two long blacks. On a long table inside, eight or ten cyclists sat and drank coffee. They were all in black Lycra, looked around 120 and were indistinguishable from each other.

'Early morning, sunshine?' one said to him.

'I'm a gardener,' Simon said. He hadn't even thought those words until he said them out loud.

'My wife's a gardener,' one said. 'We can't go on holidays in summer because she stresses over the bloody plants. We've got a watering system, love, that's what it's bloody for!'

'As soon as you finish weeding, you've got to start at the beginning again,' another said. 'Gardening is futile. It's never-ending.'

'I think that's the point,' Simon said.

'If you want a hobby, get yourself a bike,' another said. 'It keeps you young.'

'None of us look a day over ninety!' They all dissolved in laughter.

'I'll keep it in mind,' Simon said.

One by one, they stood and hobbled to the door on their cleats like drunk saddle-sore toddlers.

'Watch out for this one,' the first one said to Simon, nodding to the barista. 'She's a tiger.'

'Don't do anything we wouldn't do,' another one said, raising his eyebrows.

When they had saddled up and ridden off, the barista rolled her eyes. 'I'd like to have a garden some day,' she said. 'Or at least a room with a window.'

She was in her twenties, with vaguely pink hair and tired eyes behind huge clear-rimmed glasses. Her wrist bore a fresh stamp from a club just above a tattoo of a seahorse in multiple shades of green. She didn't look like a tiger to Simon. She looked soft and warmly cuddly; caressing her would be comforting, like a faux-fur blanket. She swayed behind the coffee machine as though she'd come straight to work from a big night. She was dextrous with the grinder and the filter basket and the tamper. She had the look of someone who could make coffee in their sleep, and sometimes did.

She was the kind of girl a single man might want to sleep with. That's what those cyclists had been implying, that leaving a man like Simon alone with a girl like that would mark the beginning of something.

All at once, Simon felt weary to his very bones. He didn't want to sleep with the barista. He wanted to give her a tulip in a pot to make her smile, to make up in some small way for the low-grade sexual harassment she must put up with every single day. She was very pretty. But she wasn't Tansy. He was a disappointment to the cyclists, to himself.

'My wife's having an affair with her best friend from primary school,' he said to her while she was making his coffees. He hadn't dared to even think the words until he said them out loud.

Her gaze darted up to his eyes. 'Man,' she said. 'I'm so sorry. That is shit.'

'It is,' he said. 'It is shit.'

'I'd better get you a cronut,' she said. *Thwack* went the portafilter against the knock box. 'On the house.'

—

When Simon arrived back at the flats, the caffeine and the food was beginning to kick in. He climbed the stairs, somehow, thighs aching. He stood at the front door to gather himself for a moment. He had no idea what he would say to his wife, his children. He had no plan.

But he couldn't stand out here all day. He put the key in the lock, opened the door.

There was no one in the lounge room, he could see no one in the kitchen.

'Tansy?' he called, as though the space was big enough for someone to hide. 'Kids?'

The flat was empty. It was vacuumed and dusted, everything was in its place, which only served to make it look dingier and more rundown. In the bedroom, he found his old suit laid out on the bed, along with an ironed shirt and a tie. And a note, from Tansy:

Where have you been? Is everything okay? I've dropped the kids at Mum's, then I'm meeting Kylie and the hire people at Naveen's. The memorial starts at 10.00 am.
See you there.
I love you.

In the shower, he leaned his head forward and let the hot water pummel the back of his neck. He scrubbed his skin with a dried-out loofah until it tingled; he shampooed his hair. He shaved with a rusty disposable and toilet-papered his nicks but (thankfully, saving Simon from himself) the aftershave in the bottle had evaporated to a thick amber and clogged the nozzle. He cut his nails and pushed back the cuticles with the clip on the cap of a ballpoint pen and snipped the hair in his nose and trimmed his ears.

How long had it been since he'd performed this kind of basic zhuzhing, the bare minimum self-care required to show respect for the person whose bed you shared? He couldn't recall. How had she put up with him for all these months? When the news of Tansy and Naveen spread, who would blame her? For all these months, Simon could barely stand himself; it should be no surprise that Tansy felt the same. He dressed, and it seemed that his skin was awake now. He could feel the fibres of the shirt and of his trousers.

When he reached Naveen's, he had to park the ute around the corner because the street was packed with cars and in the driveway, a catering van. Surely David didn't know this many people? Could there be another function today in the same street, he wondered? In front of him and beside him as he walked, people were alighting. They were single people, and couples and family groups with older children and younger ones. They wore suits and frocks and hats, mostly black but not always, and their best shoes. Church clothes for people who no longer went to church. There were many more people than he had envisaged would be there in his long dark night of imaginings. Was that only two nights ago? It seemed that years had passed.

All these people were walking up the driveway to Naveen's. Simon followed them. He overheard a conversation behind him: *How did you know David?* one woman asked. *I didn't,* another replied. *I'm a friend of Gloria's.*

As he turned the corner and the backyard opened up before his eyes, Simon stopped so suddenly a teenager in sparkly sneakers ran into the back of him. He'd worked hard, he knew. He had a modest amount of design talent – it had been his career, after all. But he had been so focused on *finishing* the backyard that he'd not fully appreciated the final result.

—

The plants, in resilient late flowering, were full and soft and luscious, and layered in pleasing yet predictable waves. The pavers were the perfect shade of silvery grey bordered by a smoky green ground-cover; the grass was crisp and new. There were surprises in unexpected places: a sandy corner strewn with succulents; spears of hot pink celosia appearing among the vivid green in one bed. In one corner, there was a fire pit surrounded by bench seats he'd made from the recycled timber. He had rigged a water feature in a large rustic pot, resting on its side, and the faint tinkle of the little pool was cool and calming. He'd strung fairy lights on the limbs of the established trees, and the hire people had added multicoloured paper lanterns. The grass was covered in rows of white folding chairs, and in front of the podium were pots of freesias on a stand, filling everything with a gentle perfume.

Simon released a deep breath. He hadn't even realised he'd been holding it. Not only had he finished the backyard on time, but it was perfect. It was beautiful. It was quite possibly the most beautiful thing he'd ever made.

He couldn't remember the last time he'd achieved anything at all, much less something so splendid. He felt his shoulders fall back and his gaze lift. He felt taller. *He* had done this. Him. Simon.

There were eighty or a hundred people squeezing between the rows, beginning to take their seats. Gloria was unmissable in the front row, in dramatic black with a black hat and veil, sitting with an empty chair on either side. On the other side of the aisle, a few rows back, was Nick in a sharp new black suit, and Kylie, holding hands with Lachie and Mia. The Chees were there, with their children. Looking over the rest of the crowd, he noticed his neighbours from the flats: Yulia, and the rest. He hadn't known they'd be coming. Then, still standing over on one side, he saw Naveen, in a pair of chinos and sports coat, talking to Lexie. At the sight of him, Simon's head squeezed as though in a vice and his hands formed into fists.

Then he saw Tansy making her way to the empty seat beside Gloria. She was looking around, turning her head. She was scanning the crowd for him, as though they were any other couple. She wore a dress he didn't recognise – a soft yellow shift, straight and sleeveless, that ended above her knees. She was somehow more animated, more alive, than any other person there.

A million thoughts buzzed inside his head like flies but for once, he didn't heed them. Instead, his heart thumped in his chest. He felt the same jolt, the same shiver spreading over his skin as he did all those years ago when he first saw Tansy across that crowded room at a party. He could not look away. And they say that lightning never strikes the same spot twice.

And then he knew why it was so important that he finished the garden. It wasn't to prove Gloria wrong, and it wasn't merely because he'd given his word. It was because he had given his word to *Tansy*. He wasn't ready to give up on her, on their marriage. There were many other women in the world – lovely women, attractive and intelligent. But none of them were Tansy. Only Tansy was Tansy.

In a flash, he saw that for all the things that had been outside of his control over the last few years – the virus, the lockdowns, the end of his business, the things that he had allowed to defeat him – there was something he could have controlled, had he decided to. That all he'd had to do was ask for help, but he hadn't. He thought of Mia and Lachie growing up without him and that he'd already given them a taste of that. He knew the names of their teachers now but hadn't a clue about Mia's at her last school. Same story for their best friends; now he knew all about them but before the first lockdown, he'd had no idea. In a blink, they'd both be leaving home for good to start their own families – whether those would be the traditional type or not. Even before that, they would hit a stage in their teens where hanging around with their parents would become torturous. He didn't have a moment to lose.

And look at his beautiful wife. See the curl in her hair, the way it kicked out at the end. The line of her calf in her heels.

Maybe it was already too late. Maybe soon she'd stand in front of him and say, *Simon, I love someone else. Let me go.*

And then he would. Of course he would. He felt his eyes swimming. He told her when they married that her happiness was the most important thing in his world. It was his responsibility to live up to that.

But she hadn't said it yet. He was still in with a chance. Maybe the lightning bolt of love had hit him twice because he was a different person now. Perhaps he could start again.

How was she not worth fighting for? She was worth fighting for.

She saw him standing at the back, and she smiled. It was that smile he loved, that one that made her seem to glow. She raised both palms and waved them around to indicate the garden, then mouthed, 'Wow'. Then she blew him two kisses and beckoned him to come up the front, and reached across behind Gloria to pat the empty seat beside her.

Simon shook his head and blinked. He motioned that he'd stay where he was, standing up the back. There were perhaps a couple of dozen people gathered around him, near the house, who hadn't found seats.

She shrugged, half-smiling, half-frowning. 'Are you okay?' she mouthed.

He nodded, looked away.

It was awkward, standing at the back among people he didn't know, waiting as though for a bus, but soon the proceedings would commence. He would think about the garden, that's what he would do. He glanced down to check the fall of the pavers – excellent, perfect angle – and when he lifted his head, Naveen was standing beside him.

'Mate,' said Naveen, 'it's just amazing. I don't know what to say. It's better than I could have ever imagined.'

Simon shut his eyes. He breathed deeply through his nose; he thought about his children, sitting not far away, and Lexie, and all the people gathered here to celebrate David's life, and how grossly inappropriate it would be to lose his cool at a memorial service. Besides, what mattered was being a good father. He was concerned about the kind of behaviour he was modelling his children? He could start being better right now. He opened his eyes.

'I can't talk to you,' said Simon as evenly as he could manage. He should have turned away, averted his eyes, stood somewhere else, but some kind of masochism had frozen him to the spot.

Naveen's brown skin paled before Simon's eyes. His lower lip buckled. 'Oh my god, you know.' He ran his hand through his thick hair and tugged, as though he was trying to pull it out by the roots. 'You know, don't you? I'm going to hell, aren't I?'

'I mean it,' said Simon. 'Get away from me. I don't want to make a scene.'

'I didn't start it, I want you to know that,' said Naveen. 'It didn't even occur to me! *She* kissed *me*, Simon. I've never in my life had a woman kiss *me* before. You're angry, aren't you?'

Simon made his hands into fists, as tight as he could. 'Of course I'm bloody angry,' he said. 'But more than that,' – he shut his eyes, and words came into his mouth from who knows where – 'I'm sad, Naveen. I'm really sad.'

'I know that, mate,' Naveen said. 'That's on me.'

'I thought you were a better person than that,' said Simon.

'But it doesn't have to change anything, right?' Naveen raised his eyebrows and grimaced. 'I mean, these things happen. We're both consenting adults. It's upsetting, I get that. But we can move past it, right?'

Simon stared at him. 'Are you deranged?'

Naveen took a swig from his glass of wine. 'You're right, of course you're right. Normally I have to construct scenarios in my head to even *touch* a woman. I even resorted to the "pretend to yawn then stretch your arm along the back of the chair" manoeuvre when I was dating Lexie's mother, which was lame I know, but that's how I usually operate. Simon, I am not what they call *smooth*.'

'Stop talking,' said Simon.

'I mean, she's so young,' said Naveen. 'How young is too young?'

Simon blinked. Tansy and Naveen were exactly the same age.

'She's in her twenties! I'm going to hell. There's some calculation, isn't there? Your age divided by something, then plus something? Don't answer that. If you have to do the sums – that's a bad sign. She's too young, that's all.'

'Naveen—'

'I have to take responsibility for my own actions.' Naveen was rambling now, gushing. 'I know that. But you need to understand, I didn't chase her. She came over here, to my house! To yell at me! Maybe that was it. No one has yelled at me since my divorce. Maybe having a woman standing there, yelling at me, made me nostalgic for my marriage.'

Tansy never yelled, thought Simon.

'She showed up uninvited, yelling at me for yelling at you on the phone on Monday! I didn't know what she was talking about. I've never yelled at you. I told her that. And then she kissed me!'

'You're talking about Monica,' Simon said.

'Of course,' said Naveen. 'Who else would I be talking about?'

Chapter 42

Tansy was not having an affair with Naveen.

This wasn't everything, he knew. The strange credit card that Tansy had used to pay for the pavers and why she'd paid for them at all; the receipt from the lawyer's office. There was still pain ahead, Simon was sure of it, but he would take his victories where he could and this had been the biggest and blackest cloud on his horizon. He felt the blood rush back to his tensed hands and he took a deep breath, the sweetest he could remember.

'I found your sock,' Simon managed.

'That bloody sock! We got dressed in the dark because you were in the yard and I didn't want you to see her, so we kept the blinds closed. It was only later I realised I was wearing one of hers.'

'You didn't come home last night.'

Naveen tilted his head back and looked to the sky. 'We drove to Phillip Island and stayed in a motel. She wanted to go to the beach! Can you believe it? Just like that, no planning. Thank god Lexie was at her mother's and Yulia could sit with your kids. I mean, who does that without making a booking? We might have had to sleep in the car! She didn't even read the reviews on Tripadvisor. I'm a single father who collects Flybuys points, Simon. I have no idea what I'm doing.'

He nodded. 'I hear you.'

'Look, Simon, does Tansy know? Can you not tell her? Is that too much to ask? It is, isn't it. It's too much to ask. Forget I mentioned it. You and Tansy have the best marriage I know, it's completely unfair to ask. But, please, don't tell her I'm sleeping with her little sister. Half-sister. Whatever. Please.'

'Where is Monica now?'

Naveen jerked his head towards the house. 'Kylie and Nick said she could sit with them, and Tansy and the kids tried to coax her down the front, but she's in the kitchen. She said she needs a moment. I think she's a little nervous about meeting Gloria.'

Oh yes. Simon scanned the kitchen windows and could see her now – a slender pale face among the catering staff, looking out towards them. He opened his mouth to say, *Hiding in the kitchen won't be good enough. If she wants to avoid Gloria, I'd be considering New South Wales.*

When Simon turned again, he caught Tansy's gaze in the crowd. She no longer looked proud and loving. She was waving at him with both hands, frantically. She grimaced. She was mouthing something to him, but he couldn't guess what she was saying. Something was wrong, he could tell.

'Naveen . . .'

'I'm going to hell,' Naveen said again. 'I know it.'

Tansy stood and walked around to the side aisle. She began stalking her way through the crowd towards them, apologising to people as she nudged them, dodging around people still to take their seats.

'Isn't your family Hindu?' said Simon, keeping his gaze on the approaching Tansy. 'Do they even have a hell?'

'Oh yes. Naraka. Yama will judge me, I know he will.'

'Simon.' Tansy had reached them; she was standing beside him now, pulling on his sleeve.

'What do you need, love?' Simon turned to her, gave her his full attention. She needed something. He could still fix things. He could still fix this.

'It's Mum. She just told me she's changed her mind. She's going to give a eulogy about Dad, in front of everyone.'

On the other hand – Simon wasn't ice cream. He couldn't fix everything.

And just then, Naveen said, 'The ceremony. It's starting.'

—

A celebrant in a black dress patterned with wild roses stood behind the podium and everyone hushed. She introduced herself, said a few words of welcome and the acknowledgement of country and talked a little about David. He had been a distinguished board member for publicly listed companies. He'd had a stellar and successful business career. He enjoyed fly-fishing and collected wine. He was survived by his children and his wife, Jackie, who wasn't able to be here today.

Above all, she told them, this was to be a celebration. David had died almost two years ago. Now that the initial mourning period had passed, this was a perfect opportunity to remember him with fondness, and with joy.

'I'm delighted,' the celebrant went on, 'to tell you there's been a change to our order of proceedings. We're fortunate to hear from someone who knew David for over four decades. Let me introduce our first speaker, Gloria Schnabel.'

'Jesus Christ,' said Simon. The thought of crash-tackling her flitted through his head.

'Oh no,' said Tansy. 'No, no, no. Where's Nick?'

He scanned the seats: Kylie and Nick, on the other side of the aisle, spun in their seats to look back at them, their faces a rictus of panic.

'Nick,' Tansy mouthed. 'Get up!'

Nick nodded, the picture of a man prepared to sacrifice himself for the good of others. But it was too late. From her seat at the front, Gloria stood. She had a natural grace, an ease that came from her years of discipline and exercise. She made her way to the podium as if in slow motion, every gaze upon her. Then she turned and faced the audience. She lifted the spotted black veil on her hat, all the better to reveal her squinched eyes. She held out her arms.

'If you want to go, just say the word,' Simon said in Tansy's ear. 'The ute's outside. No one will even see us leave. We can take Monica with us, if you like. The kids will be fine with Kylie and Nick; they didn't really know David. You don't have to listen if you don't want to.'

Tansy shook her head. She took his hand and looked deep in his eyes. 'I'm staying until the bitter end. But if we don't make it out alive,' she said, 'I want you to know I've always loved you.'

'She'll be fine,' said Naveen. 'I mean, how bad can it be?'

They all held their breath.

—

'Dearly beloved,' Gloria began, in her calm, sonorous voice that seemed to echo for miles, 'men are imperfect beings.'

'Fucking hell,' said Simon. He squeezed Tansy's hand.

'But we, collectively, have striven to forgive them. Historically, we have cared for these poor flawed creatures as best we can. We have fed them and listened to them and kept their houses and wiped their brows out of our boundless sympathy for them, for they are the weaker sex, no one can deny that. They die sooner, they have poorer immune systems, they have a lower pain threshold, their genitals hang outside their bodies.'

'I might be wrong,' said Naveen, 'but I don't think eulogies usually begin like this.'

'Men are also,' Gloria continued, 'and I'm sure you will all agree with me on this, the more *emotional* sex. You only have to attend one football match to see that. The only way they have somehow managed to label women as more emotional is because they have somehow managed to not consider anger an emotion.'

The men in the audience shifted uncomfortably in their seats.

Ahead of them, Simon could see Kylie spin in her seat to face them. 'What the fuck is she doing?' she mouthed.

'Maybe you could set something on fire?' Tansy whispered to Simon. 'Something too small to burn the house down but big enough to require evacuation.'

'And, of course,' Gloria boomed, 'those of us who are mentally strong, who are driven by logic – we need to pity men for this. These poor, emotional creatures, at the mercy of their little whims.'

'I could fake a heart attack?' Simon whispered to Tansy. 'Or some kind of embolism?'

Gloria bowed her head and clutched the podium with white, strained fingers, all the better to convey her grief and gravity. 'I can imagine what you're all thinking right now.'

Unlikely, thought Simon.

'You're thinking – you're absolutely right about men in general, Gloria. But what does this have to do with David specifically?'

The audience, open-mouthed, nodded as though they'd been hypnotised.

'Because David, my late ex-husband, did something that redeemed him. Something that made up for all his many, many, *many* flaws. Flaws, of which he had many. Flaws that I could describe in minute and vivid detail, if I were the kind of person who dwelt on the wounds of the past.'

'Thank god she's not someone who dwells on the wounds of the past,' whispered Simon.

'But I am not someone who dwells on the wounds of the past. I am here to praise David. Dear, dear, late-lamented David. I am here to talk about the things he did right, not the things he did wrong. And what did he do right?' She beamed her lasers across the audience, daring them to answer.

The audience collectively froze in fear that this wasn't a rhetorical question and that she would call upon one of them to answer.

'He gave me three beautiful children. Nick – stand up, darling, that's a good boy. And Tansy, up the back. Wave, Tansy, so we can all see you. And Kylie, where are you? Oh, right next to Nick. I didn't notice you there. Nick, Tansy and Kylie, everyone. David's children.'

The audience broke into hesitant applause.

'And, considering David is responsible for giving me my daughter, Tansy, he is also responsible for bringing Simon into my life.' Gloria raised her arm and pointed towards the back, near the house. 'Simon, Tansy's husband. My son-in-law and the father of my beautiful grandchildren, who bring light and meaning to my existence. Wave, Simon.'

The entire audience swivelled in their seats, all of them staring. Simon froze.

'I said wave, Simon,' said Gloria.

Simon bent one arm at the elbow and flopped his hand forward like a Tyrannosaurus rex patting a tall dog.

'Simon, as some of you might know, is one of the area's most sought-after landscape gardeners.' Gloria gripped the podium like a deranged televangelist. 'He and his team are responsible for this magnificent space we find ourselves in this afternoon. I cannot help but think . . .' – and here, she allowed herself the luxury of a muffled sniff that might, in a different woman, be the beginnings of a tear – '. . . that families that have the luxury of such a beautiful space would grow together and become closer and more loving towards each other. I don't think I'm overstating it to suggest that if David and I had been blessed with a garden like this, he might not have betrayed me and our vows, and our marriage might not have exploded with the heat of a thousand suns. Because, dear friends, life is short. If you truly love your family, then you should give them a garden like this one.'

Simon felt the gaze of the entire audience upon him.

'But back to David,' Gloria continued. 'If we can judge a person by what they leave behind, David's legacy of his three children—'

'Four,' came a voice from the back.

Chapter 43

It was Monica, in a black jumpsuit and black Doc Martens, her lips a slash of red. She stood at the back door of the house. Even from where Simon stood, it was clear she was trembling. The gaze of the crowd moved from Simon to her.

'Oh my god,' said Tansy under her breath.

'I beg your pardon?' called out Gloria.

Monica took a dozen steps up the aisle towards the podium until she was in the middle of the rows of chairs. 'I said, four. David had four children.'

The audience gave an audible gasp.

'I see,' said Gloria. 'Someone can add up. And you are?'

Monica's arms twisted behind her back. Her voice grew thin and shaky. 'Monica Schnabel. Child number four.'

Gloria flared her nostrils. She peeled her hands off the podium finger by finger, then she stepped around it. She took one slow pace towards Monica.

The audience leaned away from the aisle, as though buffeted by a mighty wind.

'Simon,' said Tansy.

He took a half-step towards the aisle. Should he run forward now and bodily insert himself between the two of them? From the corner of his eye, Simon could see Nick standing in front of his seat. Perhaps he and Nick could each grab one of Gloria's arms?

'So. You're this *Monica* I've heard so much about.' Gloria took another two steps towards Monica. 'You're the child he stayed for. The child who grew up with a father at home, unlike my deserted children.'

Gloria continued walking down the aisle, slowly, until she stood directly in front of Monica. *I've seen this on the Discovery Channel*, thought Simon. Monica is some kind of antelope, paralysed in the face of an approaching lion. In one minute, the camera's going to pan away and David Attenborough is going to say something about *the majesty of the circle of life* but really, someone is having an enormous chunk taken out of their neck and there is absolutely nothing majestic about that from the perspective of the antelope.

Run, Monica, run, Simon thought.

Instead, Monica widened her stance, bracing herself. She crossed her arms. Simon could see her lower lip quiver. 'Sorry not sorry,' she said, but the confidence in her words didn't fool anyone.

'I think what Monica means is—' Naveen called out.

Gloria turned to glare at him. He fell silent.

'I understand exactly what Monica means,' said Gloria. She cast her beady eyes over the audience. 'Monica has elegantly and eloquently summed up the existential dilemma of her existence. She can be sorry for my children – quite literally, she can feel sorrow for them. But she cannot apologise for the circumstances of her own birth. She is alive. She is not – she cannot – be sorry for that.'

Mon blinked.

'You are obviously a highly intelligent young woman,' said Gloria.

'I am?' said Mon.

'You are.' Gloria nodded with certainty. 'You must take after your mother.'

'People say I have her eyes,' Mon said.

'My point exactly,' said Gloria. 'Regardless, losing a parent is devastating, especially at such a young age.'

And behold! Somewhere above them, the clouds parted and a sunbeam shone down from the heavens and a chorus of angels began to sing. Gloria took a pace forward, placed her bony hands on Monica's shoulders and pulled her into her arms, hugging her.

Hugging. Her.

It was a genuine hug, a comforting one. At first, Monica was stiff. She was technically taller than Gloria, and larger, but that's not how it seemed. It seemed as though Monica was a child enveloped in Gloria's arms, supported by the tautness of her body. After a time, Monica visibly softened and seemed to deflate. She rested her head on Gloria's shoulder.

'What the fuck did I just see?' said Tansy.

'There, there,' said Gloria. 'Whatever your father did – and I could go on and on – is no reflection on you.'

Simon's mouth dropped open. He could see Kylie and Nick in the crowd, goggle-eyed and swaying.

After a long moment, Gloria released Monica and turned again to the audience. 'Thank you all for your attention,' she said, raising one arm imperiously, and she took Monica's hand and led her to the spare seats in front row.

The celebrant came to the podium again. 'Thank you, Gloria, for that . . . um . . . unique insight into David's life. Now for our next speaker.'

Simon had certainly been to funerals before but thinking back, he could recall few details of any of them. This service, though? This was memorable. It was calmer, clearer, more focused and more lyrical – and yes, more celebratory and joyful. Was it because the astonishing act of Gloria hugging Monica made such an impression that every moment seemed vivid and in a kind of slow motion? Or was it because David's death was so many months ago and the fog of intense emotion had passed and everyone had found time and space to properly come to terms with David's life and death? Simon vaguely recalled hearing about a traditional culture that held a memorial service a year after the death to mark the end of mourning and to commemorate the deceased when their memory was beginning to fade. Was it in the Philippines? Simon thought this idea had much to recommend it.

From the size of the crowd, David must have known a great many people but there were only two more speakers: in retirement, David had volunteered as a mentor for start-up businesses and as a wildlife carer, and a young woman who owned a cake shop and an elderly koala expert both spoke. Simon listened, expecting more details – but no more details came. To Simon's mind, there were vast, galaxy-sized gaps in the way David's life had been presented. And considering this entire event was allegedly devoted to the whole of David's life, Simon found these spaces jarring.

No one talked about what he'd earned, or what his stock options had been, or his bonuses. No one talked about how much business he'd brought in for his various companies and employers. And his material possessions were completely absent from every speech. No one, Simon noted, mentioned the car David drove, or what his house was worth, or if it had a butler's pantry or walk-in robe. Or when it was last renovated, or even what town it was in. No one talked about the value of his wine collection. What kind of watch did he wear? What kind of sound system did he have at home, and was it wireless? How much money did he have in super at the time of his death? Stocks? Bonds? (What even *were* bonds?) No one talked about David's boat, if there was one. All these missing details were like a web of holes, like all of these people who paid him tribute were instead playing Jenga with the dead man's life – leaving out important, no, *vital* bricks, resulting in a gap-ridden tower.

Or could it be that Simon was spending ninety per cent of his time thinking about the gaps in a man's life, instead of on the life itself?

Standing at the back behind the last row of chairs, behind all these people, Simon felt his legs begin to quiver and his breath came in gasps and shudders. He had barely known David yet it was all he could do to stand upright, to keep his head from dropping into his hands. The way he was carrying on, you'd think it was his own funeral. He thought of all the times he'd felt himself missing when there was something he should have been experiencing – his vagueness at Lachie's birth, for instance. His general abstraction from the everyday for all these past months. Yet here, at a service for a near stranger, he felt himself utterly, devastatingly alive. If it hadn't been for Mia and Lachie spinning around during the proceedings and waving at him, he might have completely lost it. Instead he forced himself to smile and wave back at them.

When the official proceedings were over, the celebrant invited everyone to stay for a drink and nibbles and to share their memories of David with each other. On cue, black-aproned waiters with drink trays appeared from the bar, set up just inside.

'Thank god that's over.' Simon squeezed Tansy's hand.

'I need a drink,' she said. 'Several drinks.'

'Excuse me,' a voice said. 'But you're Simon, right?'

A woman in an apricot-coloured dress and a long string of misshaped pearls had navigated the standing crowd and come to stand beside Simon. Her hair was smooth and black and knotted on top of her head, held in place with red lacquer chopsticks.

He nodded.

'I'm Marjorie, a friend of Gloria's? I'm in her axe-throwing team, on Tuesday nights? The Battle Axes? So you're the clever boy responsible for this wonderful garden. It's gorgeous.'

Simon murmured his thanks.

'We've been looking for someone to do ours,' she said. 'Someone trustworthy. Mature. This is exactly the kind of thing we're after. Do you have a card?'

'Oh my god, yes. It's divine.' Another woman, this one sitting in the back row just in front of Simon, spun around in her seat and joined in. 'I'd love this for my place. The fire pit especially. You're Gloria's son-in-law, right? I know Gloria from U3A – we're both studying Medieval Poisons. She said you were an absolute whiz with gardens.' She stretched behind the two people sitting to her right and tapped a man in sky-blue suit on the shoulder. 'Mitch,' she said. 'That's him. The gardener.'

'I'm not really—' Simon began.

Mitch turned in his seat and looked at Simon over the top of his Aviators. 'Oh. My. God. When can you come over and give me a quote? I want oleanders and deadly nightshades. And a pond with goldfish. The big fat ones.'

'That's very kind . . . Would you excuse me for just a moment?' he said.

Tansy had wandered to the other side of the courtyard and was looking around the garden, entranced. He followed and stood beside her, and she leaned in and kissed his cheek. Then she peeled a small piece of toilet paper away from a nick on his chin. 'You must be exhausted.'

'It's nothing. You should see the other guy.' He watched the shred of white paper flutter to the ground. 'Are you okay? Are Kylie and Nick okay? What about Mon? I can't imagine what she's thinking right now.'

'We're all fine.' Tansy took his hand. 'The garden . . . Simon, it's magnificent. It's even better than I imagined. Thank you for making everything so special. And did you know about Naveen and Monica? Look at them.'

Simon turned. Naveen was rubbing Monica's arms and kissing her hand, as though astonished she was still alive. Honestly, they were all astonished she was still alive. 'I only found out today,' he said. 'You're not upset?'

'Of course not,' Tansy said. 'They're both single. It's hard enough to find happiness in this life. You should grab it while you can. Besides, I think they're cute.'

'If by cute, you mean ridiculous,' said Gloria, who had appeared beside them in all her glory, 'then, yes, I suppose it is. She's too vibrant for him, for a start. Too much gumption. Something needs to be done about it.'

'Mum,' said Tansy.

Simon couldn't help thinking that Gloria was right. Monica was an energetic young woman brimming with potential and dreams for the future. Naveen should be dating someone whose idea of a big Saturday night was watching Michael Portillo travel by train around England on SBS.

'Old people!' said Gloria, shaking her head, as though she wasn't one herself.

As if summoned by Gloria, an older man came to stand beside them and they widened their circle to admit him. He held a glass of red in one hand and wore garish red braces under a beige linen suit. His luxuriant grey hair flopped over one eye.

'Could that possibly be the beautiful Gloria?' He held her elbow with his free hand, as though peeling her open for inspection.

'Well, well, Steve MacArthur.' Gloria freed her arm from his touch. 'Wonders never cease. I thought you'd be dead by now.'

Steve MacArthur. The name rang a bell.

Steve laughed, the way people sometimes did when they thought Gloria was joking. 'No, not yet. You know what they say – old lawyers never die, they just lose their appeal.'

Steve MacArthur, thought Simon. The letterhead, on the invoice folded inside his phone. *MacArthur Family Law*.

'You remember my daughter, Tansy?' said Gloria. 'Or has your dementia already kicked in?'

'Of course, the lovely Tansy!' Steve said, oilily. 'Seeing you standing next to your mother, it's obvious that beauty runs in the family. It's been too long, Tansy. Almost two years, I'd say. Or longer?'

'Longer, I think,' Tansy said.

'Longer indeed,' said Steve. 'Why, I haven't seen you since January 2020. I remember it distinctly, it was just before everything turned to shit. You're even more resplendent now.' Steve turned to Simon. 'And you are?'

'This is Simon, my son-in-law,' Gloria said, then, as an afterthought, 'the gardener. Simon, Steve was a particularly repellent friend of David's.'

'I'm Tansy's husband,' Simon said, louder than he'd intended, as he shook Steve's hand.

'Are you now? Well, that's wonderful news, congratulations,' said Steve.

January 2020, Steve had said. Just before everything turned to shit. Steve had last seen Tansy in January 2020.

Gloria took Steve's arm. 'Steve, dear,' she said, her voice like honey, 'let me show you the fire pit. Simon built it himself. Something like that would be perfect in your backyard – just imagine it! You and all your old cronies could sit around and drink yourselves to death while looking into the flames and imagining the ashes of your pointless lives and your own impending funeral pyres.'

Steve burst into laughter. 'You're a card, Gloria. Listen, are you doing anything after the funeral?'

They wandered off.

'Excuse me,' Simon said to Tansy, his phone in his hand. 'I have to take this.'

He stepped aside and turned his back to answer his phone's imaginary ring, and instead opened his phone case and unfolded the invoice from MacArthur Family Law. Sure enough, across the top: *20 January 2020*. Over two years ago. Like many things in his life that should have been obvious, the date had always been there. He'd just never noticed it before.

Chapter 44

Tansy had seen a family lawyer over two years ago. Before the lockdowns, before he lost everything. When he was riding high. He folded the invoice back into his phone case.

Then Tansy appeared beside him. 'I didn't even hear it ring,' she said.

A waiter in a black apron approached with a tray of wineglasses of varying hues: she chose a rosé and Simon, a tall glass of mineral water with a slice of lime.

'I'm sorry I lost your house. I'm so sorry,' he said. It was the first time he'd ever said it.

'Simon,' she said, laying a hand on his arm, 'you can't be still thinking about that. Besides, it wasn't really my house – the deposit was Mum's. You could be a little kinder, you know. Compassion? Forgiveness? You might have heard of them. It wouldn't kill you.'

'Kinder?' Simon said. 'Show more compassion, to your mother?'

Tansy snorted into her drink. 'No, Simon. Not to Mum. To yourself. People make mistakes. It doesn't have to mean punishment for the term of your natural life.'

Then a weird thought popped into Simon's head.

If this were a movie instead of real life, this entire week might well be the result of an orchestrated strategy of complex lies. Naveen, out of cash after his divorce with barely enough money to get his chicken shop off the ground and pay his casuals, unexpectedly had spare cash to landscape his perfectly adequate backyard, seemingly out of nowhere. His previous gardeners, the ones who had left him 'in the lurch' – what was their business name again? Simon couldn't recall ever having heard it. In fact, he'd seen no evidence of whoever it was who'd pulled everything out and left the backyard in such a terrible state.

And Tansy, who was not having an affair with Naveen, was nonetheless working longer hours than usual, including nights, and coming home smelling of chips. It was almost as though she was working a second job. For example, shifts at a chicken shop, like the one owned by Naveen. Which, if unpaid, would save Naveen money. Kylie was, for some reason, tutoring Lexie, which, if unpaid, also saved Naveen money. Nick, who never thought to do anything for anyone, had 'volunteered' to coach Lexie's soccer team, to save Naveen doing it and paying someone to cover for him at the chicken shop. Which saved Naveen money. The free ute Simon was driving, from Nick's 'friend' Sven, who Simon had never heard of before or since, popped up at the exact right time, with exactly the right kind of tools that someone might need to landscape a backyard. Which was a huge coincidence. Without the ute and the tools dropping in his lap so conveniently, Simon wouldn't have been able to do the work.

And holding David's service in Naveen's backyard in the first place . . . well, the more Simon thought about it, that was truly odd. They had special function centres for things like this, at cemeteries and whatnot. And there were hotels and parks, and halls of every description, all of which held events like these on a regular basis. It was bizarre and random that the memorial was held in David's estranged daughter's best friend's backyard. Doubly weird: David had died almost two years ago – surely the statute of limitations on memorials had passed. And triply weird that the whole thing had such a ridiculous and tight deadline.

And that fundraiser for the tennis club that Gloria was on about. It couldn't possibly be that the caterer was Naveen's chicken shop, could it? She wouldn't have hired him for such an important event as a quid pro quo, to go towards compensating Naveen for the money he was paying Simon? It was almost as though someone had subsidised Naveen's backyard by marshalling the entire family and every possible resource to enable Naveen to have enough free cash to pay for at least part of the garden.

However. Even with the Tansy's hypothetical chicken-shop shifts, and Kylie's hypothetical tutoring, and Nick's hypothetical coaching, and the profits from a large and generous catering job, it wouldn't have been enough money.

If all this was true, someone had to have subsidised the backyard, and bought the pavers and plants and turf, the ute and tools. That would have taken a substantial amount of cash.

And someone must have deliberately fabricated an almost-impossible timeline to create a sense of desperation and urgency, then orchestrated Simon doing the work, and then stacked the guest list with likely garden clients for the express purpose of restoring Simon's confidence and showcasing . . . what? A potential new business?

He thought about how few people at this memorial seemed to actually know David.

Simon shook his head. That's what you get for missing an entire night of sleep – faulty, crazy thinking! He'd once read an article that said missing even a few hours was the equivalent to a blood alcohol reading of 0.05. That this was all a grand scheme ... what a ridiculous idea! Real life does not evolve like a le Carré novel. Coordinating that many people, orchestrating secrets. Forcing people to donate their time to satisfy your Machiavellian will. In order to pull off something like that successfully, the ringleader would have to be a devious criminal mastermind with an uncanny ability to manipulate people to their own ends. Someone with no remorse, no boundaries. People aren't like that in the real world.

The scent of late jasmine drifted across the yard. People were chatting; he heard the tink of glasses. From the fire pit, where she was still talking with Steve, Gloria's voice carried, 'Have you considered Botox? Or have you just stopped caring?'

This was real life. Real life had quite enough drama. There was no need for him to invent any more.

He thought of the women who'd asked for his card, and Mitch, the man in the blue suit. He would find them right now and take their mobile numbers. He would follow up with them. He could begin again.

The garden was filled with people chatting now, in small and bigger groups. The hire people were stacking the white chairs to make more room for mingling and somehow a trestle table had appeared in the courtyard that Simon had paved with his own two hands on his knees in the middle of the night, and on the table was a white cloth, and on the white cloth were platters of fruit cut into shapes and wedges of cheese and crackers and small triangular chicken sandwiches with the crusts cut off. Of the people milling around, some were younger than Simon and Tansy, but most were older and their shoulders were beginning to hunch and the skin on their faces and the backs of their hands were hatched and speckled and the flesh beneath their chin was loose and wattled – some more so, some less, but all of them to some degree. All of their bodies would continue to age, as would Simon's, as would Tansy's, but Simon was sure they felt like he did on the inside.

That was the fact of ageing. Regardless of appearances, everyone still felt like a child on the inside. And all anyone could hope for, Simon realised, was the blessing of ageing with someone they loved by their side. They – these people that Simon pitied for their ageing bodies – were the lucky ones. The unlucky ones, like their guest of honour, had nothing left to fear.

'You love me,' Simon said to Tansy. He felt painfully, blissfully alive.

She raised her eyebrows. 'Don't get a big head. You're quite passable looking, in the right light.'

He took her wine and his water and balanced them both in a nearby garden bed, then he took both her hands. 'Why?'

'What a stupid question.' She breathed in and shuddered. 'Love was never in question – but for a long while, Simon . . . I didn't like you. I didn't like your friends or your hours or the kinds of things you thought were important. I didn't like the way you treated us, like we were something you collected then put in a cupboard. You were a dickhead when you had the business, frankly.'

'I was a dickhead?' He smiled wryly. 'But I wore a Longines and drove an Audi. Some people are impossible to satisfy.'

'And your friends! Dickheads. I mean, genuine wankers. And that house! God, I hated that house. I was lonely living there. I never felt like myself in that house.'

Yes, he'd been a dickhead. Okay. Fine. His friends – no arguments there. But the house! He could barely believe what he was hearing. Yes, somehow they did seem to know their neighbours in the other flats – Jock and James, Yulia, Gemma and Erin. The Chees, at the other end of the street. And now that he thought of it, the inhabitants of a number of other residences scattered across the neighbourhood. Simon couldn't recall knowing anyone in the street where they'd owned a house. Everyone was too busy working; no one had enough time to socialise with their actual friends, and definitely couldn't spare time for geographical accidents. Now the kids and Tansy went door to door for school fundraisers; last year, the kids had 'helped' Yulia make apricot jam and they'd sold it out the front for five bucks a jar to raise money for koalas.

'You hated the house? Why didn't you tell me?'

'Because you never asked. You changed so quickly, I could barely catch it from the corner of my eye.' She freed one hand from his and cupped the side of his face. 'I'm not afraid of problems. We'll fix them, we always have. What I'm afraid of is facing them with someone I don't respect.'

He swallowed. 'And at the beginning, when we first met? Why did you love me back then? You could have had any man you wanted.'

She threaded her fingers though his. 'I only wanted one man. There was only one man who didn't see me as Kylie's dumber sister or Nick's less popular sister. There was only ever one man who saw me. That was you, Simon. It was always you.'

—

Now that the ceremony was finished and all the guests had gone home and the hire people had stacked and wheeled away the chairs and the caterers had cleared away plates and glasses, Simon was sitting in front of the fire pit with a stubby in his hand. Tansy sat next to him with a glass of red; Lachie was asleep, sprawled across her lap. On the other side of the fire, Kylie, Nick and Naveen were picking from a tray of leftover sausage rolls. On the grass at the edge of the paving, Mia and Lexie were painting their toenails. It took all his self-control not to yell at them to be careful of the pavers.

'Do you think I could tidy up the backyard of the flats?' Simon said to Tansy. 'I could do a deal with the landlord for reduced rent. The guys who mow it do a shocking job. We could grow some veggies, put in a fire pit. Show the kids how to get their hands dirty.'

She shrugged. 'It won't hurt to ask.'

'Did you see the way she hugged Monica?' Kylie said. 'I don't think she's ever hugged me like that in my entire life.' She took a huge swig from her stubby.

Nick looked towards the back of the house, where Gloria was deep in conversation with Monica. 'Hilarious, the lot of you overreacting like that when Monica stood up,' he said. 'We're not the Cosa Nostra. It's not a blood feud. Mum's the most affectionate, supportive person in the world.'

'Listen, mummy's boy,' said Kylie. 'Shut up.'

'You shut up,' said Nick.

Simon was on Kylie's side in this – but then he thought of how Gloria had saved the money for their house deposit by putting aside Tansy's rent every month. 'By the way,' he said to Tansy. 'Do you remember the school fundraising drive, to buy more books for the library? Mia's class is going to make a big donation. They've been planning it for weeks.'

Tansy raised her eyebrows and shifted Lachie's deadweight to her other leg.

'I'll explain later. And we have to chat about the Visa card bill.' Then he leaned over and kissed her – a proper kiss, deep with longing. 'I'll explain that later too.'

Kylie stood and called Gloria and Monica back.

'Monica says I have a big future as an influencer,' said Gloria as she sat. 'She's going to set up my social medium. She is quite brilliant.'

'Glamorous grandmas are fashion icons,' Mon said. 'They're in demand.'

'And you,' said Gloria, 'have an exciting future ahead, I can tell.'

Monica sat next to Tansy. 'Your mum thinks I'm brilliant,' she whispered in Tansy's ear.

'Mum is always right,' Tansy whispered back.

'Charge your glasses,' said Kylie.

Lemonade was procured for Mia and Lexie. They all stood except for Tansy; Lachie was still asleep. Around them, the new plants were glowing in the sinking orange of the sun. The lawn was a vibrant vivid green, so healthy it seemed to be growing before their eyes. The cicadas were beginning.

'To David,' Kylie said.

'To Dad,' said Monica.

'To my ex-husband, who had four brilliant and caring children, and who brought us all together,' said Gloria.

At last, thought Simon, *Gloria was showing some sensitivity towards the feelings of Mon, and her own children and grandchildren.*

'Despite being a rat bastard,' she continued.

So close! Simon shrugged. They all drank.

Despite his exhaustion, Simon could see the future clearly laid out before him. He saw that he would text Flora on the way home and tell her how much he appreciated her offer, but he couldn't be away from his family right now. He would tell her how proud he was of the work she was doing. He would give her many congratulations and thanks. He would also make an appointment with his GP for a health check and a chat.

And he saw his new business cards. MiaLa Landscaping, he would call it. And in a flash, he knew it: Mia would not win the Nobel prize and Lachie would not win the Oscar for Best Actor, but they would live long and healthy lives, and they would grow to be kind people who cared about the world. Lachie will become the type of person who phoned friends and relatives just to say hello, as well as on their birthday, whether Facebook told him to or not; Mia will make chickpea casseroles for her neighbours when they're ill or grieving.

These were not small things. They were big things, and rare, and many people who deserved it were not so lucky to have kind children and a caring family and a loving, clever wife. Now, it was time for Simon to act. It was time for him to deserve it.

Acknowledgements

I'd like to thank Jane Novak, who is courageous, cool-headed and always has my back, and the brilliant Hachette team of Rebecca Saunders, Emma Rafferty, Fiona Hazard and Louise Stark, who each understood exactly what I was trying to write. Dianne Blacklock was generous with her attention to detail and Sandy Cull has designed the perfect jacket. Carrie Tiffany and Lee Falvey, my first readers, talked me down from ledges and helped fix my more egregious mistakes, and Alison Goodman listened patiently to my manuscript problems and gave me the perfect plot advice at the perfect time. And I'm still grateful for 30 April 1994, when I picked up a cute drunk guy at a party and took him home. (Longest one-night stand ever.) Thank you, Robbie, for being the source of much of my chocolate, coffee and happiness.

This book was written on the unceded lands of the Wurundjeri people of the Kulin Nation, who have been telling stories here for tens of thousands of years. I pay my respects to their elders, past, present and emerging.